SNOWED UNDER

THE LEAFY HOLLOW MYSTERIES, BOOK 5

RICKIE BLAIR

BARKLEY
B O O K S

SNOWED UNDER

To receive information about new releases and special offers, please sign up
for my mailing list at www.rickieblair.com.

Cover art by: www.coverkicks.com

SNOWED UNDER

CHAPTER ONE

IGNORING the rowdy scuffle underway in the back of his van, Mickey Doig sized up the house across the street. With its dented aluminum siding, barricaded windows, and snow drifted over the walkway, it appeared deserted.

He knew different.

While tugging down the earflaps of his tasseled wool hat, he reviewed his strategy. As usual, it hinged on a silent entry and rapid survey, followed by a little sleight of hand, and—if necessary—application of his awesome personal charm. He saw no reason to change it.

A particularly vigorous blow in the back of the van rocked the vehicle. Annoyed, he glanced at the rearview mirror. "Keep it down," he hollered, before renewing his scrutiny.

His decrepit white van was well known in the neighborhood. On its side, a magnetic sign advertised MICKEY'S DOG CARE. A detailed inspection would reveal another slogan underneath, but none of his clients cared to look that closely. He was the cheapest dog walker in Leafy Hollow, and their pets ecstatically wagged their tails when they saw him. *What more could you ask for?* the owners agreed whenever they met on the village's snowy streets.

For their part, the four dogs wrestling on the van's bare metal floor found its urine-tinged atmosphere invigorating. A standard poodle with poufed silver hair relinquished its choke hold on a chunky beagle to check out a particularly aromatic corner before returning to the fray.

Mickey paid no attention. His gaze remained fixed on his objective.

Casual onlookers often mistook the snow-covered mounds in the front yard of that house for tastefully pruned shrubs tucked under a picturesque blanket of white. Oskar York's long-suffering neighbors knew better. When that snow melted, a dozen discarded ladders, two rusted-out wheelbarrows, broken lawn furniture tangled in weeds, and a stack of worn tires would emerge. The neighbors often pleaded with Mickey to convince the old man to clean up his act. "He'll listen to you," they insisted, with more hope than conviction.

Mickey couldn't blame them. He was used to ignoring domestic situations some would consider sub-standard, but even he disliked spending time in Oskar's house. It wasn't the filth that deterred him, but the claustrophobia that gripped him by the throat after only minutes inside.

None of those neighbors were home, judging from their empty driveways. But the old man would be in. He always was—along with the most obnoxious dog Mickey had ever met. Boomer, a scrappy terrier cross, was nothing but trouble.

Not only that, but Oskar never paid *Mickey's Dog Care*. To Mickey's amusement, the old man believed he walked Boomer for the fun of it. Oskar York would be surprised to learn that exercising Boomer was Mickey's most lucrative gig. The feisty terrier was the key money maker among his "regulars," although the standard poodle, with her talent for wallet-snatching, was coming up fast.

After flattening his earflaps, he stepped onto the slippery road, slamming the van door behind him. Ice pellets stung his face, and he glanced up at the gray sky with disgust while zipping up his parka. According to the weather forecasters, the "storm of the century" was on the way. He shivered. Next winter, he was going South, no matter what he had to do to finance it.

He didn't bother knocking, because the door was never locked. Dusty planters, broken lamps, and dirty laundry stacked in the front hall reliably barred most intruders. With a muttered curse, he squeezed through the opening, stepping over a knee-high pile of old jigsaw puzzles before closing the door.

The hallway was dark. Not surprising given that the fabric shade of its wall sconce hadn't been dusted since the seventies.

"Mr. York?" Mickey called, knowing from experience that using Oskar's first name would trigger a stream of hurled insults. "I'm here to pick up Boomer."

No answer, as usual, since Oskar was hard of hearing. Mickey called out only to ensure the old man hadn't wandered into the front of the house. He cocked his head, listening.

Normally, Boomer greeted him at the front door with a barrage of abuse. Not that Mickey paid it any mind. He knew the terrier only carried on like that for the old man's benefit. Strangely, though, Boomer was quiet. Shrugging, he continued into the front room.

York often insisted he was writing a history of Leafy Hollow, but Mickey had never seen anything among the clutter that resembled a manuscript. Mounds of papers, old books, and rumpled sweaters swamped a threadbare chesterfield. An inch of dust and crumbs, mingled with mouse droppings and crumpled scraps of paper, covered the floor.

With two rapid strides, he reached the roll-top desk, where he rifled through the drawers. In the past, he'd taken fistfuls of cash from this desk—with Boomer on lookout duty —and the old man had never been the wiser. Sometimes, he found antique jewelry. The pieces rarely turned out to be valuable, but given his current situation, he couldn't afford to turn up his nose. A filigreed brooch seemed promising, and he slid it into his parka pocket along with an empty leather wallet and a gold watch that lacked a stem and a second hand.

A furious *scritch-scritch-scritch* made him raise his head. It was coming from the closed closet door under the stairs.

Scritch-scritch-scritch.

He shook his head in exasperation. No wonder Boomer hadn't greeted him at the door. *How did that stupid dog get itself locked in the closet?*

As he turned toward the stairs, a red shoebox on the desk caught his eye. He tugged it from its moorings, taking care to hold back the potential avalanche of papers that surrounded it. He flipped off the top to find dozens of old photos. Jamming the lid back on, he placed the box by the front door, where he could grab it on the way out.

Scritch-scritch-scritch.

He opened the closet door, and the terrier burst out, darting down the hall to the bathroom. When Mickey caught up, Boomer was lapping from the toilet bowl as if he hadn't had a drink in days. Then he trotted over to the closed kitchen door, scratching furiously at it until Mickey wrenched it open.

Resignedly, he followed the dog into the back of the house. Old Man York would be in the solarium, as usual. Calling it a solarium was totally bogus, Mickey thought, given its utter lack of plants. Like every other room, it was crammed with junk. Its glass roof leaked. Bits of paper stuffed into cracks along the window frames had long since wadded up, and frigid drafts chilled the air.

"Mr. York?" he called, navigating a perilous route through towering stacks of newspapers, magazines, flattened cereal boxes, and empty tins.

His foot slid on a discarded potato chip bag. Instinctively, he thrust out a hand to steady himself. The nearest wall of *Canadian Geographics* shuddered under his touch, like a volcano about to erupt. Frantically, he grabbed the pile with both hands to steady it, holding his breath.

When it finally settled, he drew back, puffing out a breath.

Somewhere ahead, Boomer was yapping.

Arf-arf-arf-arf-arf-arf...

That meant the old man was on his feet, lumbering

5

through the makeshift tunnels to holler at Mickey for whatever he was teed off about today. Mickey imagined his rant, delivered in nasal tones through discolored teeth. *"Doig! Where the hell have you been?"*

If he had disturbed the old man's treasures, God help him. He'd never hear the end of it. Honestly, if it wasn't for the cash...

He sidled around the next corner, taking care not to touch the stacked magazines.

Arf-arf-arf-arf-arf-arf...

The terrier, frantic, barreled around the corner.

And ran right into him.

Startled, Mickey tripped over the dog, falling against the nearest stack. It wobbled wildly before giving way and pitching him backward onto the floor.

As he fell, he watched with horror while magazines toppled around him. After hitting the floor with a painful thud, he closed his eyes against the clouds of dust, cringing at each thunderous crash.

When it was all over, Mickey opened his eyes. He was lying on the scarred linoleum, books and magazines digging into his back, surrounded by tattered newspapers and dented tins. Dozens of discolored ladles, rusty whisks, and scratched plastic cups spilled out of a cardboard box, covering his legs.

With a groan, he sat up. He pulled off his hat and shook it free of dust before replacing it on his head. Then he took in the scene, his mouth hanging open.

The kitchen was knee deep in the old man's ruined treasures. Magazines were ripped, china plates broken, cardboard boxes split and torn. An upended bottle of olive oil glugged over the nearest pile.

Arf-arf-arf-arf-arf-arf...

Mickey raised his eyes to the ceiling, heaving a sigh. Naturally, that odious mutt had survived. Straining his ears, he tried to hear Oskar's shouted abuse over Boomer's barking. But the terrier's yapping drowned out everything else.

He rose and shuffled through the mess, trying not to slip on the shiny *Canadian Geographic* covers. "Mr. York?"

Arf-arf-arf-arf-arf-arf...

The dog was frantically shredding a mammoth pile of fallen magazines with its front claws.

When he saw what the terrier was after, Mickey gasped.

A single foot stuck out from under a mountain of magazines and chipped porcelain bowls. Poking through a hole in its gray woolen sock was a hardened yellow toenail.

Neither the nail nor the foot was moving.

"Mr. York?" he whispered. With a shuddering breath, he crouched to grasp the foot, holding it for several seconds with his eyes scrunched shut. The skin was as cold as the drafts whistling through the leaky solarium windows.

Mickey opened his eyes. Almost hypnotically, he picked up a worn plaid slipper that lay nearby. After staring at it a moment, he slid it on to the foot. It was the least he could do.

He rose to consider his options. Since his wireless provider had long since pulled his account for lack of payment—and Oskar refused to have a phone in the house at all—he couldn't call 9-1-1. And what good would that do, anyway? No one could help the old man now.

Mickey could help himself, however—by getting the heck

out of there. He had been a good friend to Oskar York when he was alive. He'd even walked his dog for free. Why should he suffer because the old guy was dead? The police would be bound to check his record. How long would it be before they blamed him for what was clearly an accident?

Nope. He had to exit this scene ASAP.

Arf-arf-arf-arf-arf-arf...

Boomer continued his assault on the mountain of kitchen debris.

Mickey watched, pursing his lips. He couldn't take the dog with him, because that would prove he'd been here. Which would lead to uncomfortable questions about how the old man ended up dead.

"You're on your own, buddy," he whispered, shutting the kitchen door on the furious terrier. On his way out, he snatched up the red shoebox and thrust it under his arm.

Outside, he glanced warily up and down the street. The neighbors were still not home. All he had to do was get into his van and drive away.

Mickey didn't check his rearview mirror as he sped off with the dogs bouncing and quarreling in the back. If he had, he might have noticed a formerly empty sedan now had a driver at the wheel. And that when he turned the corner, the sedan pulled away from the curb behind him.

CHAPTER TWO

SHIVERING in my parka and mittens, I pushed open the red door of Leafy Hollow's favorite bakery with a sigh of relief. But that first welcome breath of warm, cinnamon-scented air caught in my throat when I saw the owner's knitted brow.

Emy Dionne was bent over the counter, dark curls framing her petite face, tapping her finger on a sheet of paper spread out over the glass. She appeared to be muttering.

At the jangle of the door's overhead bell, she jerked her chin up. "Hi, Verity. Your usual?"

"Please," I said, shaking snow from my parka before adding it to the coat rack in the corner. Then I leaned over the counter to reach for my personalized mug. As Emy's best friend, I had favored-customer privileges. "Is anything wrong?" I asked with a twist of unease, brandishing my empty mug at the paper.

"No." Emy hastily folded it and pushed it to one side. "Nothing. Listen—are you stocked up on sidewalk salt?

There's a real rush on it at Canadian Tire. Better get over there if you need any. They expect to run out by tomorrow."

"I've got plenty. But thanks for the tip."

"They're forecasting the storm of the century, Verity. Can't be too careful."

"Uh-huh." *Storm of the week,* I thought, *is more likely.* Leafy Hollow was over a thousand miles from the Arctic Circle, yet the villagers were stockpiling tinned goods, candles, and batteries as if Napoleon was on the way. Not to mention firewood—whether they had a fireplace or not.

I pointed again to the document. "What's that?"

Emy took my mug and filled it from a teapot on the counter, then plonked a raisin-butternut scone on a plate and handed it over. "I'll tell you—but don't mock."

Sputtering with disbelief, I said, "Why would I—"

"Please." She held up a hand, her lips twitching. "Save it for someone who doesn't know how cynical you can be."

Giving her my best fisheye, I bit into the scone. After dealing with a particularly chewy raisin, I reached for my mug. "I'm listening."

The bell over the front door jangled again, followed by a blast of cold air. A shivering young woman, her hair pulled tightly on top of her head in an afro puff, stamped her boots on the front mat.

Before she'd had time to take off her coat, Emy waved her over. "Shanice. Take a look at this." She held out the folded paper.

The young woman took the paper while passing Emy a brown paper bag. "Bertram's only had one jar of that lime-and-basil marmalade."

"Thanks," Emy said, tucking it behind the counter.

Shanice unfolded the paper, reading it in one hand while shrugging off her coat with the other. "Wow." She whirled around to face us with a triumphant expression. "This puts a new light on things."

Emy nodded emphatically. "I know."

I watched this exchange a little wistfully. Shanice Clarke, Emy's new assistant, had only been in Leafy Hollow one week and, already, she and her new boss had secrets. "Is somebody going to tell me what you're talking about?"

Emy shot me a sly grin. "Remember your promise not to mock."

I solemnly crossed my heart.

"It's a blank crossword contest. With a huge prize." She motioned at the paper in Shanice's hand. "One of the librarians just found a new clue."

"But I *love* crosswords," I said, putting down my mug to reach for the folded paper. "Why would I make fun of it? Wait. What do you mean—it's blank?"

"It has no clues on it."

"How do you guess the answers, then?" An all-white jigsaw puzzle that had been a childhood nemesis sprang to mind. Even my dauntless aunt had given up on that one.

Shanice grinned. "That's the best part. There *are* clues, but they're in discarded wallets. People find them all over the village, one at a time. Then they post each clue at the library." She tucked the paper beside the cash register.

"Why wallets?"

"They're easy to spot, I guess. Nobody walks away from a wallet."

"They could have used red feathers." I buttered a piece of scone.

"Too obvious," Emy said from under the counter, where she was restocking the marmalade.

"So the organizers only want determined players," I mused aloud.

"Well, sure." Shanice shrugged. "You don't give away a million dollars to just anybody."

"A million dollars?" I halted with the butter knife halfway to my plate. "Is that the prize?"

"That's what everybody says."

Emy rose, placing a dish of marmalade on the counter. Catching sight of my expression, she pursed her lips. "I see that cynical look, Verity. Cut it out."

"What do you mean? What look?"

"You think the contest is silly."

"I do not. But I do wonder who's behind it."

She shrugged. "Nobody knows. It's a mystery."

Next door, the doorbell jangled in Emy's Eco Edibles, the vegan takeout that shared the first floor with the 5X Bakery.

Shanice headed for the connecting door behind the counter. "Emy, where do you keep the recycled-paper napkins?"

"In the back room. Next to the seaweed snacks."

Once Shanice disappeared through the passage and a muffled conversation began next door, I drained the last of my tea and held out my mug for a refill. Lowering my voice, I said, "How's she working out?"

"Fabulous. She makes great sandwiches, and the

customers love her. I wish I could keep her when the semester's over."

"Will the college send you someone else?"

"Fingers crossed. I was dubious about the culinary-skills internship at first, but now I think it's great."

"I did offer to help out, you know. For the winter, at least."

"Yes, and I was grateful." Emy bit her lips in a gesture I suspected hid a smile. "But we discussed it, Verity. We decided your baking skills might not be up to the challenge."

"Ha. You underestimate my abilities."

Emy picked up the tongs. "Perhaps another scone will soothe your ruffled feelings?"

"It might," I said, accepting a second and reaching for the butter knife.

"Besides, Shanice has great marketing ideas. She thinks we should set up a parallel contest board in the bakery, so people can post crossword clues here, too." Tapping thoughtfully on the counter, she gazed into the distance. "Why should the library keep all that foot traffic to themselves? They're not selling anything."

She turned to me with a twinkle in her eye. "You should investigate it."

"Me? What on earth for?"

"You've been complaining about having time on your hands. Think of the positive publicity for your PI business if you solve a mystery the whole village is talking about."

"Not that again." I groaned. "For the last time, Emy—I don't *have* a 'PI' business."

"But you said—"

"I said I might consult on minor cases. Misplaced mementos, estranged relatives, missing puppies. That's all."

Emy nodded sagely. "Estranged relatives would be a good area to get into. Everybody has those."

"I'm not contacting my father in Australia."

"I didn't mean him," Emy objected. "And for what it's worth, I'm not contacting mine, either."

We shared a high-five. Our deadbeat dads had always been a bond between us.

"But still." Emy crossed her arms, giving me a quizzical glance. "I don't see why you won't consider it. It's the obvious solution to your problem."

"Because I promised Jeff I wouldn't do any more investigating."

"That's not true. You promised him you wouldn't do anything dangerous," Emy said with her usual precision. "Not the same thing."

I considered that while chewing. Sipping my tea, I eyed her over the rim of my mug before placing it firmly on the counter.

"Jeff says I have murder on the brain." I buttered another piece of scone before adding a dab of the new marmalade.

"Is that a bad thing for an investigator?" Emy flexed her eyebrows. "Besides, Coming Up Roses is in mothballs for the winter. From now until April, you have no lawns to cut, no leaves to rake, and no flowers to plant. Hence—no cash. Isn't that what you said?"

"Hmm." I sipped my tea.

"Tell me why you've ruled out bookkeeping."

"Because it reminds me of Vancouver."

Emy uncrossed her arms. "Verity. That was nearly three years ago. You've moved on."

Licking crumbs from my finger, I shrugged.

Emy pointed to my plate. "Do you want anything else?" When I shook my head, she put my plate into the sink.

"Okay, let's review. Snow removal is—"

"Don't even." Shivering, I drew my sweater tight around my neck. The idea of rising before dawn to push snow around for hours in my aging pickup left me as cold as the January winds outside.

"Which brings us back to my original, and brilliant, idea."

"I'm not getting involved in any more murder cases."

"Who's talking about murder? I'm only saying that, given your history, Leafy Hollow residents would happily pay you to clear up their little mysteries. You could uncover frauds, for instance."

"I'm not a certified accountant, Emy, and definitely not a forensic one."

"So what? Look how helpful you were when Mom was involved in that embezzlement thing. People don't always call in the big guns right off the bat. Sometimes they need a little advice from someone who's not going to—"

"Arrest them?" I asked drily.

"Exactly."

I must have looked doubtful, because Emy leaned in with her forearms on the counter. "The police don't investigate minor stuff. Especially when there's no crime involved."

"Then why would anyone—"

She held up a finger. "I have the perfect example. Yesterday, Henri Vartan came in for bacon-toffee shortbreads."

I snickered. "Do you want me to track down the bacon? Or is it the toffee that's missing?"

"Haha. Anyway—"

"Hang on. Didn't Henri say your shortbreads have no place in a healthy diet?"

Emy rolled her eyes. "Imagine. I use nothing but the finest butter and cream. Organic, in fact. The bacon, too. Farm-raised. Besides, he only says stuff like that when the girls are around. The rest of the time, he can't get enough of those shortbreads."

"By 'girls,' he means the two women in his artists' collective?"

"Yes."

"Hmm." I hoped Henri wouldn't call me a 'girl' the next time we met. Otherwise, I'd have to go all Krav Maga on his ample rear.

"Anyway, Henri told me how he found the oddest thing the other day outside the new Leafy Hollow art gallery—"

"Which is his house, right?"

"Yes, but listen—"

I sat back, trying to appear attentive.

"So, there he was, bending over to pick up mail off the floor in his hall, when he noticed a flash of red under a shrub. It turned out to be a red calfskin wallet. Someone left it there on purpose, Henri thinks."

"Couldn't they simply have dropped it?"

"It was tucked under the branches. No one walking past could have seen it. Henri only spotted it because when he bent down, it was visible through the sidelight by his front door."

"Any money in it?"

"Twenty bucks."

"Did it have a contest clue in it?"

"No, that's the weird part. It was a regular wallet, with ID and credit cards."

"Someone dropped their wallet. Not much mystery in that."

"Wait—I'm getting to the mysterious part. Henri went to the police station to turn in the wallet. The next day, an officer called and told him all the ID was fake. They couldn't match any of it to a real person."

"Forgeries? That is strange."

"I know," Emy said smugly.

"What about the credit cards?"

"Same thing—forgeries."

"And the twenty dollars?"

"They told Henri he could have that. He went back to the station to get it."

"Is the gallery that hard up?"

"Twenty bucks is twenty bucks. Besides, he was intrigued. He wanted the wallet back so he could look into it himself. The police kept the fake ID, though."

"Still not seeing my role in this."

"Isn't it obvious? Henri's curious. He wants to know why someone left a wallet with fake ID outside his front door. But he doesn't know where to start. I suggested you could look into it for him." She raised her eyebrows. "For a fee."

"A fee? Henri doesn't have any money." I knew Emy gave him samples whenever he came by the bakery. "He's one of those starving-artist types."

"It's possible I suggested you'd do it pro bono—you know, for the publicity. Since Hawkes Investigation Agency is only starting out."

I gaped at her.

"Sorry." She waved a hand. "Obviously, you'll come up with a better name." At my continued silence, she added, "What? It's not like you're doing anything else."

"That's not true. I'm working on designs for a client's woodland garden."

"Is that the only job you have?" Emy's eyebrows rose. "You can't plant that for months yet. Those sketches can wait."

"There's a water feature, too. A recirculating brook. Aunt Adeline is helping me plan that part. We think—"

Emy held up a hand. "It will be lovely—once the snow melts enough that you can actually work on it." She glanced at the front window, buffeted by so many swirling flakes the hardware shop across the street was barely visible. "Meanwhile, you need to make some money."

I sat back in disbelief, preparing to ridicule this incredible suggestion. But something held my tongue. I've never been able to resist a mystery. And this time, there were no dead bodies involved—a definite point in the scheme's favor.

Also, Emy was correct—I needed cash. The restoration of my nineteenth-century fieldstone cottage was on hold, but only temporarily. Carson Breuer, the laconic handyman who considered it a personal project, had lived in my driveway so long I started to think of his tent-trailer as a permanent fixture. I'd been surprised to return home one nippy autumn day to find it gone.

A selfie of Carson and Reuben posing in front of his trailer was taped to my fridge at home. Above their heads—one slightly balding, the other sporting a floppy red cockscomb—a painted sign displayed a vivid orange sunset and the words, WELCOME TO KEY WEST.

I had no idea how Carson got my pet rooster across the border. Knowing him, it was probably best not to ask. Anyway, on the photo's back, Carson had penned, "See you soon!"

Which meant a little cash coming in would be handy.

I slumped over the counter, twisting the mug in my hands while I considered it.

"You're intrigued, I can tell," Emy said.

Pushing the mug away, I stood up straight. Jeff was a trained and experienced detective—a true professional. He worked hard on his cases. Whereas I didn't even qualify as a dilettante. My only talent, if it could be called that, was insatiable curiosity.

All the same, there was no harm in paying Henri a visit.

"I guess it can't hurt to talk to him. And I am curious about the new gallery."

"There you go, then. A perfect opportunity to catch up. I'll call Henri and tell him you're on your way." Emy handed me a white box tied with a string. "Give him these shortbreads."

I eyed the box suspiciously before plucking it from her hands. "You already had that packed. Am I that predictable?"

Emy smiled. "It's an honor to be on intimate terms with Leafy Hollow's newest investigator."

CHAPTER THREE

BEFORE I COULD INTERROGATE Henri Vartan about his odd discovery, I had an errand to run at the Leafy Hollow Library. I could satisfy my curiosity about the strange puzzle contest while I was there.

Clutching my copy of *Clara Callan*, a previous book club selection, I climbed the broad stone steps and pushed open the carved wooden door. After stamping my feet on the WELCOME mat to shake off the slush, I unzipped my parka.

A second door led into the overheated main room with its twenty-foot ceiling and soaring mullioned windows. A reading area with wooden armchairs faced the worn walnut expanse of the front desk. Behind that, ten rows of tall, double-faced shelves held books, CDs, and DVDs. These open stacks, normally crowded with a dozen or more readers, were empty.

The small, closed section behind that, marked No ADMITTANCE, was accessible only with librarian approval. It housed old books and documents about Leafy Hollow. Usually, one or two visiting historians would be perusing those materials, eyeglasses pushed up over receding hairlines. But that area was also empty.

Instead, a hum of conversation drew my gaze to the bulletin board by a front window. The board normally held council memos, garage sale notices, knitting club updates, and "Free to a good home" posters—I avoided those, since Rose Cottage already had a resident feline, the grumpy one-eyed tomcat General Chang. These notices—many curled with age—were usually ignored. Not today, apparently. Judging from the chattering crowd at the bulletin board, Leafy Hollow was confronting either a glut of homeless kittens or a very unusual knitting pattern.

"Verity!" Hannah Quigley, assistant librarian, gave me a cheery wave from behind the front desk. I walked over to greet her. Hannah's gray-streaked bun and horn-rimmed glasses would have given her the look of a frontier school-marm if it hadn't been for the tattoos that swirled over her forearms. "Ready for the book club meeting next week?"

"Almost." I was way behind on this month's reading. It wasn't entirely my fault. I would have preferred a book set in a warmer climate—Bermuda, maybe. Our current choice —*Minds of Winter*, a wide-ranging novel about historic polar expeditions—made for chilly reading. Southern Ontario was suffering through its coldest winter in a decade, and I could have done without the book's descriptions of "razor-blade air." I kept putting the book down to make cocoa.

I deposited *Clara Callan* on the RETURNS HERE cart beside the desk. "How's business?"

Hannah grinned. "It's so exciting, Verity. We're contest central here." Handcrafted bangles jangled on her tattooed wrist as she pointed to the bulletin board. "The whole village is abuzz."

"Exciting" was not a word normally used to describe the Leafy Hollow Library, so it was with considerable curiosity that I turned my head to watch the half-dozen people milling around.

A slightly built woman, with skin so pale that blue veins stood out on her forehead, pointed to the board and mumbled something. The dark-haired woman beside her nodded. Even with their backs to me, I recognized "the girls," as Henri Vartan called them. It seemed a condescending label, but since Henri was at least two decades older than the twenty-something artists, I assumed he meant it in a kindly way. Unfortunately, the name had caught on, and now everyone in the village referred to them as "the girls."

The blue-veined woman was Irma O'Kay, who lived in a stone cottage at the corner of Lilac Lane, a fifteen-minute walk from my own Rose Cottage. Irma's beautiful water-colors were easier to spot in the village than Irma herself. It must be quite a contest to lure the reclusive artist out of her studio. Although, from a brief conversation once at the grocer's, I knew Irma volunteered with the elderly. Perhaps she was more comfortable with shut-ins.

Zuly Sundae, Irma's best friend, stood beside her, both of them peering at the board. With their heads almost touching, Zuly's long, luxuriant black hair contrasted sharply with Irma's thin, mousy-brown waves.

The rest of the group crowded around, chatting and

pointing. An elegant silver-gray standard poodle stood off to one side, patiently waiting for its owner—a middle-aged woman in a sheepskin coat and leather gloves. The impeccably trained animal didn't even have a leash. I wondered if it had its own library card.

One person stood out—a scruffy young man wearing a Peruvian wool hat with tasseled earflaps. Rather than studying the board, he was smirking at the contestants. Unaware I was watching him, he burrowed a finger under his hat to scratch his scalp.

Turning, Irma caught sight of him. At the sudden change in her expression, I sucked in a breath. She was giving him a look of pure disgust.

He seemed not to notice.

Zuly touched her arm, and Irma turned away, back to the board.

"Hannah," I whispered. "Who's that guy in the hat? Standing next to the girls?"

She harrumphed. "Mickey Doig. Probably posting a notice about his dog-walking business. Or some other nonsense." Hannah leaned over the desk to point to my book, which was the only one on the *Returns* cart. "Here—I can take that."

I handed it over, surprised by her zeal to keep on top of returns. Normally, Hannah would be sipping a cup of tea and talking books with one of the patrons while the volumes piled up. Perhaps she was stepping up her supervision because Emy's mom, librarian extraordinaire Thérèse Dionne, was away on a much-deserved Caribbean vacation.

Sighing with envy, I imagined myself drinking a mai tai on the beach under a blistering tropical sun.

Resignedly, I returned my attention to the contest. "Is the crossword on the bulletin board?" I asked.

"It is. Take a look. Maybe you can guess the missing clues."

Obediently, I swiveled to face the board with my elbows propped on the desk behind me. "How does it work?"

"The blank puzzle appeared on the library's front desk a few days ago. We didn't know what it was until people started finding clues all over the village. They bring them here, then everybody debates the answers and we post the best guesses on the board. It's fun."

I liked crosswords as much as the next person, but they were rarely fascinating enough to interest an entire village. "Why is everybody so engrossed? It's only a puzzle."

"Oh, that's easy," Hannah said. "The grand prize is one million dollars."

"Emy told me that at the bakery, but I find it hard to believe."

"It's on the puzzle. Take a look."

I walked over to examine the board. The crossword puzzle was posted dead center. Rows of stick-on notes adorned its borders like ruffles on a Victorian ballgown. Each note held a potential clue. And sure enough, the title across the top read, THE MILLION-DOLLAR MYSTERY. It seemed a leap to take that obvious hyperbole as truth. Perhaps the impending storm of the century was making people lightheaded.

So far, five clues and answers were filled in.

ACROSS

3 Like-minded persons
5
6
9 Ruminants' home
10
11 Betwixt and between

DOWN

1 Month of showers
2
4
7 How many toes
8

My mother had been a professor of ancient languages, so I was good at word games. I even managed to crack the Latin password on my aunt's laptop when she was missing. I couldn't help but try to fill in the missing squares in my head. For instance, it was quite possible the answers to the clues for eight down, eleven across, and three across spelled out the phrase:

KILLERS AMONGST US

Which proved I really did have murder on the brain—because, depending on the missing clue, "killers" could just as easily be "pillows." Come to think of it, pillows could be used to— Yikes. I *did* have murder on the brain.

However, I wasn't the only person to betray a flair for the

macabre. Along with *pillows*, the words *tillers*, *billets*, and *killers* were written on multiple notes.

I wandered back to the desk. "Who started this contest? The village business association?"

Hannah shrugged. "Maybe."

"How could they afford a million dollars?"

"We think it's an annuity," she said, sagely tapping the side of her nose.

As a former bookkeeper, I knew all about annuities. The only million-dollar annuity the village association could afford would be paid out over centuries. I kept that thought to myself. "But why *killers?*" I pointed to the posted notes. "Seems morbid."

"It's all in fun. No harm meant."

I wondered how she knew that.

"Oh—I have a good one," blurted a woman in a puffy parka standing beside the poodle. She plopped her tote bag onto the floor, rummaged through it for a pencil, and left it on the floor while she wrote, *Six across: B-U-T-T-E-R*. She stuck the note on the board.

Everyone nodded as she stepped back with the pencil in her hand.

"That could work," someone said approvingly.

Beaming, the woman retrieved her bag to drop in the pencil, then opened the tote wider, looking confused. "That's odd. I could have sworn my wallet was here a moment ago. Has anyone seen a wallet?" she asked, glancing around.

"Not me."

"Nope."

At the front desk, Hannah held up a jangling basket overflowing with key chains, abandoned memory sticks, and mismatched gloves. "Did you check lost and found?"

While the wallet owner rummaged through the basket, the poodle trotted over to nudge my leg. Absently, I patted its head. A tag hanging from its jeweled leather collar read *Cranberry*.

The poodle nudged me again, then sat obediently beside me. She had something leathery in her mouth. I bent over for a better look. Straightening up, I asked, "Is your wallet navy blue with white piping?"

"Did you find it?"

"It's right here," I said, trying not to snicker. But when I reached to take it from the poodle's mouth, she ran off, darting between two of the stacks and down the aisle.

"Get that dog," the tote-bag owner shouted, racing past me. "It has my wallet."

She was followed by the woman in the sheepskin coat. "Cranberry! What have you done?"

Hannah dropped the lost and found basket on the counter before dashing out from behind the desk to join the chase.

"Get her," someone yelled.

Cranberry's poufed head poked out from behind a bookcase, the wallet firmly clenched between her teeth.

"There she is," I shouted, pointing.

Cranberry bolted. A moment later, her swishing tail disappeared behind an easel with a *Library Safety First* display. The easel toppled over with a crash.

Irma and Zuly ran down adjacent bookcase aisles, colliding when they emerged at the end.

Surprisingly, Mickey Doig didn't laugh. Or even smirk. He was too busy sidling along the wall in the direction of the exit.

Returning my attention to the chase, I braced my feet and held out both arms, determined to stop Cranberry if she headed my way.

The poodle scampered out from behind a bookcase, trotted up to Mickey—who had reached the exit—and dropped the wallet at his feet.

Mickey regarded the battered object, his mouth twitching. "Will you look at that, eh?" Then he yanked open the door and swept out, tassels swaying.

I made my way over, gave Mickey's departing back a curious glance through the door's window—he was halfway down the block—and stooped to pick up the wallet.

"Good girl, Cranberry. Got it," I yelled, holding it aloft.

People emerged from all corners to surround us. They stood back to let the wallet owner through. I handed her the slightly damp billfold.

While she was turning it over in her hands, Cranberry's owner trotted up, puffing. "I'm so sorry," she said, gasping between sentences. "I'm afraid that's not the first wallet she's scooped when the owner wasn't looking. I can't imagine where she picked up such a bad habit."

I adopted a solemn look. "Poodles are natural retrievers. And smart."

"Too smart," agreed Cranberry's embarrassed owner. "Did she ruin it?"

The owner tucked it into her tote bag with a laugh. "It's fine—as long as Cranberry didn't use my credit cards."

"Luckily, she didn't have time to go next door to the butcher's," I said.

While the poodle's owner sputtered apologies, I headed over to the bulletin board to copy down the puzzle clues as well as the names of people who'd found them.

On my way out, Hannah leaned over the front desk to wink at me. "I told you it was exciting."

Nodding my head, I turned for a last look at the crossword. The same phrase leapt out at me, no matter how many combinations I tried.

Killers Amongst Us.

With a shudder, I headed for the exit. Given my history, I saw nothing in those words to be excited about.

CHAPTER FOUR

I COULDN'T RESIST a giggle when I left the library and saw my pickup truck on the street. Even three months after the big makeover, it remained a little startling. When our bookings had started to drop off the previous autumn, my landscaping assistant Lorne Lewins suggested a new paint job. "You're missing a marketing opportunity with that truck," he said. "You park it all over the village. Why not take advantage of that visibility? Let it make a statement."

Besides the fact Lorne had obviously reached the marketing module of his business classes, he had a point. So, I took the truck to our local paint shop for a refresh. I had to promise the owner free lawn care from here to eternity to pay for it, but it was worth it.

Proudly, I beamed at my Pepto-Bismol-pink pickup with the huge red roses on the doors and the gold-painted logo for Coming Up Roses Landscaping.

It definitely made a statement.

Unfortunately, when Lorne saw the new paint job, he had refused to drive it—or even be seen in it—for weeks. His beloved Emy pointed out it had been his idea, after all. "Okay," he said reluctantly. "But I'm not wearing a pink T-shirt."

Still grinning, I climbed into the truck and drove three blocks to Henri Vartan's house in the oldest part of the village. While Henri's mysterious wallet did not contain a contest clue, I was confident one would turn up in a quick search of his front yard. It was too much of a coincidence that all the other clues were found in discarded wallets. It must have fallen out.

Henri lived on a street of three-story nineteenth-century brick homes with wraparound porches that fairly screamed upper-crust—I could almost see the original signs: TRADESMEN USE BACK ENTRANCE. Carefully tended lawns and perennial gardens, shaded by massive beeches and elms, completed the picture of tranquil affluence. Even covered in snow, those sweeping gardens were impressive.

Henri's one-and-a-half-story house was dwarfed by its looming neighbors. Anywhere else in the village, the casual charm of its yellow stucco walls and brown wood trim would have stood out. On this street, it was a definite under-performer.

I strolled along the front walk and up the two stone steps that led to the door, carrying Emy's box of cookies. An engraved sign on the stucco said—HERITAGE HOME, indicating the house was at least a century old. The front half of a brass dachshund protruded from the eggplant-painted door. Gingerly, I raised the knocker by its ears and rapped sharply, wondering idly if the other half was inside.

The door was opened immediately by Henri, who must have been waiting in the foyer for me. His substantial bulk filled most of the frame, his hair was carefully combed over a shiny pate, and his ample red cheeks gave new meaning to the word "jolly." When Henri planted his stocking feet on either side of the opening, I noticed tiny knitted dachshunds cavorting across his green woolen-socked feet.

"Verity. Come on in." He stepped out of the way.

I followed, unable to resist the temptation to check the interior of the door for the dachshund's rear end. Sadly, nothing. Definitely a missed opportunity.

Plastic sheeting covered the shiny wooden floor and crunched under my feet. On the right, a staircase with an oak newel post carved with acanthus leaves led to the second floor. On the left, the entrance to the living room was cordoned off. More plastic sheets hung over the door, with a hand-lettered sign—No ADMITTANCE.

Under the sign, a real—and overweight—miniature dachshund with red pedicured nails and a Burberry plaid collar sat placidly.

"Say hello, Matisse," Henri urged.

The dachshund stared at me.

"Like the painter?" I asked, bending to pat its head.

Henri grinned, pointing to his chest. "Henri." Then he pointed at the dog. "Matisse. Get it?"

"Clever."

"Let's go upstairs. That's where I'm living these days."

I climbed the stairs after him. Matisse trailed behind, each hesitant step-hop an obvious challenge.

"Are you excited about the opening?" I asked.

"It's going to be great," Henri said over his shoulder. "The girls and I have been working hard on it."

"When's the big day?"

He waved a dismissive hand. "We haven't decided yet. We're aiming for spring, but there's a lot to do. Here we are. Let's go through into the kitchen. Oh, no—wait."

Henri swept his huge bulk around, nearly toppling me down the stairs. "I should give you a tour first," he enthused. "This is an historic dwelling. Let's begin at the front." He clomped down the hall.

I followed, maintaining a safe distance. Matisse mounted the final stair-hurdle and trudged along behind me.

Plush armchairs and a sofa with a large depression in the middle crowded the front room. Since the second-floor walls slanted to meet the ceiling, the artwork that covered them projected over our heads. Feeling claustrophobic, I walked over to the three-paneled window to look down on the street. I had to lean over the jammed bookcases that spanned the lower walls.

Matisse made a beeline for a cushioned dog bed covered in red velvet. Popping his front paws onto the edge, he willed the rest to follow. The little dog settled in, resting his head on the edge of the bed to watch us intently.

"What a lovely view," I said, wondering how a man as big as Henri could be comfortable in such cramped quarters. "Didn't you used to live downstairs?"

"Ah..." he exhaled loudly. "The sacrifices we make for art.

I still have a studio there, in the back. But otherwise"—he swept a hand through the air—"this is it. Let me show you the kitchen." He hustled down the hall.

With a sigh, Matisse hopped out of his scarlet bed and followed.

Henri ushered us into the tiny kitchen at the back. "Tea?"

After traipsing across the room, Matisse flopped onto a satin mat, also red. I sensed a color scheme at work.

"Sure," I said, tossing my shoulder bag onto a chair and mounding my puffy parka over it. I handed Henri the white cardboard box from the bakery. "Emy sent along her bacon-toffee shortbreads."

"Oooh. Nice." Henri lifted his shoulders, rubbing his hands in delight before accepting the box and rummaging around on the cluttered table for a putty knife to snip the string.

Once we were sitting at the kitchen table with mugs of tea in our hands, the box of enticing shortbreads between us, I asked Henri to tell me about the wallet.

"I'll show you. It's right here." While leaning over to root through a drawer, he repeated the story he'd told Emy. With a flourish, Henri placed the wallet—a cheap imitation-leather Alfred Sung knockoff—on the table in front of me.

I picked it up to scan the contents. "The police said these credit cards were—"

"Worthless. The ID was fake, too. They kept it."

"Emy told me. But why did they let you keep the credit cards?"

"I told them I wanted to use the cards in an art project. They agreed, finally, but insisted on punching holes through all of them." He rolled his eyes. "Kind of defeated the purpose."

"Was there a crossword clue in the wallet?"

"For that contest everybody's talking about? No. And before you ask," he raised a hand to stop me from speaking, "I double-checked the yard. There was nothing else out there."

I turned the wallet over in my hands. "Why weren't the police interested?"

Henri blew air through his lips in mock disgust. "It took them two days to check the contents. Once they realized it was all fake, they washed their hands of it. 'No evidence of wrongdoing,' they said."

I placed the wallet on the table before taking a sip of my tea. "Henri, don't you think it's odd you found a fake wallet while this contest is going on? All the clues have been found in empty wallets. None of them had ID in them—fake or otherwise—but it's a striking coincidence."

Mulling it over, I thought, *There are no coincidences— isn't that what Hercule Poirot always said?* Or was I thinking of Miss Marple? Maybe Aunt Adeline. Whatever. It still held true.

Henri's expression turned morose. "I suppose it is unlikely, when you put it like that."

"It's also suspicious. The contest, I mean."

"What are you saying?"

"Who's behind it? If there's a cash prize, as everyone seems to think, where is it coming from?" Frowning, I selected a smallish shortbread and bit off a chunk.

Henri straightened up, looking askance. "Verity, I had no idea you were such a cynic."

I squeezed my eyes shut. "I am not—"

"Everyone in the village has cabin fever. It's nice to have something to take our minds off the weather. They're calling for the—"

My eyes snapped open. "Storm of the century. Yes, I know."

"I suppose you don't believe that, either?"

Glancing through the kitchen window at the peaceful, swirling snowflakes, I said, "Not so far."

Henri merely harrumphed and plucked out a cookie.

Opening the billfold, I removed the three credit cards and spread them out on the table. "Do you know how that contest started?"

"Moi?" Surprise flashed over Henri's face. "No. I only heard about it yesterday. But it's exciting. Everybody's talking about it." After biting off a hunk of shortbread, he contemplated the wallet while chewing.

"It could be a fraud."

Henri puffed out a few crumbs in his astonishment. "A fraud? To what end?" He brushed the crumbs from his cardigan onto the floor. On his mat, Matisse perked up with interest before deciding the meager windfall wasn't worth leaving his bed for.

"I don't know, Henri. It's possible."

"Ridiculous."

With a shrug, I picked up each card in turn. The first thing I noticed was they lacked the usual heft of credit cards. The plastic was thin and bendable. "D. Smith" was the name on all three accounts, and the scrawled signature was illegible. I licked the end of my finger before running it across the magnetic stripe on the back. A smear of black ink stained my fingertip.

"The police said they've seen plenty of fake cards like those," Henri said. "A counterfeit ring in Strathcona churned out a bunch of them, they said."

"What for? You can't buy anything with fakes."

He shrugged. "Identity theft, maybe?"

After replacing the cards in the wallet, I pulled out the twenty-dollar bill. I held it up to the light coming through the window, more because Henri was regarding me expectantly than because I expected to find anything.

"This is a regular bill," I said. "They're hard to counterfeit, what with the hologram and the special features. The synthetic polymer they're printed on is fairly sturdy. That's why it didn't disintegrate in the snow." I flipped it over to scrutinize the back. Peering at it, I noticed something odd. "Do you have a photographer's loupe?"

After another rummage through the drawer, Henri handed me one. I pressed it against my eye while flattening the bill upon the tabletop.

Under the magnifying lens, tiny letters were visible.

Aloud, I read, "5 G-R-E-E-N S-P-A-C-E."

Each letter and number was etched on a different block of the First World War memorial to Canadian dead at Vimy, France depicted on the twenty-dollar bill. It would have taken a steady hand wielding a pen with a superfine nib to fit them on.

Straightening up, I put the loupe on the table and pulled out my copy of the crossword puzzle. "Look. That fits. Five across. Starts with a 'P.' Could the answer be—P-A-R-K?"

Henri's look of excitement was contagious. I handed him the bill and the loupe, so he could look for himself.

He hunkered over the table with the lens pressed to his eye. "It *is* part of the contest," he said with a triumphant air. "Green Space—PARK. Verity, you solved it. I knew you would."

I eyed the twenty-dollar bill in his hand, my brief moment of excitement already evaporating. Now the villagers would not only comb the area for wallets, they'd check every twenty-dollar bill before they spent it. I envisioned long lineups at local cash registers—including the one at the 5X Bakery. Emy might regret Shanice's embrace of Leafy Hollow's latest obsession. Far from downplaying the contest craze, I'd made it worse by finding another clue.

"I haven't solved anything," I insisted. "This is as much of a mystery as ever."

From his mat in the corner, Matisse stirred and sat up. It was possible he expected a treat since a kitchen drawer had been opened—not once, but twice. He gave a gentle yip.

"Sorry, boy." After pulling a biscuit from a dachshund-shaped cookie jar on the counter, Henri tossed it over. "You deserve a reward, considering you discovered this clue."

"What?"

He laughed. "I didn't tell you, but Matisse found the wallet."

"But you said—"

"I may have embellished that tale a bit. Truth is I felt kind of dumb for not seeing it there before. But the weather has been frightful. So, I opened the door and let Matisse pee outside. My neighbors are a bit touchy about that, but I figured nobody would notice, what with the snow and all. And when he cocked his leg, I saw—"

"Wait a minute." I gripped the billfold gingerly between thumb and forefinger while holding it as far away from me as possible. "Are you telling me Matisse peed on this?"

Henri pursed his lips, contemplating the wallet. "I wiped it off."

"Great. Do you at least have a plastic bag?"

Once the wallet and its contents were ensconced in a baggie, and I'd washed my hands, I retrieved my parka. While zipping it up, I asked, "What exactly do you want me to do?"

"I want you to find out who dropped that wallet in my front yard."

"Does it matter? It's just another clue in this ridiculous contest."

"Maybe, but I don't like the idea of strangers tossing things onto my property. Especially with the gallery's official opening coming up. I think you should investigate. Besides—" He leaned in closer. "The crossword puzzle at the library includes a rather ominous reference."

"You mean—*killers amongst us?*"

"Exactly. And now that we know this wallet is connected, I'm even more worried."

Henri's note of caution struck me as completely justified. Having been too close for comfort to more than one killer, this village mania hit too close to home for me. "You agree with me, then, that the contest could be a fraud?"

Henri's eyebrows rose in surprise. "Certainly not. I think it's perfectly genuine."

"Then why do you want me to look into it?"

"I just told you."

"I'm not sure what I can do." With a sigh, I turned to the stairs.

"Well, for starters—could you post my clue on your way past the library?"

I paused with my hand on the newel post to look back over my shoulder. "Under your name? But you said you were worried about all this."

"I am. But that's no reason to turn down a million dollars."

CHAPTER FIVE

THE PARKING LOT at Pine Hill Peak was deserted when Mickey backed his battered van into a carefully chosen spot. The pet owners who hired *Mickey's Dog Care* to exercise their dogs would be surprised to learn its daily operation involved very little exercise—for Mickey, at least. He regarded that as a colossal waste of time. Why walk animals that were perfectly capable of walking themselves?

But he liked to keep one eye on the road, in case anyone driving by might wonder why he was sitting in the van while the dogs were doing, well, whatever dogs do when left to their own devices. His standard cover story—that he ran out of bags and came back to the van for more—wouldn't work if someone found him napping. If he selected his vantage point just right, he could hear oncoming vehicles before the drivers spotted him.

Unfortunately, his favorite spot hadn't been plowed since the last storm. The van's carriage crunched, rocking, as it traversed the hard-packed snow. From the driver's seat, Mickey urged the vehicle on. Then, with one foot on the brake, he assessed his sight lines to the road. Satisfied, he leaned over the passenger's seat to prop open the far door.

"Everybody out," he called.

A black lab, silver-gray standard poodle, and border collie scrabbled over the permanently reclined passenger seat, jostling energetically to be the first to make a break for it. Once free, they bolted into the parking lot. Within seconds, they'd made their way into the field beyond.

Mickey glanced in the rearview mirror.

The final member of his regulars, a chunky beagle, stared back at him, her deep brown eyes imploring Mickey to reconsider. The embroidered slogan on her gray fleece hoodie read, *My big brother is a wolf.*

"You, too, Pixi. Move it."

Pixi whimpered, implying she was too nervous to brave the great outdoors.

Mickey sighed. He was itching to go over the contents of Oskar's red shoebox. He had no time to indulge a spoiled mutt.

Technically, Pixi wasn't a mutt. Her owners had explained her pedigree at great length when they hired Mickey. He had nodded solemnly throughout their presentation, although his thoughts soon strayed to other pedigrees. Ones that might lead to a windfall at the track.

But mutt or purebred, Pixi had to exit the van so he could concentrate on the afternoon's money-making ventures. After opening the glovebox, he rummaged about until his fingers closed on a desiccated dog biscuit covered in lint. He tossed it out the open passenger door.

"Get it," he warbled in his best approximation of a dog trainer he'd watched once on TV, back when he was hoping to pick up a few tips. He had quickly abandoned that research. Way too much pointless exercise.

The beagle scrambled out of the van. After snapping up the treat, she trotted over to check out the other dogs' activity in the field. Mickey watched her suspiciously. He could never decide whether Pixi was timid or smart.

After closing the door to keep the heat in—frost had already iced the back window even though the engine was running—he retrieved a half-smoked joint from his shirt pocket and lit it. A little dope would steady his nerves. He took a long drag, then leaned back against the seat with his eyes closed before exhaling.

It had been two days since he found Old Man York's body, and no one had reported the death. Which meant that, technically at least, Mickey was still on the hook. But he'd been over and over it in his mind, and he couldn't think of anything that pointed to him.

Once, in the middle of the night, he bolted upright in his friend Willy's basement, heart pounding, awakened by the fear that he left fingerprints on the old man's slipper. Lying there, listening to the furnace whoosh on and the overhead vents creak, he realized that, yes, there might be fingerprints. But those were easily explained, because he'd been to York's house before. Many times. With a sigh of relief, he'd gone back to sleep.

But the arrival of morning had not lessened his anxiety, because the old man's death brought another problem into stark focus—Mickey's regrettable lack of funds. Without access to York's belongings, he had no new items to sell. He couldn't risk passing on the gold watch and brooch. Not yet, anyway. What if he was being watched? He didn't think he was, but what if he was wrong? Yesterday, while he was parked at the conservation area, several vehicles had driven by on the usually deserted road. He could have sworn the same gray sedan went by twice. That was just nerves, though. Gray sedans were everywhere.

He puffed a few more times on the joint before deciding he was being paranoid. If no one had found York's body yet, how could *anybody* be under suspicion, never mind Mickey? Nobody was following him, either. That was a—what had that medical guy called it? A *delusion*. Drug-induced, the guy had claimed, but that was nonsense. It was more likely brought on by old Uma always watching him and complaining under her breath. Who wouldn't have delusions if they had to deal with that all the time?

As for the financial embarrassment issue, he might have a solution for that. Before Cranberry pulled her ill-timed stunt at the library, those artists had been talking about a new gallery. Wouldn't a gallery need photographs? Village history and so forth? Sucking on the last of the roach before stubbing it out between his fingers, he mulled this over. Sadly, there was bad blood between him and those artists. He'd need a go-between. The perfect person had been right there in the library, yucking it up with those annoying artistic types— Verity Hawkes, the village's self-styled private eye. She claimed to be a landscaper, but he could see through that smokescreen.

He would drop in on Verity at his earliest convenience. Later today, possibly.

Flicking the joint into the ashtray, he retrieved the red shoebox from under the driver's seat and flipped off the lid.

Photos. Photos. More photos. He shuffled through the contents quickly until he reached the bottom. A printed paper appeared promising. When he unfolded it to take a closer look, his mood darkened. It was a crossword puzzle. A dumb old crossword puzzle that Oskar probably copied from —wait. Why would the old man bother copying a crossword?

He rubbed his forehead with both hands, trying to think, then examined the puzzle again. Obviously, his lack of sleep was catching up with him. He yawned, shook his head, and refocused on the paper. Several clues reminded him of the puzzle posted in the library. His finger traced through the tiny boxes.

Killers.

Amongst.

Us.

Yes—it was the same. But in this version of the puzzle, all the clues were listed, and all the answers filled in. What a find! If Mickey had the answers, what was to prevent him from winning the contest? It was worth a million bucks, according to those busybodies at the library.

He leaned back, yawning. He really was getting sleepy.

Closing his eyes, he wiggled slightly, trying to get comfortable. Before long, snores echoed off the van's metal walls.

Scritch-scritch-scritch.

Mickey twisted restlessly in his seat. "Stop," he muttered.

Scritch-scritch-scritch.

Groggily, he opened one eye. "Stop it."

Scritch-scritch-scritch.

In the passenger window, the flapping ears and sad brown eyes of a beagle appeared. Disappeared. Reappeared.

Mickey flopped over on the seat to push open the door, yawning so heavily the joints in his jaw cracked. Chilly air flooded in. He massaged the sides of his face and straightened up. With a wince, he realized his head was aching, too.

Pixi the beagle clambered inside, followed shortly by the black lab and the silver poodle, with the border collie bringing up the rear by nipping at their heels. The dogs lined up expectantly in the back of the van.

Mickey got out to stretch his legs, stamping his feet to ease the tingling. While there, he swiveled to face the snow-bank. The van's tailpipe was neatly shoved into the ice.

Get a load of that, he thought admiringly. Couldn't do that again if he tried.

He got back into the van and pulled out of the parking spot, the vehicle's rear end crunching as the tailpipe pulled free of the snow.

CHAPTER SIX

EVEN THOUGH I'D promised to investigate the origin of the crossword clue on Henri's twenty-dollar bill, it would have to wait. I had a more pressing appointment—in my kitchen, preparing a surprise dinner for Jeff. It was our four-month anniversary, and I planned to mark it with his favorite dishes.

Not only that, but I wanted to make Emy eat her words. *We talked about this, Verity.* Ha! Wait until she saw the photo of my finished spread. She'd soon change her assessment of my culinary skills. The bakery's loss was Jeff's gain.

To be honest, he was a far better cook than me. His lasagna was to die for.

I glanced at the clock in the pickup's dash. Assuming Leafy Hollow's criminals took the afternoon off, Jeff would arrive for dinner at six. That gave me two hours to make meatloaf, scalloped potatoes, roasted daikon—I'd never eaten Japanese radish, but it was home cooking to Jeff—and apple pie. Plenty of time. I'd have to pick up ice cream, though. And chocolate sauce—in case my first attempt at piecrust was less than perfect and I had to ditch the pie.

Just thinking about that pastry made me nervous. I wasn't sure why I considered it important to prepare a perfect meal. Jeff was never less than complimentary about my cooking. And it was such a girly thing to do—so unlike me. One of Jeff's former dates—a blonde in four-inch heels—flashed before my eyes. I bet she knew how to make a piecrust.

Oh, my gosh. I drew in a breath. Was I... jealous?

I thumped my hand against the wheel.

Think about something else, Verity.

Instead of recipes, I reviewed my plan to interview the other crossword clue finders. The list I'd copied from the bulletin board was a good start. I didn't recognize the names, but Emy would. First thing in the morning, I'd go by the bakery and enlist her help. With any luck, Shanice would have set up the duplicate board and lured the clue holders into the bakery. That was a cheerful thought, since it meant I could begin my first official investigation with a coconut-lemon scone and a mug of piping-hot coffee.

I considered buying a laser pointer at the office-goods store in the morning. Too officious? Maybe, but it couldn't hurt. A package of sticky notes wouldn't go amiss, either. Not to mention a yellow highlighter, a box of 2B pencils, and a sharpener. I should make a list.

After my stop at the convenience store for ice cream, where I waited in line at the cash register behind four lottery-ticket buyers—honestly, the biggest mystery in Leafy Hollow was why no one ever won the lottery, given the number of tickets sold—I took a shortcut, so I could skip Main Street on my way to Rose Cottage. Normally that detour shaved several minutes off my journey, but today a police cruiser blocked the route.

Halting my truck, I peered through the windshield for the cause of the holdup. I glanced at the dashboard clock. My convenience store visit had taken ten minutes longer than expected. Should I reverse and take my chances with Main Street's flashing pedestrian crossings? If the seniors' Sit & Fit class had just ended, I might be there a while.

The cruiser's driver was directing traffic up a side street. After turning off the engine, I slid out of the cab and strolled over to the constable. No harm in asking for details.

"What's wrong?" I asked.

Two more cruisers and an ambulance were parked outside a house with dented aluminum siding in the middle of the block. Another officer was unspooling yellow caution tape across the front yard, threading it over the rusted legs of a wheelbarrow sticking out from the snow.

I let out a low whistle, because I knew whose house this was. Everyone did. It was notorious, according to Hannah, the Leafy Hollow librarian.

"Has something happened to Oskar York?"

The constable's frown was grim. "I can't say."

I recognized him—and his expression. Fred was a member of Jeff's darts team. Many times, I'd seen the same display of grim determination over missiles poised for flight at The Tipsy Jay.

I flashed my most winsome smile. "Come on, Fred. You can tell me."

49

He lowered his voice. "Okay, Verity. But this is between us."

I crossed my heart in a gesture of solidarity.

"They found him dead this morning."

"Heart attack?"

Fred winced. "Crushed."

My indrawn breath was immediate. "Crushed? That's horrible." I'd never been in Oskar York's house—or even met him—but from all descriptions, it was jammed with stuff. Mountains of it, apparently, some reaching to the ceiling. Irma O'Kay, the reclusive artist, had once told me she delivered Meals on Wheels to Oskar. We had been lined up at the grocer's cash register, and Irma must have recognized a fellow introvert. Or maybe she was just anxious to get out of there. Anyway, she babbled on about claustrophobic tunnels that snaked between towers of magazines and newspapers, boxes of clothing, tangled bric-a-brac, and flattened plastic bottles. What had she called his house? *A death trap.*

I narrowed one eye. "Are you saying something fell on him?"

Fred nodded glumly.

"When did this happen?"

"We were called in this morning, but his body had been there for several days."

I glanced over Fred's head. Since I was five-ten, and he was one of the force's shorter constables, it wasn't hard. With a sinking heart, I saw Jeff's cruiser parked across the street from Oskar's house. "Will the detectives have to work late?"

"I doubt it. It's going to be classified as an accident—Oh. Don't repeat that."

"Never." I crossed my heart again.

"The scene's been photographed." He shrugged. "But I expect we'll maintain a presence on the street until it's cleared up."

"Which could take days."

He nodded.

That meant dinner was still on. I felt bad about Fred's enforced guard duty, not to mention Oskar's horrible death, but none of that changed my dinner plans. An unexpected encounter with a dead person would make my stomach heave —and had, in the past—but it took a lot to turn seasoned police officers off their grub.

I got back into the truck, abandoned my detour for the usual route—no sign of the senior fitness enthusiasts, fortunately—and arrived at Rose Cottage fifteen minutes later. The trees that lined Lilac Lane were heavy with ice. I'd never seen the branches of the magnificent chestnut a few doors from Rose Cottage lean so low. Several were brushing the power line strung underneath.

While staring at the sagging branches in my rearview mirror, I wheeled the truck into my driveway. I had to slam on the brakes to avoid running into a battered white van parked in my usual spot—*Mickey's Dog Care*, according to the faded sign on its side.

That was weird. No dogs here.

As I turned off the engine, a scruffy young man wearing a parka and a wool hat with earflaps got out of the van and offered a languid wave. It was Mickey Doig, the smirking onlooker from the library.

I jumped out of the truck, turning to slam the door before asking, "Can I help you?"

"Verity Hawkes? Coming Up Roses landscaping?"

"Yes." I didn't mean to be rude, but there wasn't much call for lawn cutting in January. If this guy even had a lawn, which I doubted.

Plus, as I'd already mentioned—no dogs.

"I'm Mickey Doig. And, like, I need your help." The tasseled earflaps bobbed as he held out his hand.

In January? I thought as I grasped his outstretched fingers. He was wearing mittens with a flap that folded back over the hand. I had a pair myself—it was the best way to keep your hands warm when doing precision work in cold weather, like pruning small branches in early spring. Or picking up after dogs.

I gave his hand a tepid shake. "It's a little early in the season for lawn care."

"Pretty much, yeah." He glanced vaguely at my snow-covered front yard, then added with a chuckle, "Like, where the frick is the lawn, eh?"

"So—why are you here?"

"I was hoping... could I come in? To explain?"

"I'm in a hurry. Can it wait?" I struggled through the snowdrifts over the front walk. Not much point in shoveling it, since there was more on the way. Snow shoveling was a little like housework—it was never done. Unlike housework, however, if you waited long enough—snow melted on its own.

Mickey followed me up the steps to my new porch, which had been replaced after an arson attack the previous summer. It was holding up well, I noted with satisfaction as I stamped my boots by the front door.

"Like, it's a bit tricky." Mickey gave me a forlorn look. "But I really need your help."

Momentarily, I reviewed the wisdom of inviting a total stranger into my home. But apart from a battered red shoebox he held under one arm, I saw no weapon. Also, Mickey was scrawny. In fact, that was a generous assessment. By the looks of him, a square meal was not at the top of his daily to-do list. Any one of my Krav Maga moves would take care of this guy.

And if that wasn't enough, an armed police officer would be here before long. If Mickey tried anything on Jeff's girlfriend, he'd be minus a head—I pictured his tasseled hat rolling across the yard, and giggled inwardly. Then the phrase "Jeff's girlfriend" momentarily distracted me, and I giggled again. It just had that effect on me.

Mickey's forlorn expression escalated to one of utter despondency. I didn't fall for that, naturally, but it was annoying enough that I wanted it to stop.

"Okay. But five minutes is all I have."

I opened the door, motioning him across the threshold. Once inside, I tossed my parka over the nearest armchair and turned to face him with my eyebrows raised.

He held out the shoebox with both hands. "It's about this."

I hesitated. "What's that?"

"Old photos, mostly. Knickknacks. Jewelry and stuff." He gestured for me to take the box.

I heaved a sigh. "Put it on the coffee table. And sit down."

After plunking the box on the table, Mickey perched on the edge of the armchair.

I sat on the sofa across from him, then pulled the box toward me. "Photos, you said?"

"And jewelry."

"And you want me to look at it because?"

"You're an investigator, right? I need your opinion."

My brow furrowed as I considered this request. How could Mickey know about my new venture? I hadn't even bought accordion file folders yet. "When did you—?"

"I heard about it at the bakery."

Ah. Emy must be trying to drum up business for me.

I assessed the worn edges of Mickey's parka, his unkempt hair, and his two-day stubble—long enough to be visible, but not groomed enough to be deliberate. I also detected a faint whiff of... Was that *weed*?

This guy was never going to pay me—that was obvious. But it appeared the only way to get him out of Rose Cottage was to take a look at his "stuff." I flipped open the box.

It was, indeed, filled with photos. A few were faded pictures from the seventies and eighties, others older. But none were recent. The cell phone camera put an end to printed photos. Everything was online now, in the cloud.

At the bottom of the box lay a bracelet, two rings, and a child-sized chain necklace with dangling charms that spelled Lucy. Even with my uneducated eye, I could see they were worthless.

"Are these your photos? Family, maybe?"

"No. I picked them up at a flea market, like. Pretty much. That one by the highway that's only open Sundays. I think."

"You think?"

He shrugged. "Can't really remember."

Dropping the lid back on, I slid the shoebox across the coffee table to him. "What do you want me to do with them?" I glanced at the clock. Ninety minutes to dinner. And I hadn't done anything yet. Even my easygoing boyfriend wouldn't consider triple-chocolate ice cream a meal.

I leaned forward on the sofa, hoping to impart some urgency to Mickey, and raised my eyebrows again.

"Those photos are valuable," he blurted.

I gave an involuntary start of surprise. "I don't think so. But I'm not an expert," I added quickly.

"You'd be surprised at the things people will pay for. Old pictures can be useful. Artists, for instance. They need them for, like, those mixed-up things that have all those other things on them."

Wracking my brain to make sense of this, I finally offered, "Collages?"

"Yeah." He brightened. "Collages."

"Mickey." I adopted my most professional tone. "What exactly do you want me to investigate?"

His expression changed again, this time to a near-perfect depiction of *shifty used-car salesman.* "I was hoping you'd ask that artist guy if he'd buy them from me."

I sat back, confused. Clearly, my anxiety about making dinner had caused me to lapse into momentary unconsciousness. When did we go from *please investigate* to *please pimp out my stuff?*

"What artist are you talking about?"

"You know, that Vartan guy you saw this afternoon."

"Do you mean Henri Vartan?"

He nodded. "That's the guy."

"How do you know I saw Henri this afternoon?"

Shifty used-car salesman made a reappearance. "I might have witnessed said visit."

"Witnessed—as in stalked? Were you *stalking* me?"

"No! Not... exactly."

"Not exactly? But you did follow me, correct?"

"No. Maybe a little."

"A *little*?" My professionalism faltered as I consider the effectiveness of various Krav Maga moves. One that involved heaving the recipient across the room came to mind. Rising to my feet with a commendable lack of violence, I said haughtily, "I think it's time you left."

Mickey slid the shoebox over to my side of the coffee table. "I really need your help."

"No, you don't. You can visit Henri yourself. Now, if you don't mind—" I pointed to the front door. Leaning over, I grabbed his upper arm to heave him out of the chair.

He resisted. "I can't. Vartan won't listen to me. I have a... rep with those artists."

Despite my desire to get him out of there, I was intrigued. Momentarily, I relaxed my grip. "For what, exactly?"

"It's, like, so harsh. They threw me off their bowling team over a little mix-up."

Since I had an unfortunate bowling incident in my own past, this piqued my interest. "Go on." Straightening, I folded my arms, regarding him silently.

"They claimed I threw a tournament. For money. Imagine." He gave a wild wave of his hand. "After that, stuff got weird."

Before I could ask for details, he continued, words spilling out. "It's all BS, of course. But it means I can't ask the guy directly. On the other hand, Verity Hawkes is a respected member of the community. Famous, even. You could give him the box, all serious like, and not tell him where it came from. Then, after he pays you—"

I held up a hand to halt this stream of nonsense. "Absolutely not. That has nothing to do with investigating, and I'm not your patsy."

"I'll give you a cut."

I picked up the shoebox and shoved it at him. "No. Time to go." Leaning over, I grabbed his arm again and tugged him upright.

But instead of turning to the door, Mickey twisted out of my grasp and crumpled into the armchair, clutching the shoebox to his chest. His earflap tassels swayed as he shook his head.

"I'm not taking no for an answer," he muttered.

"You're not—wait, what?"

He hunkered in the chair, shoulders raised, clinging to the shoebox.

I could have forcibly tossed him out, but time was running out and I didn't want to waste any of it rearranging the living room.

"Fine," I snapped. "Leave the box here, and I'll see what I can do. But you have to go."

Dropping the box on the coffee table, Mickey leapt to his feet. "Thanks, Verity. You're a pal."

After marching to the door, I wrenched it open. "Out."

Once he was gone, I picked up the shoebox, shoved it into the bookcase in the dining nook, and promptly forgot all about it.

A decision I would live to regret.

CHAPTER SEVEN

WHEN ARMY GRUNTS peeled potatoes in old-time Hollywood musicals, they always managed an endless strip of peel that practically jumped off the spud and into the bin. In real life, peeling potatoes was arduous work. And finicky. After poking out my hundredth potato eye with a paring knife, I assessed my progress. The aluminum bowl beside me was barely half full, and the potatoes I had successfully peeled were already turning brown. Emy's scalloped potatoes were always perfectly white, perfectly peeled, and perfectly sliced. And her cheese sauce—I sucked in a breath, staring wide-eyed at the potatoes. I'd forgotten to buy cheese.

My gaze drifted to the pile of apples sitting next to the unpeeled spuds. I hadn't started the piecrust yet, either. In fact, only one component of my fantasy meal was done—the meatloaf, which was bubbling away. *Maybe I should check on it again.* Opening the oven, I admired the perfect brown crust forming on the top before shutting the door and turning back to the counter. The pile of potatoes had not gotten any smaller while I'd been checking the meatloaf.

From his perch on a kitchen chair, the General watched me intently, head tilted. "*Mrack?*"

"Where's the piecrust, you're asking? Me, too."

"*Mrack?*" General Chang hopped off the chair and strutted, tail swishing, to his empty dish.

After retrieving a bag of kibble from the cupboard, I topped up his dish. The General took a delicate sniff before sitting down to gnaw at a troublesome claw on his hind leg.

Rolling my eyes, I returned the kibble to the cupboard and reassessed the potatoes. I had to start the piecrust, peel the apples, and get the daikon into—uh-oh, where was the daikon? It was one of Jeff's favorite dishes, and I wanted to get it right. Hastily, I filled a pot of water in the sink and transferred it to a burner set on high to blanch the daikon—when I found it.

My cell phone rang while I was transferring plates and cutlery from the cupboard to the last clear space on the kitchen table. After pushing flour, sugar, and butter out of the way, picking up the General—who had returned to his perch on the chair—and plonking him on the floor, I found the phone. "Yes?"

"Verity. Thank goodness I caught you."

"Aunt Adeline? Is something wrong?"

"I hope not. It's the storm. I forgot to tell you—"

My aunt launched into a lengthy list of bad-weather preparations that might have included building an igloo in the backyard. I couldn't say for certain since my attention kept wandering to the unpeeled potatoes. And the piecrust recipe I'd taped to the fridge door, under Carson and Reuben's Key West selfie. Inwardly, I cursed my failure to check call display before answering. My aunt was halfway through a warning to check the eaves for icicles before stepping outside—"A falling icicle can kill you"—when I interrupted her.

"I'm really busy, Aunt Adeline, making dinner for Jeff."

"The well has an electric pump, Verity. Don't forget. When the power goes out, you won't have any water. Make sure you've filled the bathtub and several buckets."

"I will. But I'm really busy—"

"Making dinner for Jeff. I got that. Why can't he make his own dinner? He's not an infant."

Sometimes my aunt's feminist side got the better of her.

"He's perfectly capable of making dinner, but I wanted to do it tonight. Because..." My voice faded. Aunt Adeline was fond of Jeff, I knew that. She didn't need an explanation.

"You sound stressed."

"I didn't leave enough time, and nothing's ready."

"Can't you order pizza?"

"It's our four-month anniversary."

"Four months?" asked my puzzled aunt. "Is that even a thing?"

"Umm..."

"Never mind. We can fix it. Tell me what you've done so far."

While I was explaining about the unpeeled potatoes, the unpeeled apples, the missing daikon, the forgotten cheese, and the total lack of piecrust, I noticed the General peering intently at the stove. With a sniff, I realized that something was... *burning*.

Dropping the phone and diving for the oven mitts, I opened the oven door. Puffs of smoke emerged. The meat-loaf's lovely brown crust had significantly deepened in color. All the way to black.

"What happened?" came a tinny voice from the floor.

"The meatloaf," I wailed. "It's burnt." After placing it on the stovetop, I pulled off the mitts and picked up the phone. "It's only been in the oven for half an hour."

"Verity." My aunt's voice was calm and reassuring. "What temperature did you set the oven at?"

"Four-fifty."

"That's a little high for meatloaf."

"I know, but I'm running late and I wanted it to cook faster." I swiveled to assess the peeled potatoes in their metal bowl. At the rate they were discoloring, they'd match the meatloaf before long. A hissing caused me to whirl back to face the stove.

The pot of water was boiling over.

Dropping the phone on the table, I grabbed a tea towel to slide the pot off the burner. Hot water slopped over the side and onto the meatloaf.

"Oh, no," I moaned.

"Verity," came a calm, but still tinny, voice from the table. "What have you done?"

Picking up the phone, I explained.

"It's not too late to order pizza," Adeline said.

"I guess."

"Don't sound so dejected. I was kidding. You can fix this."

"How?"

"Put the phone on speaker, and I'll walk you through it. First, dump those potatoes into the boiling water."

"They're not peeled."

"Doesn't matter. Roughage is popular these days."

"What about slicing them?"

"You're no longer making scalloped potatoes. You're making mashed potatoes. If you add enough butter, Jeff won't even notice the difference."

I did as she instructed. Once the potatoes were bubbling away, I asked: "Now what?"

"The meatloaf. Set the oven to three-fifty, drain off the water, scrape away the burnt layer, and put it back in the oven. It'll be ready in an hour."

"Done."

"Now we make dessert. Core and slice the apples—don't peel them—mix them with brown sugar and butter, then put them in a baking dish. Remember my crumble recipe?"

"Sort of."

"I'll walk you through it. It's easy."

Once the apple crumble had joined the meatloaf in the oven, and I was mashing the cooked potatoes, I brought Adeline up to date on Oskar York.

"I heard about it," she said. "Poor man."

"I don't know why I bother telling you anything. And I've run out of time to set the table."

"Eat in the kitchen, kiddo. Men love that."

Outside, a car horn beeped.

"Jeff's here. Gotta go. Thanks for your help."

"Verity. About the storm—"

"I'll be careful. And thank you." I clicked END CALL on my way out of the kitchen.

Before Jeff got out of his black pickup, I was at the front door. I waved from the doorway, not willing to step outside and ruin my new down slippers in the foot-high drifts on the front walk.

Jeff bounded up the walk and the stairs until he reached the door, where he swept me up for a big kiss.

"Wow," I said a few moments later, trying to get my breath back. "That was something. I only saw you this morning."

"I missed you," he whispered, his lips brushing my ear.

I settled in for another kiss, even though the door was wide open, the wind was howling, and the snow—

"What's with all the snow, by the way?" Jeff asked, taking a step back to assess the front porch.

Biting my lip, I evaluated the frosty boards. "I haven't shoveled yet."

Jeff grinned. "You really hate snow, don't you?"

"You would, too, if you'd been living in Vancouver for years. I'd almost forgotten what snow looked like."

"I'll do it," he said.

"No." Grabbing his arm, I pulled him through the door and closed it. "You had a busy day. I drove by Oskar York's house earlier. What happened?"

He grimaced. "Later."

"Are you still going to Strathcona tomorrow for that two-day departmental meeting?"

"Yeah. It's bad timing, though. If this storm gets worse, I'll have to come back early."

"I made meatloaf," I said, trying to cheer him up.

He brightened. "What's the occasion?"

I took a step back, feigning disappointment. "Have you forgotten?"

"Ah... maybe?"

"It's our four-month anniversary."

"Oh." His brow wrinkled in confusion. "Four months? Is that even a thing? Because—I didn't get you a present."

I heaved a sigh. "So much for the 'love that shall not die.'"

"Shakespeare? Are things that bad?"

"Maybe not. I'm impressed you recognized that quote."

"You used it at our three-month anniversary."

"Which you also forgot. I'm detecting a pattern here—and it's not good."

Grinning, Jeff held up a finger. "I do have something for you." He ran back to the truck and opened the back door. When he turned around, he held a wriggling tan-and-white bundle in his arms. Four tiny feet pawed the air.

Arf-arf-arf.

"A dog? Seriously?"

"It belonged to Oskar York—it's some kind of terrier. The shelter was full for the night, and I couldn't leave him at the station."

"Bring him inside. It's cold out here."

The little dog squirmed when Jeff handed him over, but once I had hold of him, he snuggled against me. "He's shivering. Didn't you have a blanket in the truck?"

"Yes," Jeff patiently replied. "I wrapped him up in it, *and*

I warmed the truck before I put him inside. He wiggled out of the blanket and tried to jump into my lap. To be honest, I think he's a bit of a drama king."

I chucked the little dog under his chin. A worn metal tag, *Boomer*, was riveted onto his frayed leather collar.

"Are we a widdle dramah king? Are we?"

Jeff cocked his head, appearing incredulous. "Is that baby talk?"

I ignored this silly question. "Are we a good boy? *Are we? Yes, we are.*" I turned my attention to Jeff. "Did you pick up dog food?"

"Sorry. You'll have to make do for tonight. Tomorrow, I'll try the shelter again. Oh. Wait." He slapped his forehead. "I won't have time. I have to leave first thing in the morning for that meeting in Strathcona. Can you—"

"Keep him an extra day or two? Sure. We'll have fun. Won't we, Boomer? He won't be any trouble."

And with those laughable words, my fate was sealed. After adopting a one-eyed tomcat with an attitude, followed by a vicious rooster with a mean right beak, I should have known better.

"Thanks." Closing the front door, Jeff sniffed appreciatively. "Something smells good." He wrinkled his nose. "And it isn't that dog."

I turned to the kitchen, snuggling Boomer's face against mine. "It's a good thing I made meatloaf. Isn't it, Boo-Boo?"

"While you two"—Jeff shook his head, retrieving his parka from the armchair—"do whatever it is you're doing, I'll get started on the front walk. The weather's only going to get worse." He paused on the threshold to zip up his parka. "They're calling it the—"

"Storm of the century. I heard," I called from the kitchen door. "Let's find you some food, Boomer."

Keeping the door open with one hand, Jeff leaned in to call, "You're not feeding that dog my meatloaf, are you?"

"Come on, Boo. Let's see what we've got for cute widdle doggies."

The door closed on Jeff's audible sigh.

I turned toward the kitchen, holding Boomer, but stopped dead at a loud *hissssssss*. A throaty growl followed. I'd forgotten about General Chang. The scruffy tom was clinging to the top of an armchair with his back arched, channeling his namesake, a notorious *Star Trek* villain.

Hissssssss.

I'd seen the old boy angry, but never at me. In fact, he once thwarted an assailant who was threatening me. The General spent the bulk of his time snoozing atop the sofa and jonesing for liver treats, but he could move fast when circumstances required.

As, apparently, they did now. Canine interloper and all that.

"It's only for tonight, honest," I said, carefully giving the armchair a wide berth on my way to the kitchen.

Which was when the dear little terrier in my arms transformed into a deadly ninja dog, leaping from my grasp to lunge at the cat.

The blur of paws that followed could have been lifted straight from a martial-arts movie. No blows found their mark, however. This seemed to be more of a getting-acquainted bloodbath.

Within moments, the General had retreated to a safe perch atop the fireplace—after making a bold leap across the back of the sofa and scrabbling for purchase on the mantel's edge.

It was not so safe for the framed photos and knickknacks on the mantel. One by one, they crashed to the floor. Boomer ducked each fresh missile, continuing to press his assault on the main target.

"Stop," I yelled, worried someone would get hurt, and afraid it would be me. "Stop that."

Atop the nearly cleared mantel, the General flopped down and stretched, reclining comfortably as if that had been his objective all along. Nonchalantly, he licked a paw, ignoring the frenzied dog at his feet.

Boomer darted back and forth, tongue lolling and tail wagging so hard his entire hindquarters shook. This was clearly the most fun he'd had in ages. Repeatedly, he leapt for the General's swishing tail, which dangled enticingly over the edge. Finally, he sat, whimpering, urging the old tom to come down and continue sparring.

I decided not to chance a closer encounter for the time being. Scooping up Boomer, I hurried into the kitchen, kicking the door shut with one foot before placing him on the floor. Taking a step back, I studied the little animal.

His badly matted fur was a filthy white with brown patches. Despite the collar, he hadn't had a bath in months. At least he wouldn't have fleas, given the current weather. The shelter would have to bathe him, though.

Amazingly, he had no fresh scratches. Not one. The General had definitely pulled his punches.

"You got off lucky, Boomer. I'd watch that in the future, if I were you." The meatloaf was in the oven, so I scooped a helping of cat food onto a shallow dish before placing it on the floor. I figured the General wouldn't object, since he hadn't yet touched the food in his own dish.

Boomer tore into it. The cat food no soon disappeared than it reappeared.

I turned to grab paper towels to clean up the regurgitated meal. By the time I twisted around, it was gone again. Boomer stared at me with what amounted to a grin.

"Does that mean you're not hungry anymore?"

He trotted across the floor, then started in on the General's dish.

"No," I shrieked, grabbing the cat's bowl and holding it above my head. Boomer hopped energetically, trying to reach it. I placed it on the far end of the counter, next to the back door. "Let's see about a bed. Shall we, Boomer?" I harrumphed. "A *temporary* bed."

After tucking him into a blanket-lined box under the kitchen table, I heard the front door open. I ducked out of the kitchen, with one foot held up to deter the terrier from following me, and slammed the door shut.

As I passed the mantel, the General swished his tail and averted his gaze.

"Sorry, fella." I stopped to chuck him under the chin. "Maybe tomorrow, too. But that's definitely it."

Hunching his shoulders, he shot me a look of pure disgust.

In the foyer, Jeff was taking off his parka and snow boots. Standing on tiptoe, I wrapped my arms around his neck for a quick kiss. "Thanks for clearing the walk."

"No problem. I'd shovel a lot more than that for meatloaf." He paused. "We still *have* meatloaf, right?"

"No, sorry. Boomer ate it all."

Jeff paused with his parka in one hand and a coat hanger in the other, a forlorn expression on his face. "Really?"

I snickered. "You are *way* too easy. He's a small dog, Jeff. He couldn't possibly eat an entire meatloaf in under ten minutes."

That was an out and out lie, of course. That dog could eat an entire cow in under ten minutes. But why was I covering up for an animal destined for the shelter? It wasn't like Boomer was listening. I gave the kitchen door a wary glance.

Jeff hung up his parka, then closed the closet door. "I wouldn't be surprised if he did. I don't think that animal has had anything to eat for days. The dish on Oskar's kitchen floor was empty."

"Was there water at least?"

He shrugged. "Toilet."

"He gobbled down the food I gave him so fast that it came right back up. And then he *ate* it. Can you imagine?"

Jeff grinned. "You've never had a dog, have you?"

"*Mrack.*" The General hopped off the mantel onto the sofa, sashayed across the coffee table, and leapt onto the back of the armchair. "*Mrack.*" He lowered his head to be patted by Jeff, his second-favorite person in the world.

Who was I kidding? He was his *most* favorite person in the world.

Jeff scratched the General's head. "How did the big guy react? Not happy, I bet?"

"That's putting it mildly."

General Chang head-butted Jeff's arm. Jeff reached into his pocket for a liver treat.

"You're spoiling that animal," I said, grinning.

The General butted again, and was rewarded once more.

I rested one hand on my waist. "What about me?"

Jeff wrapped an arm around me, pulling me close. "Treats for you later," he whispered into my ear, then lowered his face for a lingering kiss.

I melted into his arms.

"But first—" Jeff released his hold. "Meatloaf!"

CHAPTER EIGHT

"THAT WAS DELICIOUS." Jeff held out his cup for coffee.

"There was supposed to be roasted daikon. Sorry."

"I had it for lunch."

"You did not."

He leaned over to drop a kiss on my head.

I picked up the carafe, then moved to fill his cup. "You're easy to please. It was only meatloaf and mashed potatoes."

"I could eat that every night." He raised an eyebrow over the edge of his mug.

This wasn't a conversation about meatloaf. And it wasn't a conversation I wanted to have. Not now, anyway. I replaced the carafe on the table.

"You know darn well you're a better cook than me."

"True."

"Hey. You're not supposed to agree."

Boomer had been banished to the living room while we'd

been eating dinner at the kitchen table. It was the only way we could get in a forkful without having a lap full of terrier.

He had been scratching at the kitchen door ever since, trying to pull it open. I assumed it was secure. Right up until the moment the faulty latch gave way. The door flung open with a crash, and Boomer burst through the doorway. He was moving so fast he skidded past the kitchen table and bounced off a cupboard on the far side of the room.

"Oh," I said, startled. "Is he—"

"Hurt? Not likely." Jeff chuckled at the dog, who had whirled around and jogged back to the table, where he sat, looking expectant. "I think he's indestructible."

I mentally added *fix kitchen door latch* to Carson's never-ending list of Rose Cottage repairs. And realized that would only matter if Boomer was staying.

With a yawn and a stretch, Jeff dropped a piece of apple crumble on the floor. Boomer snapped it up.

"I saw that."

"Saw what?" Jeff sipped his coffee, innocence painted across his handsome face.

"Uh-huh. Okay, we've eaten—tell me what happened to Oskar York." I eyed Jeff intently. "Was it really an accident?"

He settled his coffee cup on the table, absently running a thumb down its side. "We think so, but the ME said he's been dead for several days, so we're not sure. We'll get a more detailed estimate for time of death after the autopsy. And the forensic team isn't finished."

"Could it have been deliberate?"

Jeff had been lifting his cup to his mouth but halted, arm

extended, to give me one of those no-nonsense professional police looks I knew from experience.

I made a face at him.

His lips twitched in a smile. "You could be harboring the killer right now." He inclined his head at Boomer, who matched the movement in an almost eerie way.

"You two could be twins," I said. "And what do you mean, *the killer?*"

"I mean—Boomer's excitable. He could have crashed into a stack of magazines and knocked it over. We found thousands of *Canadian Geographics* all over the floor and all over—"

"Oskar?"

He winced.

"Could old *Geographics* really have killed him?"

"One cubic yard of magazines weighs nearly a thousand pounds. So, yes, depending on how they were stacked and how they fell—they could. Easily."

We turned our heads to study Boomer.

Shifting his glance between us, he raised a paw in that universal begging motion all puppies learn from television ads.

"You were kidding about Boomer, weren't you?" I asked.

"You are *way* too easy."

"But Jeff, seriously. It's unlikely to be an accident. Oskar York lived for years with that stuff. Why would it suddenly fall over?" I frowned. "And don't tell me the dog did it."

"Verity—"

"I know. I've got murder on the brain. But there's a story

in the village that Oskar kept money and valuables in his home. Could it have been a robbery gone wrong?"

"Oskar York had nothing of value in that house."

"It doesn't have to exist. Just the rumor might be enough for someone to rob him. Maybe they tried to get Oskar to tell them where it was... and things got out of hand."

"Verity. Leave the detecting to the—"

"Detectives. I know." Rising to my feet, I picked up our dirty plates to take them to the sink.

Jeff pushed back his chair. "I'll help."

"No. I'll take care of the dishes. You must be exhausted after all the hours you've been working. Sit. Finish your coffee. Why don't you take it into the living room, where you'd be more comfortable?"

"I'd rather talk to you. We haven't seen much of each other this week. And I'll be gone for two days."

"There is something I've been meaning to ask you." After scraping the leftovers into the compost pail, I set the dishes in the sink and returned to the table. Sitting across from Jeff, I rested my chin on my hands and took a deep breath.

"That's good," he said. "Because I've been meaning to ask you something, too. But—you first." He smiled, twisting the coffee mug handle in his fingers.

"You know I've been worried about my finances."

"Yes, but there's no need—"

I held up a hand. "Emy thinks I should start an investigation agency. To solve little mysteries around the village." I paused, waiting for his input.

Jeff merely appeared dazed. "Investigation of what?"

"Nothing serious. Small stuff. Missing pets, estranged relatives, lost wallets. What do you think?"

Jeff leaned forward to take one of my hands from under my chin, then clasped it in his own. "You don't need to worry about money. If the two of us—"

"I have a case already," I blurted, pulling my hand back. "Henri Vartan hired me to investigate a mysterious wallet he found in his front yard."

"A wallet? Verity—seriously, there's no need for this. Landscapers obviously can't work in the winter. It's not a problem. I have plenty of money."

"It's not about money. I need an occupation."

"No, you don't."

"Yes. I do."

Jeff pressed his lips together for a moment. "Let's not argue," he said. "Whatever you want to do is fine with me, that's all I'm trying to say."

"As long as it has nothing to do with investigating crimes?"

"Crimes? You said, 'small stuff.' Lost pets. Wallets. Missing... books."

"Books? Why—never mind. I *was* talking about small stuff. You're right. And you can help me."

"I could help you better if I was living right here in—"

"No," I blurted. "I mean—not *no*, exactly, but—let me tell you about Henri's case."

"You mean it's a real case? You don't have a license."

"I know that. These are little domestic mysteries, remember? Not actual crimes."

Jeff seemed confused. "Is Vartan paying you? Because you don't have to worry about money."

"Stop. Listen to me. Please."

"Sorry. I'm all ears."

I explained about Henri's wallet and the crossword puzzle contest. And how I suspected it was a fraud. "So." I crossed my arms. "What do you think? What should I do next?"

"Does this mean we're not going to talk about—"

"No. I mean—yes. We're not going to talk about it."

"I'm confused. Is that a no?"

"The wallet, Jeff. What should I do?"

"When Vartan turned it in at the station, they told him the ID was fake?"

I nodded. "Could you ask them about it? See if they know where those counterfeit IDs may have come from?"

"Do you have any idea how many wallets are turned in every week?"

"If you think it's inappropriate." I stuck out my lower lip and dropped my head, running a finger along the edge of the table. "You shouldn't do it."

Jeff smiled. "Nice try. Stop being coy. I'll ask around."

"Thank you. And what about Oskar's death? Do you think that's related? Because I think—"

Jeff shook his head emphatically. "Stay out of it, Verity."

There was an obvious note of caution in his voice, and I pounced on it. "You *do* think it's suspicious, don't you? Was I right about the money?"

"I can't talk about it. You know that." Jeff ran a hand over his head, leaving his straight black hair uncharacteristically rumpled, and yawned.

Immediately, I felt guilty for pressing him. Placing a hand on his arm, I squeezed. "Why don't you switch on the game? I'm going to walk that dog." At the sound of the "W" word, Boomer leapt up to frantically pace the floor. "Then we can talk some more."

Jeff yawned again. "I am a little tired."

It only took a few minutes to clean up the sink and make a leash for Boomer from kitchen cord, but Jeff was already asleep in an armchair. General Chang perched on the chair's back, one paw resting on Jeff's shoulder. The cat swished his tail as I edged past with the terrier, but otherwise ignored him. It was a truce of sorts, but only because Boomer was more interested in going outdoors than in lunging at the cat.

As we walked along Lilac Lane—Boomer did more peeing than walking—I stopped to gaze at the picture-perfect crescent moon and the thousands of stars sparkling overhead. The snow had stopped falling, and the ground was crisp and crunchy underfoot. The silence was broken only by the far-off hoot of an owl. It was hard to believe a "storm of the century" was on its way.

I turned around to head back, tugging on Boomer's makeshift leash. He followed happily, trotting along beside me. I found myself almost hoping the shelter would have no room for him after all.

Despite the tranquility of the setting, my mind was in turmoil. Why couldn't Jeff accept I might have a talent for investigating? He'd praised me for it in the past.

I should rephrase that. Not *praised*, exactly, but he

admitted I'd been helpful. When he wasn't scolding me for putting my life in danger, that was. Which was not my fault, by the way. There had been a rock-climbing incident that even I had to admit ended badly. And the arsonist's attack—poor General Chang had taken the brunt of that. Not to mention a misguided expedition to Niagara Falls—or, to be more exact, the deadly whirlpool at its base. But honestly, how could I have anticipated *that*?

Stopping outside Rose Cottage, where only a faint light shone through the drawn curtains, it hit me maybe that was the problem. A real detective would anticipate disasters like those. Jeff was right. I should stick to landscaping. Even crossword puzzles were no longer a safe pastime.

Killers Amongst Us.

Ridiculous. I had to rein in my imagination and drop Emy's far-fetched idea. Tomorrow, I would contact Henri Vartan and tell him I couldn't help.

Resolutely, I mounted the front steps and pushed open the door. I'd admitted defeat. I should have felt relieved. But instead, a wave of disappointment swept over me. I had ridiculed Emy's idea from the beginning. Why did it make me sad to give it up?

Boomer waited impatiently for me to untie the cord from his collar, then vigorously shook off a few flakes of snow before trotting into the kitchen. No doubt he was checking to see if more food had materialized in our absence. On his way through the living room, he nuzzled Jeff's hand, which was draped over the side of the armchair.

Jeff mumbled, but did not wake up.

I stood for a moment beside his chair—admiring his

strong shoulders and long legs, the straight black hair that tickled the back of his collar, the black lashes that brushed his sharp cheekbones. I remembered his concern for a dog he didn't know. Recalled the touch of his lips against my ear as he whispered, *I missed you.* And felt again his comforting arms, holding me close.

Joy surged within me.

Followed immediately by confusion. Given how much I cared for him, why was I so reluctant to discuss our living arrangements? What was I afraid of? Emy's voice echoed in my brain. *That was nearly three years ago. You've moved on.* But had I? Then why couldn't I accept Jeff's assessment of my abilities? Why didn't I fully trust him?

After slipping off my boots and parka, I trod noiselessly on stocking feet toward the bookcase in the dining nook. In his chair, Jeff was gently snoring. The General watched me cross the room before lowering his head and closing his one good eye.

I searched the bookcase, running my fingers across the titles, until I found the one I wanted. *Risk Mitigation and Threat Assessment.* It was my aunt's book. When I first arrived in Leafy Hollow, I noticed it while combing her shelves of gardening volumes for pruning tips. At the time, I thought "threats" referred to garden pests. Later, I assumed it was an accounting textbook.

Now that I knew about my aunt's extracurricular activities, I reviewed it with fresh eyes.

Stretching out on the sofa, I turned to the front page to scan the list of contents.

Part 1: Vulnerability assessment.

Part II: Cyber-risk Mitigation and Threat Assessment in Military Intelligence.

Part III: Potential strategic responses.

This was not exactly the how-to book I was hoping for. I needed something more along the lines of *Sleuthing for Beginners.* Tomorrow, I would visit the library and see what they had. And since I was going to be there anyway, surely it wouldn't hurt to get an update on the crossword situation. And perhaps see if anyone else had found a wallet like Henri's.

I closed the cover, then set the book onto the coffee table.

Maybe I wasn't cut out to be an investigator, but that didn't mean I should give up.

CHAPTER NINE

THE 5X BAKERY was bustling when I dropped by early the next morning, hoping to avoid the usual crowd of midmorning caffeine addicts. I must have timed it wrong, because a dozen customers were huddled in the back of the tiny shop, peering at an easel.

I sidled over to the counter, where Emy was restocking the baked-goods trays.

"What's with all the clientele?"

"Hello to you, too," she said, rearranging a display of scones.

"Sorry. Hi. But seriously, you never have that many people in here at this time of the morning."

Emy shot me a wry grin. "Thanks for the vote of confidence. But you're right. That," she tilted her head at the crowd, "has more to do with Shanice. Remember her idea to lure in more customers? Take a look."

I had no problem seeing over the dozen heads

surrounding Shanice's project. Even from ten feet away, I could make out a giant crossword puzzle surrounded by sticky notes. A few steps nearer and I heard scraps of conversation.

"I think you've got that one," said a woman pointing to a note on the board.

"I think she's right." Another woman leaned in to move that note from the sidelines.

Stepping back to the counter, I leaned an elbow on it while watching the crowd. "How long has this been going on?"

"Since yesterday. Shanice went to the office-goods store to pick up supplies. I paid for them from petty cash."

"Isn't it a copy of the clues already posted at the library?"

Emy grinned. "It's identical. Hannah keeps me updated." She finished making a café latte.

"Why don't people just go there, then?"

"Theresa," Emy called. "Your order's ready."

A lithe young woman pranced over, grinning, to claim her coffee and walnut-toffee scone with clotted cream before returning to the group.

Emy lifted an eyebrow. "You have to ask?"

That was when I noticed the extra chairs in a row along the far wall. I pointed. "When did you add those?"

Emy beamed. "There are tables coming, too. Lorne found a style that attaches to the wall. They hardly take up any room at all."

"Scandinavian?" I asked, eyebrows raised.

She nodded.

"Do they come with a key wrench and recommended curse words?"

"Dunno. That's Lorne's department." Eying the chairs, Emy smiled. "I doubted there was room for more seating, but turns out I was wrong. What can I get you, Verity?"

"I wouldn't say no to a green tea. But I really came in to ask your advice."

"Ask away." After flicking on the burner under the kettle, Emy placed a teabag into a mug.

I pulled the crumpled list of names from my pocket, then smoothed it out on the counter. "These are the names of people who found clues to the crossword. I want to interview them to see if they can shed any light on Henri's mysterious wallet."

Emy nodded. "Good thinking. And you want to know—"

"Who's this?" I pointed to a name on the list.

Emy looked grim. "Rick Armstrong? I know who he is, worse luck." The kettle boiled behind her, and she turned to fill my mug. "He's the new owner of Lucky Lentil. My competition."

She placed my mug on the counter with a thud. A trickle of green tea splashed over the side.

"The new restaurant?"

"Yes. Want a scone with that?"

"No thanks. Trying to quit."

"You are not. Hey, speaking of food—how was the big dinner last night? Did you make my piecrust recipe?"

"No." I sighed, watching the group around the bulletin board debate the next clue.

"Why so glum? Jeff didn't complain, did he?"

"He would never. You know that. But I wanted it to be special."

"Don't put so much pressure on yourself. Jeff's not interested in your *baking*." She winked.

I turned around with my elbows on the counter and my back to Emy, to hide the flush rising on my cheeks.

"You're turning red, like always," she teased.

"I am not."

But when I whirled around to pick up my mug, Emy was staring out at the street, chewing on her lip.

"What about this other name?"

She didn't look at me.

"The list?" I asked, leaning over the counter to poke her arm. "Emy?"

With a startled jump, she said, "Huh?"

"Who's this other person? Rebecca Butterfield?"

"Oh." Emy shook her head as if she was brushing away a bad memory. "She's married to Noah Butterfield, the investment adviser. They have an office up the street, across from Lucky Lentil. I guess you've never met them."

"I've never needed an investment adviser," I said ruefully. "How do you know them?"

Emy ignored me.

I poked her arm again. "Emy?"

She jerked. "What?"

"How do you know the Butterfields?"

"They've lived here over a decade. Mom knows them. She says Noah never misses a day's work. I'm sure you've seen him around—the middle-aged man in the Italian suit and expensive loafers? Tall, perfectly groomed, brown hair combed back? He comes in here midmorning for a green tea and a toasted half-bagel, no butter. Oh, look, here's Lorne."

The front door opened with a whoosh of frigid air and a tinkle of the overhead bell. Lorne pulled off his wool toque, revealing a bad case of hat head, and brushed snow off his parka. After stamping his boots on the mat, he walked up to the counter and leaned in to give Emy a kiss.

"How's it going?" He aimed an inquisitive glance on the crowd around the bulletin board.

"Lorne, tell Verity about Noah Butterfield. She's never met him."

"Noah's a good guy. He advised me which business courses to take at the college. Babe, can I get a coffee to go, and—" Lorne peered through the glass wall of the counter, his brows furrowed in disbelief. "No sausage rolls?"

"Sorry, hon. I've had quite a run on them this morning. How about a cheese cruller?"

Lorne nodded enthusiastically, and Emy prepared his order for takeout.

I pointed to the waiting chairs. "Brilliant suggestion for the tables, Lorne."

"Yeah. Emy needs to monetize that wasted space."

"Hmm-hmm." The transformation of my formerly tongue-tied landscaping assistant into a jargon-spouting businessman made me smile. I had no doubt Lorne would fulfill his dream of presiding over an entire chain of bakeries, with Emy at his side.

For now, though, he had to pass his exams. Lorne was painfully conscious of being older than the other students in his class, and anxious to make up for lost time.

"Gotta get back to studying," he said, picking up his takeout bag and leaning over the counter for a farewell kiss. "See you later, babe."

Brushing past me on his way to the door, Lorne leaned in to whisper out of the side of his mouth. "A word?"

Mystified, I followed him to the door.

Emy shot us a puzzled glance, but was soon busy filling more orders from crossword contest contestants.

"What's up?" I asked.

"Have you noticed Emy's a little preoccupied?"

"Now that you mention it—" Turning my face away from Emy, I lowered my voice. "I have."

"Any idea what's wrong?"

"I don't know that anything's wrong. Exactly. Can you be more specific?"

"She's been looking up stuff online, scowling at it. And when I ask her what it is, she slams the laptop shut and refuses to talk about it."

"That doesn't sound like Emy." With a workday that started at four AM, she didn't have time to surf the Internet. Lorne had told me that on many nights, he found her asleep on the sofa in her apartment above the bakery, still wearing her apron. My chest tightened. "She's not ill, is she?"

He shook his head. "I don't think so. But something's on her mind."

"What are you two whispering about?"

We jerked around with guilty expressions. New assistant Shanice had moseyed up behind us.

"Nothing."

She glanced between us. "I thought maybe you were

discussing—" After a glance back at Emy, she leaned in to whisper. "The rumors."

Lorne and I exchanged surprised glances.

"What rumors?" I asked.

"You haven't heard?" Shanice had the expression of someone who knew a juicy secret and was dying to tell.

"No," I said impatiently. "What rumors?"

"Somebody—" Shanice stretched out the word, building anticipation. "Has been posting on restaurant review sites that Eco Edibles uses butter."

"No." My jaw dropped. "That's outrageous."

Lorne screwed up his face in confusion.

"Vegans don't eat dairy products," I said. "They would be horrified to learn there was butter in their food, even the tiniest amount."

"I knew that," he hastily added.

"Emy would never do such a thing. It's nonsense." I pointed to the sign posted above the pass-through to the vegan takeout—YOU ARE ENTERING A MEAT AND DAIRY-FREE ZONE. "She's extremely careful."

Shanice nodded. "I know she is. But it looks bad. Negative online reviews can destroy a business overnight. It's hard to fight them."

"Even when they're obvious lies?"

She nodded ruefully.

"Who would post something so hateful?"

Shanice pulled her cell phone from the pocket of her white apron, and scrolled down before handing it to me. "Take a look."

Someone called ButterUpTripleX had posted: EMY'S

ECO EDIBLES IS A FRAUD. I SAW A CASK OF BUTTER IN THE COOLER. AND THE AVOCADO ROLLUPS DEFINITELY HAD BUTTER IN THEM. MILK, TOO. I HAD A REACTION THE NEXT DAY, SO I KNOW IT'S TRUE.

"Emy?" I marched up to the counter, flourishing the phone. "Have you seen these?"

She gave the screen a cursory glance. "Yes." She turned to make another latte.

"What are you doing about it? It's slander."

"Henrietta," Emy called. "Your order's ready."

A smiling, red-cheeked woman in a plaid blazer hurried up to collect the latte. Once she returned to the group huddled in front of the crossword—their voices getting louder as they debated the merits of each new guess—Emy turned to face us.

"Nothing. I'm doing nothing."

"But—" I spluttered.

"You can't respond to online reviews, Verity. It only makes them worse."

Next door, in Eco Edibles, the counter bell dinged sharply.

"Shanice." Emy said. "Customers."

Shanice snatched back her phone, ducked behind the counter, and dashed through the connecting door. We heard her say, "What can I get you?" Followed by a muffled conservation.

"You can't just ignore this, Emy," I said, keeping my voice low.

"Verity's right," Lorne added. "Someone's trying to hurt your business. We have to take action."

"No." Emy's retort was sharp. "You two should do nothing."

At Lorne's hurt look, she apologized. "Sorry, hon. I appreciate everything you've done, I really do. But leave this to me. It will blow over."

"What if we try to find out who's responsible?" I asked.

Emy wrinkled her brow. "How exactly would you do that?"

"Well..." Temporarily baffled, I tried to work up a course of action. "For starters, we could explain that nobody gains access to your storage room except staff. So, obviously, this person who claims to have seen anything there is lying."

I straightened up with a triumphant air.

Lorne nodded aggressively. "That's true," he said.

Emy heaved a sigh. "Apparently, you haven't seen the online review with the photograph of my storage area. With an industrial-sized tub of butter in it."

"What? How is that possible?" I whipped out my own phone and did a quick search, then halted at the incriminating photo. "Oh." Morosely, I studied the screen. "How did that happen?"

Lorne leaned over my phone, adding helpfully, "Photoshop?"

"That must be it." We nodded together, sagely. "Wait—it *does* look like your storage area, Emy." I tapped on the part of the picture that showed the butter cask's delivery label. Eco Edibles was clearly visible.

"You see why I told you to leave it alone?" she snapped. It was obvious she immediately regretted her tone. "Sorry."

Lorne ducked behind the counter to give her a hug. "Don't worry, babe. It'll all work out."

My confusion grew as I stared at the picture. "But if this wasn't photoshopped"—and I had to admit it looked real —"who could have taken this if no one goes back there?"

Emy winced. "That's not exactly true."

"What do you mean?"

"I mean—the delivery guys have a key." At my look of surprise, she added, "They deliver my orders in the middle of the night. Once a week, on Wednesday usually. It's easier that way. They don't have to fight traffic to make their rounds."

"How long have they been doing that?"

She shrugged. "Years. It's never been a problem. And honestly, I don't believe they would do something like this."

Lorne pursed his lips. "Somebody did."

"We need to talk to them," I said.

"No," Emy said firmly. "Please? Leave it alone. Now, shoo—I have to get back to work."

Lorne turned to the door. I followed. Out of the side of his mouth, he said, "We have to help her."

"I know," I whispered. "I have an idea—"

"I can see you two, you know," Emy called as she wiped down the counter. "You're up to something."

Indignantly, I sniffed. "Can't I chat with a friend without you thinking we're planning a reconnaissance mission?"

"No. Because usually you are planning a reconnaissance mission."

"That's... not true." I refrained from mentioning two such missions—one involved a roasted chicken—that had gone terribly wrong. But those debacles could be chalked up to inexperience. Surely by now we had the protocol down pat.

Emy turned her raised eyebrows on Lorne, knowing he would never lie to her.

He shrugged apologetically. "We were talking about curling."

I regarded my assistant with newly appreciative eyes. Curling was a passion of his, but one Emy didn't share—so this was an excellent bluff on his part. Emy barely knew a bonspiel from a butter knife.

She twisted a fist at her hip. "Okay, I'll bite. What *about* curling?" she asked.

"You know, babe. I told you. The rink has a couples' night every week, and I thought—"

Emy resumed wiping the counter after tossing him an incredulous glance. "Not a chance."

"Forget I mentioned it." Lorne assumed an appropriately humbled air. "Although—Verity and Jeff are going."

Giving him a thumbs-up behind my back, I muttered, "Nice save."

Dropping her cleaning cloth into the sink, Emy straightened up, astonishment widening her eyes. "Really?"

I nodded enthusiastically. "We sure are."

"That's okay, babe," Lorne said. "I'll just watch from the stands."

Emy bit her lip. "I'm sorry, hon. If it means that much to you, of course I'll come. With Shanice helping out, I have time. I warn you, though—I'm not much of a curler."

That was an understatement. With the Dionnes' extended family being curling fanatics, Emy had had her fill of the sport. She went out of her way to avoid it. Only for Lorne would she brave the slippery ice and noisy catcalls of the curling rink.

"I'm not wearing those ridiculous pants, though," she added.

Simpering, I made a heart shape with my thumbs and forefingers. "Not even the ones with the pink hearts?"

Emy gave me a cautionary glance. "You. Stop." While we watched, she bustled around—rearranging the baked-goods trays, lining up the coffee cups, dusting the top of the spotless coffeemaker. Emy halted, turning to give us a suspicious stare. "Are you still here?"

Lorne and I exchanged glances, zipped up our parkas, and headed for the door. Once out of view of the bakery's front window, we huddled together, eyes narrowed to keep out the stinging wind.

"We need to talk to those delivery guys," I said.

"Agreed. But we don't know their names."

"We know where to find them."

"Aha. Undercover work." Lorne grinned. "I like your thinking."

Silently, we exchanged a high-five.

CHAPTER TEN

MICKEY TUGGED on his earflaps to keep out the biting wind while he sized up the promising crowd outside the pet-food store. He'd been out of the van for only five minutes, and already his day was looking up. His regulars wrapped themselves around his legs, wrestling and mock growling at each other. He ignored them. His attention was focused on the three women talking on the sidewalk outside the shop.

The tallest woman, who wore a bright orange coat buttoned up to her scarf-wrapped neck and gray cropped hair, held the loose leash of a small cinnamon poodle.

The second woman, who was much younger and chunkier, and dressed in form-fitting ski pants and bulging jacket, held the taut leash of an equally chunky bulldog.

A Jack Russell terrier hopped on two legs to paw at the side of the third woman—a stylish matron in a puffy down coat, cross-body bag, and huge sunglasses. She brushed the dog away with a muttered "Stop it." Her protests had no effect.

Having run into this woman before, Mickey knew her Jack Russell—inexplicably named Darling—was a natural troublemaker.

All he needed now was a diversion. And Leafy Hollow delivered.

A tall, well-groomed man in a camel overcoat, brown fedora, and galoshes stepped out of the pet-food shop onto the sidewalk. His leather-gloved hands jerked anxiously on the leash of a boxer that wasn't moving rapidly enough for its impatient owner.

Mickey recognized Noah Butterfield, the village's investment adviser, and his nervous boxer Axel. He turned his head to hurry the dog along, without slowing his own stride. With Noah's attention on Axel's dawdling, it was obvious to Mickey what would happen next.

Noah and his dog stepped right into the center of the women's group.

The Jack Russell whirled to snarl and snap at the boxer, whose jowls flapped as he jerked back in surprise. The chunky beagle started baying, as only a beagle could. His owner tried to silence him, but a sudden rearguard action by the little cinnamon poodle caught the beagle unprepared and he went down with a yelp.

Mickey plunged forward, yanking on the leashes of his own charges. Within seconds, Pixi the beagle and her friends —the border collie, silver-gray standard poodle, and black lab —were haunches deep in the melee, their leashes wrapped around multiple pairs of human legs.

Shrieks and curses echoed off the brick storefronts.

"Get out of the way!"

"Get off me!"

"Get that monster off my dog!"

"Eeeeek—"

The orange-coated woman toppled backward, propelled by a leap from the panicked boxer. Mickey shoved Noah Butterfield, Axel's owner, out of the way with both hands to catch the woman just in time.

"Thanks," she said gratefully as he helped her to her feet.

The little cinnamon poodle nuzzled her leg while eying the other dogs with disdain.

"No problem," Mickey said. "That guy was moving so fast he walked right into you." He jerked a thumb toward Noah, who had freed himself from the group with a quick *sorry-sorry* and was dashing away along the sidewalk, Axel trotting after him.

The woman gave a snort of disgust as she tracked Noah's rapidly departing back with her flashing eyes. "People should be more careful."

Mickey solemnly nodded. "They certainly should."

The second woman was patiently explaining to her terrier the need to "behave yourself when Mommy's talking to her friends." Unconcerned, he cocked his leg on the nearest lamppost.

Mickey bent to untangle the leashes of his own pack. Smiling, he straightened his hat and patted his earflaps back into place. "So long as everybody's all right, I'll be on my way." With a brisk wave, he strolled off in the opposite direction from Noah Butterfield.

Once around the corner, he jerked on the leashes and turned into the alley that led to his parked van. Pleased, he patted the pocket of his ragged parka. He'd wait until the parking lot at the Pine Hill conservation area before checking his haul.

Best be out of sight before Butterfield reached into his pocket to pay a bill.

———————

With the dogs romping in a field—which field, Mickey wasn't sure—he resumed his scrutiny of the recently acquired calfskin wallet, flipping it over to examine both sides of the hand-stitched item. Nice workmanship. Always a good sign.

The interior didn't disappoint, either. Mickey extracted five credit cards, six hundred dollars in cash, a Tim Horton's gift card with a colorful iced doughnut on the front, and a booklet of car-wash coupons—a nice bonus, since the van hadn't been washed in over a year.

There was also a brochure for a cruise, which he spread out on the steering wheel. Mickey's brows arched in envy at the price. Nice for those who could afford it.

A folded piece of notebook paper fluttered into his lap when he turned the page. Mickey read it with considerable interest. It appeared to be notes for a personal conversation.

Tell her it has to be the last time. That it was a good time, fun maybe? probably better to say it meant a lot—but we both knew it couldn't last. Should have met earlier, etc. If she cries, say something mushy.

Mickey chuckled. How about that Noah Butterfield, eh? Not so straitlaced after all.

He tucked the note into his pocket, followed by the cards, cash, and coupons. The driver's license he tossed onto a discard pile—after guffawing at its photo. After pocketing the government health card—he had a client who'd pay good money for that—Mickey dropped the empty billfold into a manila envelope and tucked it under the driver's seat. Normally he'd dump it into in a trash can, but recently he'd had reason to collect empty wallets. *Never turn down cash,* was his motto. It hadn't failed him yet.

CHAPTER ELEVEN

LUCKY LENTIL WAS ONLY a block from Emy's bakery, so I decided to make Rick Armstrong my first interrogation. Or friendly chat, depending on who was asking.

Leaning into the wind on my way there, I tried to puzzle out who in Leafy Hollow might want to destroy Eco Edibles. Its companion business, the 5X Bakery, was the village's favorite destination for all things sweet. Of course, Emy used butter at the 5X. Fake buttercream would have elicited a shudder of horror from her. Also, her famous maple-bacon butter tarts contained farm-raised bacon. But in Eco Edibles, meat and dairy were banned. Customers could order soy milk, almond milk, coconut milk, even hemp milk—but never cow's milk or butter. Emy wouldn't store it in the vegan shop's cooler, either.

I'd been called a cynic occasionally, but two facts were obvious. Those nasty rumors started after the opening of the village's newest restaurant, Lucky Lentil. Its proprietor could be involved.

That might be unfair, I thought. *No*—I chided myself—*it was definitely unfair.* I had absolutely no proof that anyone at Lucky Lentil was involved.

Not yet, anyway.

I stopped on the other side of Main Street, across from the Lentil, to study the posters in the window. No ANIMALS HARMED boasted one hand-lettered sign. Its edges were decorated with cutout pictures of wide-eyed sheep, cows, and small children holding angelic fowl under their arms. Obviously, they'd never met my rooster, Reuben.

The previous restaurant in this location had been an upscale place, complete with an indoor fountain, pricey "tasting menu," and Irish linen napkins. Unfortunately, someone intimately connected with that eatery wouldn't be back in the village for a while. Twenty-five years, in fact. I hoped the menu behind bars was up to their standards, but I doubted it.

The four-foot-wide window boxes that graced the front entrance, however, remained. The flowers were long gone, replaced with foot-high mounds of snow, but spring would eventually come—or so I'd been told. Coming Up Roses had filled those window boxes in the past. I could drop in to offer my services and welcome Rick Armstrong to Leafy Hollow. All while checking for evidence that the new restaurateur might have it in for Eco Edibles.

To be honest, I had no idea how to determine that, but it couldn't hurt to check him out. Maybe he'd unwittingly give the game away—he wouldn't know Emy and I were friends. I could ask a few leading questions and see what happened.

While I pondered my next move, the restaurant door opened and a woman stepped out. Her outfit caught my attention. A bitter wind tore at her hair, but this woman wasn't even wearing a coat. Or boots. She had on four-inch heels, a trim pencil skirt, and a bulky mohair pullover. When she turned her head, blonde curls whipped back from her face, revealing earrings gaudy enough to reflect the single ray of sunlight breaking through the clouded sky.

Behind her, the door remained open. A square-jawed man wearing a white chef's apron, one hand on the door handle, leaned out to beckon her back with a crook of his finger.

After a quick glance at the street, as if to check if anyone was watching, she complied with a smile, lifting her face for a kiss. It wasn't passionate exactly—how could it be, with the wind threatening to knock her over?—but it wasn't one of those peck-peck smooch-smooch fake kisses, either. These two shared something.

Mentally, I reviewed the timeline. Lucky Lentil had been open for only two weeks. Either the proprietor was a fast worker or—more likely—he knew this woman before arriving in the village. Thing was, I knew her, too—at least, her face was familiar. Wracking my brain, I tried to remember where I'd seen her before. The library? Bertram's grocery?

My confusion soon cleared up. As the aproned man tugged the door closed against the wind, she darted across the street, disappearing into the office of investment adviser Noah Butterfield. No wonder she hadn't bothered with a coat and boots. It was a three-second dash, at best. Although, one had to admire the fact she did it in heels. I would have been sprawled on the sidewalk.

But it sparked the question—why was Rebecca Butterfield, Noah's wife, kissing the proprietor of Lucky Lentil?

The Lentil was snug and cozy, a welcome respite from the miserable weather outside. While stamping my boots on the entrance mat, I scanned the interior. The earlier restaurant's pretentious decor was gone. A wainscoting of weathered barnwood warmed the walls, and the mismatched tables and chairs were obviously secondhand. Sorry —*reclaimed.*

I made my way to the counter, where multicolored signs proclaimed—ORDER HERE, NO PLASTIC CUTLERY, and PLEASE RECYCLE. Hand-lettered arrows directed attention to blue recycling bins along the back wall. Lucky Lentil must order its felt markers from Costco.

The square-jawed man behind the counter turned vivid blue eyes in my direction. "Why, hello." His sensual baritone conveyed surprise that such a beautiful creature would grace his establishment, and how lucky for him that I had. "Here for lunch?"

Ignoring his blatant overture, I scanned the day's specials on the chalkboard. "The soup looks good."

"It's delicious. Black bean pineapple with chili. One of our best sellers. And particularly suited to our current weather." He nodded at the front windows. Between the recycling signs and the bulletins from a local cycling group that papered the glass, the snowy street was barely visible.

"Brrr." I shivered. "You're not kidding. I'll have the pineapple-chili soup, thanks."

While he ladled the steaming broth into a bowl, I began my interrogation.

"You must be Rick Armstrong."

"Correct."

"Have you lived in Leafy Hollow long?"

"Nope. Just arrived. It's a wonderful place. Great people." He winked.

"You should see it in the summer. The view from the Peak is famous."

"I intend to." He smiled while placing my bowl on a pressed-cardboard tray. "Crackers?"

"Sure."

"Gluten-free?"

"Not necessary, but—okay. Also," I pointed to the soup, formulating a white lie, "I'm lactose-intolerant, so..."

"No dairy products here." He gave me an amused glance while tucking crackers under the edge of the bowl.

"Just checking. No butter, either?"

"Never." He chuckled while adding my bill to the tray. "We're totally vegan."

"Great," I enthused. "I'm sure you'll be busy. There's only one other vegan takeout in the village."

He leaned in conspiratorially while handing over my lunch. "If you can call it vegan."

My grip tightened on the tray, but I kept my tone light. "What do you mean?"

"Oh, nothing." He grinned broadly, those blue eyes riveted on mine, instantly disarming my suspicions. Rick was quite the accomplished flirt.

"No, really. What do you mean?" I asked.

"A true vegan might find it distasteful, sharing space with a bakery that buys bacon in bulk. Not to mention all those dairy products. I've heard..." He straightened up. "It's not for me to say."

Rick Armstrong had heard the rumors. Had he also started them? I decided to change tack before I lost my temper and gave it all away.

"I run a small business myself." I pulled out my wallet, counted out enough change to pay my bill, added a hefty tip, and handed over a business card.

VERITY HAWKES

COMING UP ROSES LANDSCAPING

LAWN CARE, SEASONAL CLEANUP, GARDEN DESIGN

Rick read the card carefully before looking up. "No snow removal?"

"No," I answered firmly, before adding, "But we do window boxes. In fact, the previous occupant hired me to fill the ones out front. I can email you a picture if you like."

"Can you provide organic?"

"Absolutely."

Rick tucked my card into the breast pocket of his bamboo shirt and patted it with another blinding smile. Then he reached beside the cash register to retrieve his own card. He handed it over. "I look forward to hearing from you."

As I took it, Rick held on to it longer than necessary while gazing directly into my eyes. This from a guy who had been kissing someone else's wife not ten minutes earlier.

I wrested the card from his grasp. "Would it be a lot of trouble to change my order to takeout?"

"Not at all." His lips curled up disarmingly as he continued gazing into my eyes. "Verity."

I felt as if I'd just been to the optometrist's. I decided to give him the benefit of the doubt and assume he treated all his customers this way.

While Rick transferred my soup to a cardboard bowl, then tucked it and my crackers into a paper bag, I remembered that one of the clues posted on the library's bulletin board had been attributed to the restaurant.

"Did you find one of those wallets with a clue in it that everybody's talking about?"

He cocked his head, seeming puzzled. "No. Why do you ask?"

"I heard about it at the library."

"Oh. That might have been Gloria." He pointed to a photo of a young woman taped to the wall under a banner that read—LUCKY LENTIL EMPLOYEE OF THE MONTH. "She works for me part time, and I asked her to mention the Lentil any time she could. Word of mouth is important, you know." He nodded sagely, business owner to business owner. I ignored that, too.

I peered at the picture. Gloria had dyed green hair, multiple piercings, heavy black eyeliner, and a thumb raised up in front of her grinning face.

"How many employees do you have?"

"One."

I nodded. "I see. And Gloria found a wallet?"

"She did mention something like that."

"Do you know where she found it?"

"Sorry, no." He handed me the paper bag. "We have a five-percent discount if you bring your own containers."

"I'll remember that."

"Also"—he reached behind the counter—"tell your friends." Rick handed me a dozen bonus cards, each reading —LUCKY LENTIL, FEBRUARY SPECIAL—TEN PERCENT OFF.

"I sure will."

I took my soup back to the truck, where I ate it—with the motor on to heat the cab—while watching Noah Butterfield's office. The crackers were dry and tasteless, but the black bean-pineapple soup was delicious, with just a hint of tang. Rick's food was good enough that he didn't have to resort to name-calling—or flirtation—to entice customers. Maybe I'd been wrong about him.

After carefully wrapping my containers for the recycling bins, I pulled out the list I'd copied in the library—with Emy's comments in the margins—to study. Halfway down, I found the name I was looking for.

Rebecca Butterfield.

Might as well check her out while I was here.

When I pushed open the front door of BUTTERFIELD INVESTMENT ADVISERS, Rebecca, red cheeked from her dash across the street, looked up from behind the reception desk. With a smile, she rose to greet me, stepping from behind a gurgling fish tank to extend her hand.

"Verity. We haven't seen you in a while."

"That's because I don't have enough money to hire an investment adviser." Since that statement was painfully true, my attempted wry chuckle came out more like a strangled cry for help. Clearing my throat, I added hopefully, "Yet."

"I'm sure Noah could help you with that."

"Maybe he could. Is he here?"

"Not today, I'm afraid."

Rebecca's suddenly furrowed brow, plus her glance over her shoulder at Noah's office down the hall, seemed strange. Noah never missed a day's work—at least according to Emy's mom, the formidable Thérèse Dionne.

"Is he ill?"

"No. He's fine." She rubbed her hands together, but offered no explanation for her husband's absence.

"I won't keep you, then. It's just... I've been doing a little sleuthing for a friend—"

"You're good at that." Rebecca nodded, apparently welcoming the change in topic.

I chuckled nervously. "I don't know about that. Anyway, I heard you found one of those wallets with the clues."

"I did. It was fun. I posted it at the library."

"That's where I saw it, actually. Do you mind telling me where you found it?"

"I'll show you." Rebecca led me to the front window, where she pointed at a sandwich board advertising the village's secondhand record shop. In a nod to the inclement weather, the sandwich board was strapped to the nearest lamppost, three feet off the ground. I wondered if the village council had seen that sign. They were proud of the replica antique lampposts that dotted Main Street. The only allow-able embellishments were hanging summer baskets of asparagus ferns and flowers. Oh, and the Christmas wreaths that magically appeared after Halloween.

"The wallet was jammed between the two halves of that sign," Rebecca said. "It was right at eye level, so it was easy to spot."

"When was this?"

She scrunched up one eye, thinking. "Couple of days ago, I think. Not long, anyway. I took it to the library the same day." Her face brightened. "Did I win anything?"

"I'm not involved in the contest, sorry. I'm only curious. Does Noah have an opinion about it?"

"What do you mean?"

"Does he find the contest a bit—suspicious? It could be a fraud."

Rebecca took a step back with a jerk of her neck. "Verity. How did you get to be so cynical?"

Finding several dead bodies might have something to do with that, I thought, but kept that sentiment to myself.

"I'm not cynical. Really, I'm not. It's just odd. Who started this contest? And why?"

Rebecca shrugged. "Does it matter?"

"It might. Do you still have the wallet?"

Stepping behind the reception desk, she rooted through several cubbyholes before extracting a tattered brown billfold and handing it over.

Turning it over in my hands, I said, "This is pretty beat up."

"There wasn't anything in it except a scrap of paper with the clue written on it. I don't think anybody was using it as an actual wallet, do you?"

"Doesn't look like it." I handed it back. "Did you see who put it there?"

"No. And the wallet itself wasn't obvious unless you looked right at it. But I'm in and out of here so often, for lunch and so forth, that I naturally noticed it."

"Have you tried the new restaurant across the street?"

"Do you mean the vegan place?"

"Uh-huh. I had their soup. It was good."

She nodded thoughtfully. "I've been meaning to go over to welcome them to the neighborhood. Noah thinks we should offer them our services."

"You've never been inside?"

She shook her head. "Never."

Baffled by this obvious falsehood, I moved on. So far, my reconnaissance mission had been futile. "A Lucky Lentil employee found a wallet, too."

"Really?" Rebecca, who had turned her head to gaze indifferently out the window, didn't seem interested. The wind had picked up. The restaurant was barely visible through the swirling snow.

Scouring my brain for something to keep her talking, I hit upon the death of Oskar York. I'd seen Oskar coming out of the Butterfields' office once, months earlier. Even though I'd never met him, his shuffling, overweight bulk and thatch of unruly white hair had been instantly recognizable. Judging from the descriptions of the inside of his home, he wasn't wealthy enough to need investment advice. Maybe he and Noah were friends.

I rearranged my face into what I hoped was an expression of sorrow. "Sad news about Oskar York, isn't it?"

This topic definitely caught Rebecca's attention. She jerked her head back to face me. "Did you know him?"

"No, but I heard about the investigation."

Rebecca narrowed her eyes. "The police told Noah there was no need for an investigation. It was an accidental death."

I paused to analyze this sentence. Why would the police talk to Noah Butterfield about the death of the village's most notorious—and penniless—hoarder? Unless Noah knew him?

"Was Oskar one of Noah's clients?"

"I can't discuss our clients." Rebecca's attitude turned even frostier.

"Sorry. Only, it sounded as if your husband was advising him." I locked gazes with her. "Was he?"

"I can't answer that. Our clients insist on their privacy."

"So Oskar was a client?"

"I didn't say that."

"But if he was—"

"I can't talk about our clients."

I inclined my head. "Even the dead ones?"

Rebecca's eyebrows rose.

"I meant no disrespect," I hastily added.

She said nothing, but her expression was clear. I gestured weakly at the door. "Maybe I should get going."

"Maybe you should."

Turning to the entrance, I plunged a hand into my parka

pocket to retrieve my gloves. My fingers closed on Rick's discount cards. "Oh, wait." I turned to face her with one in my outstretched hand. "Next time you visit Lucky Lentil, you can get ten percent off." Regarding her intently, I tried to gauge her response. I wasn't disappointed.

Rebecca gawked at me, but didn't take the card. "What do you mean—next time? I told you, I've never been there."

"Sorry. I forgot." I dropped the card on the reception desk before turning to leave. At the door, I shot her a backhand wave and added, "Say hi to Noah for me," before stepping out and raising my parka's hood against the biting wind.

I'm not cynical, really. But I have been a little petty at times.

My bit of snark did nothing to raise my spirits. The day's "sleuthing" had been a waste of time. I didn't know who planted the wallets, or how to solve the crossword puzzle. Nor did I know why someone wrote a clue on a twenty-dollar bill and left it outside Henri Vartan's house.

Returning Henri's wallet seemed the logical next step. Another visit would allow me to scour the rest of his yard. Also, he may have recalled a vital clue that would shed light on his case. If it even was a case. Jeff's comment came to mind.

Do you have any idea how many wallets are turned in every week?

I climbed into my adorable pink pickup. As I started the engine, my mind swirled with questions. Such as—when did Rebecca Butterfield get so cozy with the village's newest arrival?

And where was her husband?

CHAPTER TWELVE

AFTER PULLING up outside Henri's house, I leaned over to pull his mystery wallet from the glovebox. Ruefully, I slipped it into my parka pocket, ready for the handover. My first case was a bust. I had nothing to report to my client, and no idea what to try next.

But Jeff always stressed the importance of "grunt work" to the constables who helped with his cases. I shouldn't give up so easily. At the least, I could interview anyone who'd found a mystery clue. Maybe that way, I could solve the puzzle. If I worked out the rest of the answers, it might become clear who planted the wallets—and why. It was worth a try.

I got out of the truck and slammed the door. Verity Hawkes, intrepid investigator of lost wallets, missing keys, and overdue books, was on the job.

My boots crunched on the unshoveled snow—I shook my head in sympathy—that led to Henri's eggplant-painted door.

I kept my head down so I wouldn't slip on the ice. Big mistake.

As I climbed the three stone steps that led to the entrance, the door flung open. I jerked my head up to see a figure in a hooded parka with a navy scarf over his face barrel down the steps, vaulting them two a time. Before I could react, he crashed into me.

With a strangled "Oomph," I flew backward, landing with a thud on my rear end in a snowbank. The more I flailed, the deeper I sank into the crusty snow. Eventually, I gave up struggling and flopped back, blinking snowflakes off my eyelids as I stared at the gray sky.

"Verity? Is that you?"

I managed a pitiful squeak. "Yeah. It's me."

Henri's round, red-cheeked face hung over me, his mouth agape. "Are you all right?"

"I think so." I flexed my fingers and toes. Nothing broken, at least. I wrenched one arm free and thrust it into the air. "Can you help me up?"

Grabbing my hand, Henri pulled.

My torso broke free with a loud crunching sound, and I struggled to my feet.

"Who the heck was that?" I asked, brushing snow from my arms and legs as I glanced around. My attacker was nowhere in sight. "He could have killed me."

"I have no idea, believe me," Henri said, massaging the side of his head.

"Is that blood?"

Henri lifted his fingers from his scalp, staring at them as if hypnotized. "I think it is." He raised his astonished eyes to mine. He was not wearing a coat. Or boots.

"Let's go," I said, firmly taking his arm and directing him to the door. "It's freezing out here. You can tell me the whole story inside."

While limping up Henri's front steps, I grimaced. Snow was working its way inside my boots and between my frozen toes. "I wrenched my knee when that thug knocked me over."

Henri pushed open the front door. "Wait till you see this." He closed the door behind us.

I halted in the foyer, stunned into silence.

The plastic sheets across the opening to the gallery hung in slashed ribbons. Easels were toppled, and an open tin of paint dribbled onto a drop cloth.

"When did this happen?"

"A few minutes ago." He heaved a sigh. "I was just about to check the second floor to see if they damaged anything up there."

"I'll come with you."

I slipped off my wet boots. We plodded up the stairs, my soggy feet leaving prints on the wooden steps.

At the top, we gasped. Every cupboard door and drawer in the kitchen gaped open, and crockery and utensils were strewn across the floor. Down the hall in Henri's bedroom, bedclothes were heaped on the floor and the bare mattress was flung against the wall.

In the living room, we chose our steps carefully. Almost every book in the room was now on the floor. Henri bent to retrieve a massive illustrated volume on *Truth or Dare in*

Twentieth Century Art. "This was a gift," he said, forlornly looking around for a place to put it.

I took it from his hands and slid it onto the nearest shelf. Then I flipped over an upturned armchair and patted its back. "Sit here and tell me what happened. Did you phone the police?"

He slumped into the chair. "Yes. Once I woke up."

"Were you sleeping?"

"No." He dropped his forehead onto his hands, elbows resting on his knees, fingers raking his hair. "I must have blacked out after he—ouch." Henri pulled his hands away from his head, staring in shock at his sticky fingers.

Fumbling in my parka pockets, I pulled out a tissue and bent over to check his scalp. "It doesn't look too bad. A flesh wound. I bet it hurts, though." I dabbed at it with the tissue. "You need to go to emergency to have that checked, especially if you blacked out. They should observe you for a concussion, at least. What did that guy whack you with?"

"I don't know."

"Tell me what happened, from the beginning."

"I went out to Bertram's, to get a little air—"

"In a snowstorm?"

Henri was not the type who exercised every day without fail, weather be damned. In fact, I'd spotted him more than once sitting on a park bench on a beautiful summer day, bemoaning the heat. A threatened snow flurry should have had him running for cover.

"It's not that bad," he said. "Besides, they always have those nice cheese danishes mid-week."

I raised my eyebrows, but he merely waved a hand.

"I wasn't gone more than an hour. I left Matisse at home, because the salt on the sidewalks always stings his—" Henri's eyes widened in horror, and a strangled cry came from his throat. "No-no-no..." He leapt to his feet, flinging me and the tissue aside. "Where's Matisse?"

I followed as he bolted downstairs.

"Watch the water on the stairs," I yelled. Too late.

The thump-thump of his body hitting wood was my answer.

On the first-floor landing, I grabbed Henri's arm to help him up.

"Matisse," he moaned.

"Listen," I said. "Is that—whimpering?"

We cocked our heads. Henri darted to the cupboard under the stairs, then flung open the door.

The little dachshund bounded out, excitably scrabbling into his owner's arms.

"*Mattie,*" Henri shrieked in a voice that must have been audible on Main Street, a block away. "I was so worried."

Tucking the dog against his chest, Henri went back upstairs, practically cooing at the dog.

I followed. "So, what happened? You came home and surprised an intruder, is that it?"

"I must have," Henri said over his shoulder, putting Matisse down on the linoleum. "I didn't see anybody. I came in, turned around to lock the door, and then—something hit me on the back of the head. When I opened my eyes, I was on the floor and the front door was wide open. When I got up to close it, I saw you in the snowbank."

After a fruitless search for the cookie jar on the trashed

kitchen counter, Henri patted all of his pockets in turn until he found a dog biscuit.

Matisse snapped it up. He seemed none the worse for his stay in the closet.

"So, I stepped outside to see if you were all right," Henri continued. "Are you all right, Verity? How's your knee? I'm so sorry."

"It's not your fault. And my knee is fine." I gave it a trial bend. "See? But your house is in shambles. What do you think this guy was looking for?"

"I couldn't say. We don't have anything valuable, other than the art, and he didn't take any of that."

"It was a man?"

"I guess so."

"You didn't see him?"

"No. I have to sit down." With a flutter of his hands, Henri plunked onto the nearest kitchen chair, breathing heavily.

I bent over with my hands on my knees, watching his face. "Breathe. You'll be fine. The police will be here soon."

After a few moments, his breathing slowed, and he looked up with a hand resting on his chest. "But why are you here, Verity? News on my case?"

"I'm afraid not. Sorry." Sliding the mysterious wallet out of my pocket, I handed it over. "I brought this back."

"Thanks." He placed it on the table, where it nearly disappeared in the clutter. Henri pointed at the wallet. "The intruder couldn't have been looking for that, could he?"

"I don't see why, unless he needed that clue on the twenty. But I compared it to the other clues and it's a duplicate, so it's not helpful in any way. That answer is already posted at the library. Besides, we don't know if there's even a prize."

I wasn't sure he'd heard me.

"No," he muttered, staring at the wallet. "That can't be it."

Turning to the stove, I filled the teakettle and flicked on a burner. After a short search, I found two unchipped mugs and a packet of tea bags.

Matisse plonked down next to Henri's feet.

That was when I remembered Mickey's strange request.

"There is one other thing, Henri. I was approached by someone who owns a shoebox full of old photos. They suggested maybe you could use them for a collage—Leafy Hollow historic lore and so on. This person wanted to know if you'd be interested in buying them. I meant to bring them by before this, but I forgot."

Henri shot me a surprisingly sharp look for someone suffering from a head wound. "This person wouldn't happen to be Mickey Doig, would it?"

"Maybe." To hide the growing flush on my cheeks, I bent over to rub the dachshund's silky ears. For an aspiring PI, I really needed to develop a better poker face. I straightened up. "What if it was?"

Henri's expression hadn't changed. "Mickey Doig is a two-bit crook and a scoundrel."

"That's a bit severe."

"Any photos of his will be worthless, Verity. Or worse, stolen. Did he say where he got them from?"

"Not exactly."

"Plenty of vintage photos have been donated since we announced the new gallery. So many, in fact, that we don't have time to sort them. All were offered free of charge. Unless old photos depict famous subjects, they're valuable only to the person who took them. Or their descendants."

This tirade seemed to drain the last of his resources. Henri slumped forward with a groan, holding his head.

I filled a mug with a tea bag and boiling water from the kettle, added milk from a carton in the fridge, and passed it to him.

After taking a sip and clearing a spot on the table for the mug, he continued. "Even if by some miracle they were valuable, Mickey's wrong if he thinks we can pay for them. Our budget doesn't allow for that. We're operating on meager donations. In fact..." Miserably, he picked up his tea. Matisse jumped onto his lap. Henri wrapped his other hand around the dog, staring vaguely at the contents of his mug.

I regarded him with a sudden stab of worry. It wasn't like Henri Vartan not to boast and bluster his way through a potential marketing opportunity. "Henri," I said softly. "Does the gallery have enough money to open?"

Wincing, he placed his mug on the table and shook his head.

I leaned over to give his shoulder a quick squeeze. "I'm sorry. That must be discouraging."

"Irma and Zuly are so excited about the opening. I haven't had the heart to tell them."

"What are you going to do?"

"Before this happened"—helplessly, he waved a hand at the mess—"we planned another fundraising drive. There were local businesses we hadn't tapped yet, like the village's investment adviser. So, I approached him."

"Noah Butterfield?"

Henri nodded. "Noah was helpful. He even suggested someone who might back our opening exhibit."

"Like who?"

"I don't think I should say." He let out a despairing moan. "Besides, there's no point. It's too late."

"You can tell me. I'll keep it to myself, I promise. Why is it too late?"

A siren blast whirred on the street outside, and car doors slammed. The police had arrived.

Henri leaned forward, dropping his voice to a whisper. "Because Noah told me to ask Oskar York."

I stepped back in surprise. "You're kidding. The rumors about him having a secret stash were true?"

Bang, bang, bang.

Booming knocks reverberated through the house. "Police!"

Bang, bang, bang.

"It's not locked," I called down the stairs.

As the front door opened, I tried to get more answers from Henri. "What did Noah say about Oskar's money?"

"I can't tell you," he whispered. "Don't ask me." Rising, he turned to the staircase.

I grabbed his arm. "No, please," I hissed. "Just tell me that one thing. What did Noah say?"

"Police!" a baritone voice called from the landing. "Anyone here?" Footsteps thumped on the steps, accompanied by a gust of freezing air.

Henri tugged his arm away, scooped up Matisse, and went down to greet the officers. I followed, stopping in the first-floor gallery to peer out the front window. An ambulance had pulled up, and two paramedics were headed for the front door.

I watched their approach while I puzzled over Henri's remarks. If Oskar York had indeed been wealthy instead of penniless, and if that wealth was hidden in his crowded house—that meant only one thing.

His death was not an accident.

CHAPTER THIRTEEN

JEFF CALLED me from his Strathcona conference within ten minutes of the police arriving at Henri's house. He insisted on returning immediately to check on me.

"Don't do that. I'm fine. Really. There's absolutely no reason for you to leave your meeting."

"I can be there in an hour."

"No, you can't," I said, bemused. "Unless you speed the entire distance with your siren on."

"It is an emergency," he replied defensively.

"No, it's not. Someone ransacked Henri Vartan's house and knocked him on the head, but he's going to be fine. The paramedics are checking him out, and then they're taking him to the urgent care clinic. Meanwhile, I'm dropping his dog off at a friend's place, so I won't even be at home. Stay where you are."

"Then I'm coming back tonight. Tomorrow's meetings aren't that important."

"Jeff, listen. I'm absolutely fine. Henri was thumped on the head, yes, but I wasn't. I want you to stay there until the end of your conference. I'll feel guilty if you come back."

I decided not to tell him about my encounter with Henri's intruder and my forced snow angel. It would only provide more ammunition for his case against my fledgling PI business.

There was another reason I didn't want him to return early, but I obviously couldn't tell him about that, either.

"Are you sure you're not hurt?"

"Positive. I mean it, Jeff. Stay where you are."

"Only if you promise to stay with Emy tonight. And take Boomer with you. He's a good guard dog."

Crossing my fingers behind my back, I said, "Okay. I promise."

After agreeing to call Jeff later, I set about packing doggy essentials. Henri was adamant about which coat the little dachshund required, and his preferred food.

"Matisse has a sensitive stomach," he said, waving an arm. "And please see if Bertram's has any more of those homemade organic dog biscuits—the ones with the cheese," he implored, frantically texting on his cell phone with his other hand.

"Hold still," cautioned the paramedic who was wrapping a temporary bandage on Henri's head wound.

"And don't give him licorice, whatever you do," Henri beseeched with an outstretched hand.

"Sir. Please," the paramedic chided.

Nodding, I repeated, "Grain-free food. Organic biscuits. No licorice." I held up a tiny red snowsuit with four tiny red legs, an artificial fur-trimmed hood, and "Canadian Canine" embroidered in white on the back. I'd found it tossed into the cupboard under the stairs. "Is this the right one?"

Henri nodded vigorously. The paramedic sighed loudly, but refrained from giving his patient a cuff on the head.

"Did you find his winter booties?"

"I'm afraid not."

"Well, don't let him walk on any salt."

"Check."

As I left holding Matisse in my arms, the little dog whimpered anxiously, looking over my shoulder at Henri. But once I got him into the truck, he sat placidly on the passenger seat until we were underway. Then he jumped up to plant both paws on the windowsill for a better vantage point.

Zuly Sundae lived above a convenience store on Main Street, several blocks from the village's center. Her second-floor one-room unit overlooked a parking lot at the back. When we pulled up outside, she was waiting downstairs with the front door open to the sidewalk, a cardigan pulled tight with her other hand.

She brushed her black hair over her shoulder before taking Matisse from my arms with a squeal. "You poor widdle ting. What an awful day for you."

Matisse frantically licked her face.

I followed Zuly and Matisse upstairs, closing the door behind me and edging past a dripping parka hanging from a wall hook at the top of the stairs. "Did you go out in this weather?"

"I didn't realize it was so awful. I wanted to see if any more clues had been posted at the library. The contest is fascinating, don't you think?"

I nodded, watching Zuly settle Matisse into a makeshift bed in the kitchen. "I guess."

"You sound dubious."

"I am, a bit."

"We can talk about the contest later. Tell me about Henri. He sounded hysterical in his texts. Is it true the gallery was ransacked?"

"I'm afraid so. But none of the art was taken, according to Henri."

"I rushed back from the library as soon as I got your call about Matisse. Did they take him all the way to Strathcona Hospital?"

"No. He's under observation at the urgent care center. I'm sorry I couldn't take Matisse home with me, by the way. I'm already hosting a visiting dog."

Boomer, I suspected, would not take kindly to interlopers. And I knew for certain the General wouldn't. I was on thin ice with the ornery old gentleman as it was.

"That's no problem. I love Matisse. I'll drop by the center later to let Henri know he's okay. And I'll send him a pic right now." Zuly rummaged around on the counter, shoving aside a plastic-wrapped loaf of bread, a carton of orange juice, and a stack of advertising flyers before finding her cell phone.

Plucking the dog from his new bed, she held him next to

her face with one hand. "Say cheese, Matisse," Zuly instructed, holding up her phone for a selfie.

At the word "cheese," Matisse yipped excitedly.

I slapped a hand on my forehead. "Darn. I forgot to check Bertram's for those organic biscuits Matisse likes."

Zuly issued an amused snort. "Yeah, like we're going to pay fifteen dollars a bag for those. And a tiny bag, at that."

I scrunched up one eye. "That does seem excessive." However, given Bertram's reputation as the village's highest-end food peddler, I wasn't surprised.

"No kidding. Listen, pup." Zuly nuzzled the little dog. "I have perfectly nice cheese right here."

She placed Matisse on the floor. Then she pulled a package of processed cheese slices from the fridge, slapped two on a plate, and set it down in front of him.

The dachshund tucked in ravenously. Luckily, I wouldn't be cleaning up after him.

After pulling a chair opposite mine, Zuly sat down. She leaned in, fixing me with an intense look. "Now. Tell me the truth. Why are you dubious about the contest? Don't you think it's a good thing for Leafy Hollow?"

I puffed in exasperation. "It could be a fraud, Zuly. How is that a good thing?"

Eyes widening, she straightened up, tossing her hair back with one hand before replying. "It's just a bit of fun, Verity. You're such a cynic."

"I'm not a cynic. Why does everyone keep saying that?"

"Have you been telling people it's a fraud?" Red spots of color on her cheeks announced her rising indignation.

"No, I haven't said anything. But it's suspicious, don't you think?"

She smoothed the front of her vintage blouse with both hands as she rose to her feet. "No, I don't think."

"And you're right—we don't know anything about it. Why is that? When I was a bookkeeper, I saw plenty of questionable transactions. Not everybody can be trusted. I'm sorry, but it's true."

Zuly bit her lip.

"Why would someone start a contest for no reason at all?" I continued. "What's the point? If there's a prize, what is it? Where is it?" My thoughts couldn't help returning to a previous crime in the village. "What if it's a decoy, to cover up something else?"

Zuly moved in jerky, almost angry movements to the sink, then twisted the hot water tap. With her back to me, she dumped a stack of dirty dishes into the sink with a clatter and added a stream of liquid soap. "You're from a big city," she said, raising her voice over the sound of the running water, "so you don't know how rarely anything exciting happens here. Maybe that's why you're so quick to heap scorn on us." She turned off the tap with a vicious twist.

"That's spectacularly unfair," I spluttered. "I love Leafy Hollow. I spent years of my childhood here. Vancouver is no longer my home. I left all that behind. I live here now."

Zuly showed no sign she'd heard me. "Or maybe you consider us country bumpkins who don't know any better than to be taken in by scam artists? And we need Verity Hawkes to save us?"

"How can you think that?"

I slumped against my chair, a hollow feeling in my chest. Did the villagers really see me as merely the latest interloper telling them how to run their lives? On my neck, a vein throbbed, a sure sign an anxiety attack was on the way. Shutting my eyes, I tried to slow my breathing. The anxiety that kept me a virtual prisoner in my Vancouver apartment after Matthew's death had tapered off during my time in Leafy Hollow. I wanted to keep it that way.

Zuly whirled around, making my eyes snap open at the sudden movement. She wiped her hands on a kitchen towel more viciously than I thought necessary. "Not everyone lives your charmed life, Verity. You've only been here a few months, yet you've already snared your own home and your own business and the most eligible bachelor in town. It all landed right in your lap. Things are pretty sweet up there in Rose Cottage, as far as I can tell."

She threw the towel onto the counter and crossed her arms, glaring at me.

Matisse's wide brown eyes swiveled from Zuly to me and back again.

A wave of indignation rose in my throat. *Wow.* Where to start with the description of my so-called charmed life? The deadbeat dad who abandoned my mother and me when I was a child? The husband who died much too young, making me a widow in my twenties? Or the aunt who disappeared for months, scaring me half to death?

"Listen," I said, struggling to form words. "That is so—"

Before I could finish my sentence, Zuly burst into tears.

On the floor, Matisse tilted his head in confusion as he stared up at her.

My mouth hung open in disbelief. Wordlessly, I pulled a tissue pack from my pocket and handed it to her.

Zuly took it, sniffling, then turned to face the window and blew her nose. After several deep breaths, she faced me again. "Sorry," she said.

Matisse pawed at her leg. After another swipe at her nose with the tissue, she picked him up and swiveled back to the window and its mundane view of a parking lot, sighing heavily.

"What's going on, Zuly? What's wrong?"

No reply. The soap bubbles in the sink gradually dispersed, leaving only a slick on the surface of the water.

Finally, she straightened her shoulders, smiling weakly as she spun toward me, clutching the dog to her chest. "This attack on Henri and the gallery has been upsetting. Not to mention Oskar York's horrible accident. It's been an awful week." She took another deep breath. "I shouldn't have said those things, Verity. I'm sorry."

"Did you know Oskar?"

She shrugged. "Not really. But he's a Meals on Wheels client, and Irma's a volunteer. It's too bad she wasn't there that day..."

Letting her observation hang there unfinished, Zuly put Matisse on the floor and sat in the chair opposite me. She lifted the lid of a teapot sitting on the table. "Shall I boil some water?"

"Not for me, thanks."

She replaced the lid and pushed the pot away.

Since our pleasant conversation seemed beyond repair, I decided to go for broke. "Speaking of Oscar York, did you ever hear rumors that he hid money or valuables in his house? Or that he was secretly wealthy?"

Zuly's eyes rivaled tea saucers at this line of questioning. "Who told you that?"

"Henri mentioned it. Today, after the attack." I tried to recall if I'd promised not to tell anybody, but came up blank. Despite my assurances to Jeff that I was fine, I was rattled. The vein in my neck continued to throb. *This was no time for an anxiety attack*, I thought. I forced myself to concentrate on the soothing bubble bath I intended to slip into at the end of this trying day.

Meanwhile, Zuly was talking.

"...so I don't know anything about that. Irma delivered meals to Mr. York, sure, but they never talked about his money as far as I know. Or even if he had any, come to think of it."

"No rumors?"

She ran a hand along the edge of the table, not meeting my eyes. "Not that I heard."

Rising to my feet, I said, "Let me know if you need any help with Matisse."

"We'll be fine." Her brisk tone told me my help wouldn't be needed.

Back in the truck, I turned on the engine to heat the cab and sat there, thinking. Something in Zuly's reply when I asked about Oscar York's rumored riches didn't sit right. She knew something about the old man, something hidden. But what?

I didn't want to think about it anymore. I wanted to go home to an early dinner and that soothing bath. And then, I intended to curl up on the sofa in front of a roaring fire and thumb through Mickey's shoebox of photos.

I recalled Henri's question. *Did he say where he got them from?* Remembering Mickey's suspicious claim about the flea market, I thought—*no, he didn't. And why was that?*

My phone beeped with a text.

ARE WE SET FOR TONIGHT?

I texted back a thumb's-up emoji.

CHAPTER FOURTEEN

LATER THAT NIGHT, I parked the highly visible Coming Up Roses truck in a side street two blocks from the bakery and trekked the rest of the way, my head bent against the bitter wind. Main Street was deserted. Even The Tipsy Jay had long since sent its last drinker home. The bar's hanging sign creaked in the wind, making its giant bird sway. After a cautious glance around, I ducked into the alley beside the 5X.

At the back entrance, Lorne was huddled over the lock. He turned his key. A moment later, we were inside with the metal door closed behind us.

"Did you bring your flashlight?" I whispered.

"Right here." Lorne switched it on. "I taped over it," he said, pointing to the lens, where duct tape blocked all but a tiny stream of light. "That way, it can't be seen from the street. But we should hold it facing the floor at all times."

"That's impressive, Lorne."

"I saw it on a rerun of *It Takes a Thief*."

"Even so, it's quite professional."

In the feeble gleam, I saw him shrug modestly. "We should take our coats off, so we'll be ready for action in case we have to tackle anybody."

"Why would we be tackling anybody?"

"They might try to escape."

"Why would they—wait, why are we whispering? Emy's a sound sleeper."

"Yeah," Lorne said in his normal voice, with a glance up at the ceiling. "True."

After shucking off our parkas and boots and throwing them into a heap in the back room, we crept into the takeout's customer area, where we paused, surprised by the sudden light. "I forgot about the streetlamps," I said with a groan, pointing to the square of yellow on the floor facing the plate glass window. "We'll have to sit behind the counter. That way, we can hear anyone who comes in the back door, but they won't see us."

Given that I was five-ten and Lorne five-eleven, tucking ourselves out of view behind the tiny counter wasn't easy. We wiggled and squirmed for a bit.

"Ow," I said. "Watch it. That was my eye."

"Sorry," Lorne said, pulling in his elbow. "There's not much room here."

"When does this delivery person arrive?"

"I narrowed it down to a one-hour window. I couldn't ask Emy outright, so I employed an unorthodox line of inter-rogation."

"Such as?"

"Questions about her inventory methods."

133

"Wasn't she suspicious?"

"No. Inventory control is one of my college courses."

"Did this interrogation produce any concrete evidence?"

"Our target arrives between two AM and three AM. Emy comes downstairs to start baking at four, and the new stuff is always here by then."

"We don't have long to wait. Fortunately." With a groan, I rearranged my limbs. "So, Lorne—your courses. How are they going?"

"Really good. A year or two more, and I'll have a diploma."

"That's terrific. Good work."

"I never could have done it without your help. And Thérèse, of course."

Thérèse Dionne, Leafy Hollow's chief librarian and Emy's mom, had convinced Lorne to enroll in the local community college as an adult student to earn a business diploma.

"You had help, sure, but the hard work was all yours. Thérèse is proud of you. When the big day finally comes—"

"The big day? You mean graduation?"

I punched his upper arm. "No, idiot. Well, yes, graduation, but I was thinking more of a wedding day."

Lorne let out a long puff of air. "I don't know about that."

This was puzzling. I'd never met anybody crazier about someone than Lorne was about Emy.

"I know your parents have that nice rental unit in their basement, and you're comfortable there, but..." I took a deep breath. "Shouldn't you be living here, with Emy?"

"I can't," he said wistfully.

"Why not? It's not Emy, is it?" I knew it wasn't, but I didn't want Lorne to know that my best friend and I frequently discussed his reluctance to commit.

"I don't want to talk about it," he said.

"Okay, then. How about those Leafs, eh? Did you see that game against the Bruins on Tuesday?"

"Yeah. That third-period save by Andersen was amazing, wasn't it?"

"Yeah. For sure. It was—amazing."

The digital clock on the wall ticked over. Then again.

"Oh, come on, Lorne. I don't want to talk about hockey. I want to know why you're not living with Emy." I flicked a hand in annoyance.

"*Ow.* Watch it. That was my ear."

"Sorry. But—"

"I have no income, no job, and no prospects. I'm not going to live off Emy's money."

"She doesn't care."

"I do." The light streaming through the windows revealed the stubborn set of his jaw. Lorne wasn't kidding. He wanted to be the provider. *Men.* I recalled Jeff's earnest declaration—*It's not a problem. I have plenty of money*—and my heart gave a little twist. That led to memories of my deadbeat father and the realization that wanting to be the breadwinner wasn't a bad thing. In fact—

With a sudden start, I placed my hands on my hips. "What do you mean, no income? I pay you to work at Coming Up Roses."

"Not in the winter," Lorne said, then added hastily,

"Which isn't your fault. I'd be happy to help with snow-plowing if it wasn't for my classes."

"I know. To be honest, I'm not that keen on snow removal myself. As for future prospects, I'd bet on you any day. In fact, in the future I fully expect to holiday on your yacht in the Mediterranean."

He snorted with laughter.

"But I won't visit you in the south of France if Emy's not there," I added in a warning tone. "You better decide what you're doing, buster. She's not going to hang around forever."

Actually, I suspected Emy would hang around forever waiting for Lorne, but that was a different argument. Meanwhile, my knees were throbbing after half-an-hour crammed into that tiny space. "Enough heart to heart. Let's stand up and stretch our legs," I suggested.

We were jogging lightly in place when a key turned in the back door.

"Get down," I blurted. We dropped in our tracks.

"*Ow*," I said. "That was my—"

"Shh," Lorne hissed.

The door opened and then closed with a clink of metal.

I expected the new arrival to switch on the overhead light, but nothing happened. Poking Lorne with my finger, I whispered, "No light."

"I know," he whispered back.

Shuffling footsteps came down the short hall. A delivery person would have turned into the refrigerated storage area by the back door to drop off their goods, but this one continued on until they reached the public area of the shop where we were hiding behind the counter.

I poked Lorne again. "Burglar?" I whispered.

"Maybe," he whispered back.

More shuffling footsteps. A hooded figure paused, outlined in the light from the streetlamps. It was almost as wide as it was tall, with both hands clasped on a massive belly as it waddled forward. If this was a delivery person, he or she was badly out of shape.

"On three," Lorne whispered. "One. Two—"

We darted out from behind the counter to tackle the newcomer.

Well... Lorne tackled the newcomer. I caught my toe on the edge of the counter, then screamed in pain before jumping about on one foot. "*Oww-oww-oww*," I squealed. "That hurts."

"Verity—help, please," Lorne called from the floor, where he was grappling with the intruder. "What the blazes?" he yelled. One of his hands hit the vinyl flooring with a loud slap.

I hurried over to assist, surprised the athletic Lorne couldn't handle an overweight delivery boy on his own. But before I could apply my planned headlock, my foot stepped into something slippery and slid out from under me.

I hit the floor. "What the blazes?" I muttered, unconsciously mimicking Lorne.

"Verity—get him," Lorne yelled.

Lorne was crawling across the floor in an uncoordinated way. Every so often, a knee or hand slid away from him. The hooded figure was also scrambling on all fours, trying to evade Lorne. They were both moving with the speed of turtles.

Sore toe forgotten, I dove for the intruder with a guttural cry rarely heard outside a Wimbledon forecourt. My arms closed around his torso at the approximate location of that enormous belly. I expected it to be, if not exactly firm, at least wobbly. Instead, it collapsed beneath my hands, almost as if the entire figure was dissolving.

With a horrible squelching sound, I slid off the intruder and onto the floor, face-first.

When I tried to raise myself up on my hands and knees, my arms slithered out in front of me. When I lifted one hand, it came away from the floor with a sucking noise. "What is this stuff?" I asked in disgust. "Where did it come from?"

"Get him," Lorne called.

Not much chance of that. I was mired in place.

"Show yourself," I demanded—trying, and failing, to stand up. "Who are you? What are you doing here?"

"Verity?" came a tremulous voice. "Is that you?"

My jaw dropped at the sound of a familiar voice. "Shanice? What are you doing here?"

"I can explain. Really."

Lorne clapped his hands against the nearest wall, one after the other, to pull himself up. He shuffled to the back door, without lifting his feet, and flicked on the overhead light.

I took a good look around, hardly believing what I saw.

"Son of a bee sting. Shanice—what have you done?"

The tiled white walls and floor of Emy's pristine vegan takeout were covered in yellow swirls, mounds, and splashes. As were all three of us.

I lifted the back of my hand to my face for a quick sniff,

followed by an exploratory lick. "It's butter, isn't it?" I asked. "There's butter everywhere."

Shanice tossed her parka hood back, shooting me an apologetic look. "I'm sorry."

Sighing, I closed my eyes.

"It's unsalted," she added hesitantly.

The room went silent.

Finally, "I can't believe you'd do this to Emy," I said. "Bring a pail of butter in here, I mean. You posted those photos online, didn't you?"

Shanice's eyes were wide. "No! I didn't. Please believe me, Verity. It's not what you think."

"It was bad enough that you planned to store another pail of butter in Emy's back room. But why did you leave the lid off? Look at this mess," I wailed.

"I didn't. It's not what you think."

Lorne spoke up from his position by the light switch. His eyes narrowed at Shanice. Lorne was slow to anger, but this was too much, even for him. "You better start explaining."

Shanice swiped butter from her face, leaving one eye partially closed. "I wanted to cheer up Emy. And it wasn't a pail of butter. It was a sculpture." She gestured at a black garbage bag muddled in a heap at her foot. "I had it in there, on a board, and when you tackled me—"

"A what?" I asked, my voice cracking. "It was a what?"

"A butter sculpture," Shanice said. "I made it for Emy."

I scrambled to my feet by clutching the edge of the counter and stood, clinging to it. After a few seconds of wordless staring at the mess, I managed only, "I have to sit down."

Lorne skated slowly forward, sliding a stool my way. I

plunked onto it. "Thanks." Slumping forward with my arms on my thighs, I regarded the muddled garbage bag. I raised my gaze to Shanice. "Explain it to me again."

"When our class checked out the food exhibits at the fall fair last year, one of the displays had these cool butter sculptures. Ever since, I've wanted to try making one. And now, with all those horrible reviews online, I thought it would be a way to have fun with the whole butter thing. I imagined Emy would display it in the bakery and everybody would —laugh."

"I'm not laughing."

"No, not after this. But it was so cute, Verity. I thought Emy would like it. I thought it would give her a chuckle. Maybe take her mind off things."

"Is this the truth, Shanice?"

"Yes," she wailed. "Would I make that up?"

Lorne puffed out a stream of air. "She's got a point there."

"Why were you delivering this sculpture in the dead of night?"

"Because I wanted it to be a surprise when Emy came downstairs, and she always does that at four, so I had to get here early, and I have a key, naturally, so I thought—if I just let myself in, I can go into the bakery and leave it on the counter and—"

I held up a weary hand. "I'm not saying I believe you, but what did this sculpture look like?"

Shanice brightened, just a little. "Emy standing behind the counter with a tray of cookies. I have a picture. I can show you. It's on my phone."

"All right." I stumbled to my feet. "Better wash your

hands before you get out your phone," I said, pointing to the sink.

While Shanice was cleaning herself up, I asked, "Have you ever sculpted butter before?"

"Not exactly. I practiced at home first." Shanice dried her hands, then retrieved her phone. While she scrolled through the photos, she added, "That nice artist woman, the one from the library, helped me."

"Zuly? Or Irma?"

"The one who does the beautiful watercolors."

"That would be Irma." After Shanice handed me the phone, I studied the sculpture in the picture. Lorne leaned over to take a look. Sniffing, he stood up again.

"It was rather good," I said, handing back the phone. "Too bad it's all over the floor." I turned to Lorne. "What do you think? Should we call the police?"

Shanice started forward with pure terror on her face. "Don't do that. Please. I'm so sorry."

Lorne knew I was kidding. His mouth started to twitch. "Sounds like a good plan to me."

Shanice whimpered, clapping a hand over her mouth.

I let her dangle for a few moments.

Then I said, "We're not doing that. But you'll have to help clean this up. Before Emy sees it."

Shanice carefully shuffled off to get mops and pails from the back room.

Lorne, who had winced at the mention of his beloved, glanced at the clock. "We'll never get it done in time."

"We have to try."

With all three of us mopping and wiping, we almost

missed the arrival of our true quarry. It was after three when we heard the telltale sound of a key in the lock.

We froze. Gripping my mop handle, I whispered, "The delivery guy."

The door opened, and a young man in a parka with a logo on the chest entered. He was carrying a large box with both hands. He kicked the door shut behind him with one foot.

Whistling, he headed for the storage area.

Suddenly, he froze. He slowly turned his head to face us.

"Hi," I said.

"Whoa. Normally, there's no one here."

"Sorry if we startled you." I propped my mop handle against the wall. "We were hoping to ask you a few questions."

"Can I just—" He tilted his head toward the storage area. "Put this away first? It's heavy."

"Go ahead. Meet you back here."

He returned a moment later, smiling feebly. "I'm in kind of a hurry. Lots of deliveries tonight. So, if you don't mind—"

"This will only take a second. Did you bring a tub of butter in here and photograph it?"

"No. I would never do anything..." His voice trailed off as he flicked his gaze between us. "Like that."

It took only a few seconds of Lorne towering over him with a grim expression before Harry—the name was stenciled on his parka under the logo of a wholesale grocer—came clean.

"Look," Harry said. "They told me it was a practical joke. Some kind of birthday thing. It wasn't serious."

I adopted my most earnest tone. "Let me get this straight.

An unknown person paid you fifty dollars to plant a vat of butter in Emy's storage area, snap a photo of it, and then take the butter away again?"

"That's right. Like I said, a practical joke. That's all."

"Then you emailed them the photo—and they posted it online?"

"I don't know what they did with it. I just sent it to them. I never met them in person."

"How did you get the cash, then?"

He cocked his head, raising an eyebrow. "You've never heard of online banking?"

"Don't get snarky with me." I'd spent nearly an hour mopping up butter at that point, and I was in no mood for chitchat about our financial system. "You must know their real name."

"I don't. Sorry. Can I go?" His gaze zeroed in on a point over my shoulder. "Emy. How ya doing?"

Lorne's eyes, also fixed on something behind me, widened.

Cringing, I turned around.

Emy was wearing a fleece robe and slippers. Her hair was rumpled. "What's going on here?"

Her voice was eerily calm—the kind of calm that must have been in evidence right before the passengers on the Titanic said, "Why is there so much water in this stateroom?"

Lorne, Harry, and I stood rooted to the spot.

Shanice stepped forward. "It's my fault."

That was when Emy noticed our pails and mops, and the butter we hadn't reached yet. Her mouth opened and closed a few times like one of those little aquarium fishes while she surveyed the scene. No one spoke.

Finally, Harry cleared his throat. "Can I go?" When no one replied, he added, "Invoice's on the counter, Emy," and backed out, closing the door behind him.

"Well?" Emy asked.

With all of us talking at once, it took ten minutes to fully explain.

Finally, Emy handed Shanice back her phone, her demeanor tense. "I'm going upstairs. When I come back down here in an hour, I want all of this"—she swept a hand to indicate the remaining mess—"gone."

"We were only trying to help," I said, helplessly.

"I asked you and Lorne to leave it alone. Once this story gets out—" Emy raised a hand to curb the rebuttal rising on my lips. "Oh, yes, Verity. It will get out. This is Leafy Hollow, don't forget. Then, those rumors about Eco Edibles will *really* take off." She swiveled on one slippered foot before disappearing through the connecting door and up the stairs to her apartment.

Lorne slumped on to the stool, face crumpled in devastation.

"She'll get over it," I said hopefully, feeling totally inadequate to the task of cheering him up.

CHAPTER FIFTEEN

THE FLIMSY PAPERS rustled in his fingers as Mickey Doig lined up cigarette wrappers on the threadbare sofa, counting them under his breath. Hopefully he could sell enough joints to tide him over until his more ambitious scheme bore fruit.

In the far corner of the basement, behind the furnace, a clothes dryer rattled and bumped, almost drowning out the television that faced the sofa. Uma was doing laundry. She'd be back down with another load before long, so he should hurry. After tugging a plastic bag from behind a cushion, he untwisted its tie and placed it beside a stack of dirty plates on the packing crate beside the sofa. He sprinkled a mound of dried weed onto each paper, glancing up at the TV when a new contestant walked out to face The Dragons.

The reality-show panel of investors frowned as the latest arrival explained his sure-fire business plan for "foreign driving gloves. You can wear them on either hand, depending on whether you're driving on the right-hand side of the road or the left side."

The panel fell silent. Ominous music blared on the show's soundtrack. Mickey was unable to tell whether the panelists were stunned by the brilliance of this idea, or simply stunned. "Wait—what?" one of them finally asked.

Mickey returned to his task.

He wasn't thrilled to be sleeping in the basement of his friend's house. But Willy had offered, and Mickey accepted. He knew that Uma Wilkes, Willy's mother, wouldn't approve, but he'd already settled in before she learned of the new arrangement. *He's got nowhere else to go*, Willy told her. Which was true—until Mickey landed a job, his finances would be under pressure. And since a job wasn't really his style, he'd be here for a while.

Not forever, though. He had plans.

After rolling and licking each paper in turn, he lined up the joints with a surge of pride. Then he pulled off his woolen hat and dropped it on the sofa, scratched his head vigorously, and parted his hair with his fingers. Once that was completed to his satisfaction, he pulled a folded page from the hat's inner pocket. While the clothes dryer rumbled on, he studied the list of crossword clues he'd found in Old Man York's shoebox. Quick to realize the list gave him a leg up in the competition, he had removed it from the box before giving the photos to Verity Hawkes for resale.

Ever since, he'd been trying to work out why the old man had a copy of the solved puzzle. Eventually, he decided the contest must have been York's idea from the start—a way to distribute his hidden riches. It seemed a crazy way to give away money, but there was no denying that Oskar York was a crazy guy.

The crossword answers made no sense to Mickey, but that seemed appropriate, given their source. It didn't matter, anyway. All he had to do was wait for the appropriate moment and then "solve" the final clue in the puzzle. Wouldn't Leafy Hollow be surprised?

Snickering, he fingered the half-dozen photos he'd also saved from the box, fanning them out on a sofa cushion and turning them over one by one. He didn't recognize most of the people in any of the photos. Except for one. He held that picture under the cheap metal floor lamp by the sofa for a better look.

Oskar York had been much younger when the photo had been taken. Mickey had never seen a smile like that on the old man's face. Mostly, Oskar only scowled and complained during Mickey's visits. Once, he'd demanded that Mickey go next door and, "tell them to stop running around in their skivvies."

The old man had never been sociable. So, who were the people in the picture with him? Mickey tapped his fingers on the photo before tucking it back into his hat.

Come to think of it, why hadn't he heard back from Verity about the other pictures? Just because that blowhard Henri Vartan was laid up—he chuckled at the image—was no reason to delay a potentially sweet deal.

The dryer's buzzer beeped, making him jump.

Seconds later, Uma Wilkes, her trim figure clad in running shoes, yoga pants, and a navy Maple Leafs hoodie, descended the stairs with a laundry basket perched on her hip.

Mickey scrambled to a sitting position while flipping the edge of the afghan over the newly rolled joints. He eyed Uma appreciatively. More than once, he'd fantasized about what was under those yoga pants. She was a little older, sure, but experience was a good thing, right? She'd probably be interested in hot young stuff such as himself, given the opportunity.

"How ya doing, Mrs. Wilkes?"

Uma halted mid-step with a look of disgust. "Mickey," she said tersely, before continuing down the stairs and into the laundry room behind the furnace.

Mickey sniffed. *Doesn't know what she's missing,* he thought. He resumed his study of the crossword. Given the looming legalization of marijuana, he needed a new source of income. But it would take way more capital than he had to crack the hard-drugs market. How much did those loony librarians say this contest was worth? A million? He twisted his lips, contemplating this potential windfall.

The dryer started up again with a rumble. Moments later, Uma passed him on her way upstairs.

Mickey shot her a friendly wave, which she ignored.

The door at the top of the stairs opened, and footsteps much louder than Uma's rumbled down. Willy Wilkes took two steps at a time as he descended, barely avoiding the dangling laces of his turquoise Adidas. When he turned sideways to sidle past his mother on her way up, she grabbed his arm. Uma jerked her head at Mickey, who was intently watching the Dragons humiliate the driving-gloves guy and pointedly ignoring the pair on the staircase.

"How long is he staying?" Uma's query was conveyed at a volume that might have been meant as a stage whisper—if the listeners were deaf, which Mickey definitely wasn't. In fact, he was proud of his excellent hearing. If he'd wanted to, he could have been one of those whisperer guys.

Willy glanced guiltily at Mickey. "I dunno."

Uma switched the laundry basket to her other hip with a flourish of irritation and marched up the stairs, adding over her shoulder, "Find out." The door at the top closed with a hollow thud.

Willy thundered down the rest of the steps, managing to reach the bottom without tripping over his laces. He hustled over to the sofa to exchange a complicated handshake with his friend.

Mickey gave him a hurt look. "Your mom is like, really cold, dude."

Willy shrugged. "She can be that way sometimes. No worries. Aren't you supposed to be walking dogs today?"

"Came back to fill a few orders. Didn't know old Uma was home, sorry." After flipping the edge of the afghan, he selected a joint and handed it to Willy. "Your cut."

Willy's face fell. "One? Come on, man—like, I gave you fifty bucks."

"It takes money to make money, dude."

"I know, but—"

"Willy—"

"Stop calling me that."

"Dude. It's your name. What's wrong with it?" Chuckling, Mickey carefully inspected the other joints before selecting the largest. "Hardly anybody calls you Wee Willy anymore."

His friend slumped onto the other end of the sofa, petulantly twirling his unlit joint between his fingers. "Most guys call me Viper."

"They do not." At Willy's truculent expression, Mickey amended his comment to, "Whatever." Sliding the joint between his lips, he pulled a lighter from his pocket and flicked it on.

Frantically, Willy waved his hands. "Not here, dude. Mom's been like"—he adopted a strident falsetto—"'What's with all that smoke in the basement?' And I'm like, 'Nothing,' and she's like, 'Are you smokin' weed down there?'"

Mickey shrugged. "Your mom should chill. It's legal now."

"Almost."

Mickey shrugged.

"Seriously, dude, she wants you to leave. For real this time."

The joint between his lips flapped as Mickey pointed to the TV. "I'm going to be on that show."

"Dragon's Den? Like, seriously?"

"Yeah. The producer loved my idea for spray-on underwear." Mickey tilted his head to indicate the rumbling dryer. "No more laundry, eh?" He pulled the unlit joint from his mouth, then dropped it into a plastic bag. After adding the others, he tucked the bag behind the sofa cushion.

"How do you get it off?"

"Peel it. Easy."

"Cool."

Mickey nodded gravely. "I know."

While Willy babbled on about his own business plans, Mickey feigned interest. But really, he was trying to decide what to do about those photos in his hat. Because while he'd been mulling it over, he realized someone in those pictures looked familiar.

Which was weird. Because if they were friendly with Old Man York, why hadn't they come forward when his body was found? Why were they pretending not to know him?

He sucked in a breath as another notion hit him. What if this other person had been in York's kitchen when that mountain of junk fell on him—the first time? What if that "accident" had been deliberate?

"Lend me your phone, Willy." Mickey extended his hand.

Willy shot him a look of annoyance. "No way. Last time, Mom was all"—he switched to a falsetto again—"'What are these extra charges on our phone bill? Have you been watching porn again? We talked about this.'"

Mickey flashed his fingers in a *gimme* motion. "I need to send a text."

Scowling, Willy handed over his phone. "One text. Like, one."

Mickey keyed in a message.

GUESS WHAT I FOUND IN THE OLD MAN'S HOUSE?

And hit Send.

It took only moments for the phone to beep. After reading the message, Mickey sent a reply.

Smiling, he handed the phone back to Willy. Things were looking up. And—bonus—old Uma would finally realize that *Mickey Rules*. And show him a little respect.

CHAPTER SIXTEEN

I NEVER SAW IT COMING.

One moment, Boomer and I were strolling along the woodland path behind Rose Cottage, admiring the snow-covered spruce trees glistening in the sunshine and the vivid red cardinals flitting from branch to branch.

The next, I was face down in a snowdrift, struggling to breathe, with an unfriendly knee in my back and one arm pinned behind me.

From my Krav Maga training, I knew it was better to flee than fight. But sometimes there was no choice.

First, the feint.

I stopped struggling, forcing my body to relax. The moment the pressure on my back eased, I shoved against the ground with my unpinned arm and flipped over.

Even with one hand behind my back, I was able to knee my attacker in the groin. He barely had time for a muttered oath before I followed that up by slamming the heel of my palm into his nose.

Then I was on my feet, ready to run.

"Blast," came a muffled voice from the figure bent over beside me. Red drops stained the snow at his feet. "I told you this was a bad idea."

"No, it was a good idea. You're just too old and too slow," a woman said.

I recognized that voice.

With both hands planted on my hips, I abandoned my planned flight and swiveled around on one foot to scowl at the pair who stood before me.

My next-door neighbor Gideon Picard, a hand clapped to his bloody nose and a parka hood pulled over his gray topknot, glared accusingly at me through his blue-tinted octagonal glasses.

"Sorry about that, Gideon. But you surprised me."

"You could have broken my nose," he said with a distinctly nasal tone.

"No. My aim was off."

The woman beside him was Aunt Adeline. She tilted her bare head, with its pixie-cut streaked gray hair, in amusement. One finger was looped under Boomer's collar, holding him in place.

The terrier was looking up at her with undisguised awe.

Figured. Even animals fell under my aunt's spell.

I scanned her winter outfit. The fur-trimmed parka, leggings, and snow boots were pure white. "Is that your Alpine disguise?" I asked. "Because we're about a thousand miles from any mountains."

Her gold-flecked gray eyes twinkled. "Don't you be smart with me, young lady." Aunt Adeline smiled sweetly at me while handing her companion a crumpled tissue.

Gideon held it to his nose with his head tilted back, muttering under his breath.

"Excellent work, by the way," my aunt enthused. "Glad to see you haven't lost your edge, Verity. Although—" She narrowed her eyes. "You should have noticed we've been tracking you for half a mile."

"How could I hear footsteps in the snow?" I pointed to the fresh dusting of white that covered the path I'd taken through the woods on my way back to Rose Cottage. *Hang on —why was I making excuses?* "Tell me why you were trailing me."

Aunt Adeline looked surprised. "To keep your skills sharp, of course. There's no telling when you might have to defend yourself. Snow is no excuse. Villains don't take the winter off. Also"— she gave Gideon a pointed look—"you're not the only one who's slowing down. Someone needs to hit the gym more often."

Gideon, having known my aunt for decades, did not waste his breath on objections.

I, on the other hand, was indignant. "I have not been slowing down. You try cutting lawns and clearing brush for a living, then see whether you're fit or not." I straightened up to my full height, glaring down at her.

"I didn't mean you, Verity." My aunt bestowed the same benign smile on me she'd been using since my childhood. "Of course, *you're* fit."

Gideon emitted a strangled cry of protest.

Adeline ignored him. "We only want to keep you on your toes. Especially since the attack on Henri Vartan. Have the police uncovered any motive?"

I eyed her suspiciously. "How would I know?"

The corners of my aunt's mouth twitched, but she said nothing.

"Jeff does not share details of police investigations with outside parties, and that includes me."

My aunt raised her hands in a conciliatory gesture that didn't fool me for a minute. "I'm not fishing." Her voice lowered a register to her most serious tone. "You have to be careful, that's all I'm saying. Promise me you'll be careful, and I'll back off."

My irritation vanished, and I held out both hands with a muttered, "Aww."

I wrapped her in a hug, inhaling the comforting, familiar aroma of lavender tinged with a whiff of cheroot. After fearing my aunt was dead, I was not used to the pleasure of having her back in my life—and in one piece. It had been months since our reunion at Niagara Falls and the tumultuous case that brought us together. But I could not forget the overwhelming joy of seeing her face again, and of being given a second chance to mend our relationship.

I'd recently dropped by the cottage she shared with Gideon, hoping to catch a movie while seated in the *Star Trek* command center that spanned their living room. When my aunt and her partner greeted me at the door, I was stunned to see they both sported bruises, and Gideon was using a cane. He'd tried to tuck it behind the captain's chair, so I wouldn't see it.

They attributed their injuries to a cross-country skiing mishap. I was fairly sure that was a lie, but what could I do? My aunt had promised me they were retired from their "freelance security work," and I had to take her at her word.

So, actually, it was a relief to know the only person she was currently tracking was me. It felt good to have someone worry about me, to be honest. Someone else, that was. Jeff also considered it his job to repel any and all potential attackers. Between Aunt Adeline and my new beau, I feared for any villains who might have me in their sights.

"You're bored, aren't you?" I asked before releasing my aunt with a grin.

"A little."

"How about we do some sparring next week? We can go to the gym."

She returned my grin. "Excellent idea." Leaning in, she whispered loudly, "Let's leave the men at home. That way, we can get in a good workout without worrying about hurting them."

Behind us, Gideon snorted.

"Only if you promise to stop ambushing me," I said.

"I'll think about it."

We set out for Rose Cottage, Boomer bounding ahead and racing back, over and over. Occasionally he left the path to chase a squirrel, only giving up when he was chest deep in snow.

Adeline smiled at his antics. "Silly dog," she said. "Are you keeping it?"

"Dunno. Maybe."

At a fork in the trail, Gideon turned toward their house. "Are you coming?" he asked my aunt.

"You go on. I'm going to walk Verity home first." She slid an arm under mine.

Home. I was still getting used to that. For decades, Rose Cottage had been my aunt's—until she insisted on giving it to me and moving in with Gideon.

"How are the gardening plans going? Have you thought any more about that recirculating brook?" she asked.

"I've been working on something else. Not garden-related."

She squeezed my arm gleefully. "I know. Emy told me all about it when I dropped by the bakery. How's it coming? The case, I mean?"

"It's not really a case—merely an odd coincidence. It's these strange wallets people are finding. And then there's Oskar York."

Adeline nodded sorrowfully. "So sad."

"Did you know him?"

"Years ago, before he became a recluse."

"He wasn't always that way?"

"No. He was a respected academic at one time. Oskar was never what you'd call a party animal, but he did leave his house from time to time."

I winced. This was hitting close to home. After Matthew died, for the next two years I rarely left our Vancouver apartment. I spent most of that time kicking aside dust bunnies and devouring self-help books. Maybe I'd be there yet if Adeline hadn't gone missing.

"Oskar was nothing like you," my aunt quickly added,

noting my discomfort. "He was always eccentric. I don't believe any one thing pushed him over the edge—if that's what happened. His death was probably unavoidable."

"Do you believe it was an accident? Because—"

"Jeff told me you're suspicious."

I halted, giving her an intent look. "He shouldn't have said that."

"He worries about you," Adeline chided, squeezing my arm again. "It's a good thing."

"He doesn't think I'd make a good investigator."

"I'm sure he didn't put it like that. He wants you to be safe, that's all."

I sighed. "He's probably right, anyway."

"Verity." My aunt's tone had turned no-nonsense. "You're smart, resourceful, and brave. Don't doubt your abilities." She narrowed her eyes. "Do you hear me?"

For an instant, I was ten years old again, balking at chowing down on an edible insect. "Yes," I said, kicking my toe into the nearest snowbank like a spoiled child.

My aunt raised her eyebrows.

"Sorry." I lowered my foot to the ground. "Yes. I will believe in myself."

"That's better." Without warning, she jabbed her fist into my upper arm.

"Ow," I exclaimed, rubbing the smarting area. "What did you do that for?"

"You need to keep up your training. I didn't want to admit it in front of Gideon, but you were a little slow."

"Thanks."

"Also, I meant to tell you—Gideon and I will be out of

town for a while. A week or two. Maybe more. We're leaving tomorrow."

My stomach did a flip-flop. "Why? You told me—"

"It's not work. Honestly. We're taking a vacation."

"Why don't I believe you?"

Aunt Adeline winked. "Because, like I always say—you take after your mother. You're a cynic."

Boomer and I walked on alone to Rose Cottage, approaching through the cedars in the rear. A black pickup was parked in the driveway, and smoke was coming out of the fireplace chimney. My pace quickened. Jeff was back.

When I reached the porch, the phone in my pocket beeped. I pulled it out for a closer look. I'd set the online restaurant review site to notify me of any new postings about Emy's vegan takeout. With growing indignation, I read:

VEGAN? NO WAY. CLEAR SIGNS OF BUTTER. UNCULTURED, TOO.

This was too much. I texted the review to Lorne.

WE'LL GET THEM, he texted back.

Followed seconds later by, DO NOT TELL E.

Inside, I barely had time to shuck off my parka before Jeff gripped me in a bear hug and whirled me about the room. He settled me back on the floor for a lingering kiss.

"What was that all about?" I asked later, still breathless.

"Nothing. Just glad to see you."

As usual, I melted. "You're adorable."

"I am, aren't I?"

Grinning, I gave his arm a backhanded tap. "How come you're back this early? You said the conference didn't wrap up until tonight."

Boomer pawed at Jeff's leg, and he bent to rub the terrier's ear. "It was supposed to, but with an ice storm on the way, the organizers decided to end early. I'm headed into the station, but I wanted to check on you first."

"We're fine, as you can see."

"I also wanted to remind you about our lesson. Couples' curling, remember?

"Yikes. Is that tonight?"

He checked his watch with a grin. "Yes, it is." His expression turned serious. "Have you changed your mind?"

Our search for a fun sport we could share had been fruitless so far. During summers as a teenager working on his grandfather's farm, Jeff developed an interest in horticulture. But our shared love of gardening was no use in the winter. Hence—curling.

However, his prior attempt to teach me another sport that featured heavy objects had ended badly.

"I haven't changed my mind. It's only... remember my bowling lesson?"

He winced. "How could I forget? Thing is, in curling, you don't pick up the stones. They stay on the ice. And if you don't pick them up—you can't drop them." His eyebrows arched.

Now it was my turn to grimace. "That was *one* time. Are you never going to let me forget it? It wasn't my fault. I never claimed to know anything about bowling." I worried my lip between my teeth while I studied him. "Besides, you got over that bruised foot in no time. You said it was 'nothing'."

"I lied. It hurt like heck."

"Why didn't you tell me?"

161

"You can't tell the woman you're wooing that she just cracked a bone in your foot. It's not—macho."

I placed my hands on my hips. "You're exaggerating. It wasn't that bad."

"The guys at the station called me 'Hopalong' for weeks."

I doubted that, but decided to drop it. "All right. Curling it is. As long as nobody gets hurt."

"Well." He dropped his gaze.

"Stop looking at your foot."

"I was only thinking—curlers sometimes slip and fall on the ice. Especially beginners."

"Oh. You were worried about *me*. That's sweet."

Jeff gave me one of those looks that implied he always worried about me before sweeping me back into his arms. "Wish I could stay," he whispered, lowering his face to mine.

Several minutes later, I reluctantly pushed him away. "One of us needs to keep their job," I said, tugging at my sweater. "Also, I want your advice."

Jeff leaned against the kitchen counter with his arms crossed. "All ears."

I recited my reservations about Oskar York's death, based on what I'd learned from Henri Vartan. "Turns out Oskar had money. Quite a lot, even."

Jeff was not convinced. "Did Henri ask Oskar for this money?"

"He didn't have a chance. But he intended to. And if Noah Butterfield told him that Oskar had enough money to foot the bill for the new gallery, don't you think it's worth checking out?"

"No."

"No? What do you mean—no?"

Jeff uncrossed his arms. "Verity, this case of yours—the mysterious wallet Henri found?"

"Yes." I eyed him suspiciously. "What about it?"

"Did Henri tell you he turned it in at the police station?"

"Yes. And they gave it back to him later."

He frowned. "I asked around. Nobody remembers Henri Vartan coming in with a wallet. And there's no paperwork on it in the files."

"But that must be a mistake," I blustered. "He was so particular about it—what was in it, what the police said to him when he got it back. Everything."

"I'm only telling you what I know."

"Why would Henri lie?" Emphatically, I added, "They lost the paperwork, I bet. Maybe they didn't even fill it out, since nothing was stolen."

"Maybe, but I think the most likely explanation is that Henri made it up."

"But why would he—"

Jeff held up a hand. "I wouldn't put too much stock in what Henri Vartan tells you."

Slumping onto the nearest chair while Jeff admired the stuffed toy Boomer had presented him with, I mulled over this development. Henri had been so adamant, his story so detailed. Jeff must be mistaken. At the very least, it was worth another trip to Noah Butterfield's office. If the Leafy Hollow police detachment didn't want to follow up on this, there was nothing stopping me from asking a few questions. I couldn't be accused of stepping on toes if there were none to step on.

A tap on my own toes caused me to glance down.

Boomer tapped again. Then he jumped into my lap.

"Do you want me to try the shelter again?" Jeff asked.

"We don't need to do that, do we?" I crooned at the little terrier. "We can keep the widdle pup a few more days."

Jeff rolled his eyes.

"By the way, where's the General?" I asked.

"Last time I saw him, he was on your bed, sulking."

"Did you give him any liver treats?"

"A whole handful."

"That mean ol' kitty will have to get over it. Won't he, Boo-Boo?"

Boomer licked my face.

"I gotta get back to work," Jeff said, shaking his head as he headed for the door. "Pick you up later for curling?"

"I'll be ready."

Once the door shut behind Jeff, I put Boomer on the floor. "Let's find your leash, buddy. This seems like a good time to continue our walk."

And if that walk should happen to take us past Oskar York's empty house for a little reconnoitering, so much the better.

CHAPTER SEVENTEEN

THE MORNING'S scattered snowflakes had turned wet and slushy, but that didn't mean the weather forecasters were right. *It could blow over*, I thought, scrutinizing the darkening horizon. No need to be all cynical about it.

Boomer enthusiastically scrambled into my truck for our hasty trip to the conservation area. I assumed he wouldn't mind a detour past his old home.

After driving down Lilac Lane, I turned onto the narrow, slippery road that ran for two miles alongside the conservation area. For half that distance, the road hugged the partially frozen river. Ice thickened the water's edge, but the surging stream in the middle was visible.

Within minutes, I was on the two-lane road that zigzagged down the Escarpment. It was plowed and salted and the way was clear.

In the village, I pulled up near Oskar York's house. I parked half a block away because vehicles jammed Oskar's driveway and the street on either side. The front door was wide open.

Two men in coveralls, work boots, and face masks walked out carrying boxes. They loaded them into a moving van parked in the driveway. I watched as they made multiple trips. This was hardly the deserted site I'd hoped for.

Making up my mind, I reached for the door handle.

Boomer planted both front feet on the dash, intently watching the work crew.

"Sorry, fella. This must be hard for you." I rubbed his back consolingly. "You curl up in that blanket, and I'll be right back. If I see any dog toys, I'll grab 'em for you."

When I got out and closed the driver's door, Boomer objected.

Arf-arf-arf-arf-arf-arf...

I tapped on the window. "No, no, no. Don't do that. Shh."

Arf-arf-arf-arf-arf-arf...

"No. Shh. I'll be back in a minute."

Boomer shot me a fleeting glance before lifting his muzzle to resume his tirade.

Arf-arf-arf-arf-arf-arf...

I threw up both hands, giving up and hurrying away. At York's open front door, I hesitated. What would I say if the work crews demanded to know what I was doing? I perked up as an excuse came to me—*looking for Boomer's toys*. I glanced at the truck. Even from half a block away, the terrier's barks were ear-splitting. These guys would happily hand over anything I wanted, just to get rid of us.

In the end, no one even spared me a glance. Methodically, the men gathered up yellowing newspapers, cracked china figurines, and ancient kitchen utensils, then shoved them into garbage bags and boxes.

While I watched, they started on a room at the front of the house. Stacks of typewritten sheets and worn, leather-bound books spilled from a huge roll-top desk. All of it was going into cardboard boxes.

"You're not throwing that stuff out, are you?"

A beefy man who was bent over with a sheaf of papers clutched in his work-gloved hand stopped, eyeing me. "Who are you?"

"A friend. I'm looking for the—dog stuff."

He shrugged, uninterested. "Our orders are to bag everything. It's going to one of those storage places."

"But those documents might be important."

He shoved the papers into a garbage bag, then bent to scoop up more. "Not our problem."

"Can you tell me who hired you?"

He shrugged again. "Don't know. Check with that lawyer."

"Wilf Mullins?" I asked, citing the village's favorite councilor and go-to attorney. He was also my lawyer, as it happened.

"Yeah. That's the one."

I appealed to the second workman, who was about to step through the front door to pitch another two bags into the van.

"You might be destroying evidence."

"Evidence of what?" His lip curled. "That this guy was a slob?" He brushed past me on his way to the bin.

I stood, fixed to the spot, watching him go.

"Excuse me." A heavy hand pushed me to one side, and a third man edged past with three more bags.

Helplessly, I surveyed the mess, thinking this was a cavalier way to dispose of a man's life. Once Oskar's belongings were packed away in a storage unit, they might be there forever.

Or until the rent ran out, when they would go to the nearest landfill.

Through the kitchen doorway, I saw another blue-suited figure at work. But there was no noise from upstairs. They hadn't reached that far yet. I had time to take a look around.

I sprinted up the steps, two at a time. At the top, I ducked into each room in turn—or as far as I could before hitting stacked furniture and clustered boxes. While the first floor smelled fresh, thanks to the frigid air rushing in through the open door, the second was musty. I picked out the odors of well-used footwear, wet dog, and crumbling cardboard.

And something else, which I decided not to probe too closely.

A small room at the front, overlooking the street, was more promising. Two chairs and a side table were arranged into a seating area. The boxes and crates that lined this room were low enough that the photos and artwork covering the walls were visible.

Slowly circling the room, I scanned the pictures—pen-and-ink drawings covered with glass, small oils in ornate frames, old photos with captions handwritten in white ink, advertisements torn from flyers. It was an eclectic collection, but included nothing valuable as far as I could tell. Many of the drawings appeared to have been made by children.

A group photo caught my eye. I unhooked it from its nail to take it down for a closer inspection. Holding it up to the dirt-encrusted window, I scanned the faces to see if I'd been correct. Yes. The tall, thin man in the back row was definitely Oskar York. Much younger, but recognizable as the man I'd seen in the village. His wild, white hair was mahogany brown and carefully combed, and he was a hundred pounds lighter —but it was him.

There were dozens of children in the photo, and other adults. Two women were dressed in nurses' uniforms. The entire group stood in front of a huge house, possibly an institution. Was this the school Aunt Adeline mentioned?

Footsteps sounded on the stairs, and I ducked my head out the door to check the hall. Two workmen, carrying a sheaf of empty garbage bags, tromped into a room at the back.

Quickly, I flipped the picture over and pried off the back of the frame—scratching a finger in the process. Cursing, I slipped out the photo and replaced the empty frame on the wall. I regarded it for a moment, sucking blood from my finger, wondering if the removal crew would notice this frame was empty. Then, after snatching the frame off the wall, I guiltily tossed it into the nearest box.

With the photo hidden under my parka, I trotted downstairs.

The workman I'd spoken to stopped what he was doing to glance up. "Find what you were looking for?"

"Not really." I forced a laugh. "Hard to find anything in this mess."

He joined in my mirth—"Tell me about it"—then resumed his work.

Back in the truck, Boomer stopped barking long enough to greet me enthusiastically. After licking my face, he clapped his front paws on the dash, staring ahead as if to say, "Let's go." I sensed the little terrier was not burdened by nostalgia.

I started the engine to get the heat flowing before tugging the photo from under my parka. As I studied it again, I knew what had drawn me to it. It was similar to one of the photos in Mickey's shoebox. I couldn't remember if it was the same people, the same pose, or simply the same building. Maybe I was wrong, and it wasn't the same at all. But something nagged at me, and I was anxious to compare it to the pictures at home.

As I drove up the Escarpment road, thinking it over, my suspicion mounted.

Mickey gave me those photos.

Mickey was a dog walker. He might have walked Oskar's dog. Meaning—that shoebox of photos could have come from Oskar's house.

What was it Henri Vartan said about Mickey? That he was a *two-bit crook*.

But Jeff said, *I wouldn't put too much stock in what Henri Vartan tells you.*

It was a conundrum, all right.

One thing was certain. Someone authorized a cleanup of Oskar's house. Since he had no apparent relatives, there was no one to complain. But what if the police decided to take a closer look at Oskar's death? With all his odds and ends gone, there'd be nothing to see.

Which left the question—who ordered the cleanup?

Noah Butterfield was the obvious person to ask. Jeff

might be right that Henri was unreliable, but I'd seen Oskar walk out of the investment adviser's office myself.

That left the problem of how to get past Rebecca Butterfield.

Aunt Adeline could have introduced me to Noah. She knew everybody in the village—and where all the bodies were buried. Normally that was a figure of speech, but in her case, it was probably true. Unfortunately, she and Gideon were *taking a vacation.* No help there.

What if I made an appointment with Noah to talk about "investment opportunities?" I could pose my questions about Oskar at the same time.

Pulling over to the side of the road, I reached for my phone and dialed his office.

Rebecca answered. "What can I do for you, Verity?"

"Could I speak to Noah?"

"I'm afraid not."

"Is he in?"

"No."

"Will he be back soon?"

I could hear the fish tank gurgling in the background while I waited for an answer.

"What did you want to see him about?"

"Oh—investment opportunities. Mostly."

"Verity. Noah cannot speak to you about his clients."

"So, Oskar York *was* a client?"

"I didn't say that."

"But you knew him?"

"No comment. I'll tell Noah you called."

"Wait, please. Has Noah been in the office since I visited the other day?"

"Why do you want to know?"

With her ability to keep a secret, Rebecca could work for MI-6. "I was hoping... that he's not ill."

The fish tank gurgled again.

"I'm sure he'll be back soon. Thanks for calling."

Click. Dial tone.

I could cross Noah Butterfield off my list of informants, unless I found a way to talk to him without Rebecca listening in. But since I didn't even know where he was, that was unlikely.

Which was another weird thing. According to Thérèse, Noah was a real workhorse, always on the job. She claimed he once came in to work with a ruptured appendix. I suspected that was a village myth, but—

My hands gripped the steering wheel. As a bookkeeper in Vancouver, I'd seen a few fraud cases. The one thing those crooks had in common was an inability to stay away from the office—even when they should have been in the hospital, like Noah. Embezzlers couldn't leave their books unattended, even for a day, for fear their crimes would be discovered.

Was Noah Butterfield stealing from clients? Clients like Oskar York?

Shaking my head, I put that idea out of my mind. It was ridiculous. Noah was a respected member of the community. Plus, he wasn't in the office. Not today, anyway. Obviously, he wasn't worried about clients checking the books.

But Oskar was dead and not able to check anything.

Stop it. Stick to the crossword puzzle, Verity. Oskar's death was an accident and none of your business. Still—what had that workman said? *Check with the lawyer.* Aunt Adeline had been one of Wilfred Mullin's clients for years, and I was, too. In fact, I considered the diminutive councilor a personal friend. Hopefully, he'd forgotten that unpleasant encounter with a roasted chicken. Yes. I should call Wilf. I pulled back out onto the road.

Beside me, Boomer caught sight of the conservation area, whimpered excitedly, and tried to climb over my lap to get to the driver's door. Which reminded me that he'd probably been here with Mickey, and I hadn't given Henri that shoebox of photos yet.

And I wouldn't, until I had a chance to ask Mickey about the photograph that was currently burning a hole in my parka. I'd like to find out what he knew about it. If nothing else, it was a strange coincidence. After that, I would definitely stop thinking about Oskar York's mysterious—make that *accidental*—death.

I turned into the conservation area, joining the only other vehicle in the parking lot, a battered white van. Talk about coincidences. The proprietor of *Mickey's Dog Care* was walking his charges. I could show him Oskar's photo without even leaving the neighborhood.

There were no dogs in sight. Mickey must have taken them out on the trail. Boomer and I could follow or wait in the truck. But with the way the terrier was drumming his front paws on the dashboard, I figured waiting around would be a tough sell.

I opened the driver's door, intending to let him out the passenger side. But the instant I opened the door, Boomer—

yipping excitedly—dove over me and hit the ground at a run.

"Wait," I called, getting out of the truck and pointing to the sign that said—ALL DOGS MUST BE ON LEASH. "Get back here."

Boomer bounded like a rabbit toward me, then stopped just out of arm's reach with his front legs bent, tail wagging and black eyes shining.

"Come here," I said solemnly, pointing to the ground at my feet.

Boomer bounced a few more times, then darted in my direction.

I reached for his collar.

He darted away.

We performed this pas de deux several times. The more I tried to grab him, the more excited he became. How had Mickey managed to corral this dog?

Finally, I gave up. "Okay, no leash. This time. But if I get a ticket"—I waggled a finger at the sign—"it's coming out of your dinner money."

Boomer didn't look worried. I slammed the truck door, then started around the back to avoid the thigh-high snowbank that surrounded the lot.

Mickey's van was parked beside the cleared path that led to the conservation area trails. But the spot he'd picked to park in was deep in snow. It reached almost to the top of the wheels.

As I passed by, something caught my eye. I swiveled my head toward the window on the driver's side, then drew back, startled.

Mickey was slumped against the seat with his eyes closed. His head was bare. For an instant, I wondered why he wasn't wearing his tasseled wool hat. Maybe he kept it for special occasions.

Since it was way too cold to be napping in an unheated car, I tapped on the driver's window to wake him. He didn't move. "Mickey," I called, rapping again. "Wake up."

No response.

Turning the handle, I wrenched the door open. Mickey's body leaned—very, very slowly—until his head and one arm flopped out of the van. His eyes were shut and his face had turned a peculiar pink, as if he'd been basking under a sunlamp.

"Mickey?" My throat tightened as I poked his motionless form. "Are you all right?"

Whipping off a glove, I pressed my thumb under his chin and waited, trying to gauge his pulse. I felt nothing. Repositioned my thumb. Waited again.

Still nothing. His non-pulsing neck was as cold as the ice under my feet.

Boomer stood beside me, his forepaws on the running board, staring intently at Mickey. He lifted a foot to paw at Mickey's coat. Nothing happened.

I slumped to my knees on the ground, feeling queasy. After a moment, I got to my feet and sprinted back to the truck.

Boomer followed.

I opened the driver's door. "Get in. Please?" I expected him to dart away, in a resumption of our game, but he obeyed at once. If a terrier could look solemn, Boomer was pulling it off.

After getting in and closing the door, I reached for my phone to call 9-1-1. After that, I called Jeff. Then I leaned over the steering wheel, head in my hands, with tears in my eyes.

Boomer nuzzled my side. I brushed him away. He nuzzled me again. With a sudden pang of fear, I bolted to an upright position.

Mickey wouldn't be here unless he had dogs to walk. Where were they?

I jumped out of the truck, followed by Boomer. After a quick jog to the path that led to Pine Hill Peak, I bent to study the ground. Trampled marks in the freshly fallen snow showed the passage of multiple canine feet. There was no way to tell how old those tracks were.

Standing upright, I scanned the surrounding trees and fields. Overhead, a hawk swooped and soared. But on the ground, Boomer and I were alone. What happened to Mickey's charges?

Where were the dogs?

CHAPTER EIGHTEEN

FOR THE NEXT TEN MINUTES, I sat in the truck cab with Boomer, with the engine on and warm air blasting out of the heater, listening to soothing classical music on the radio and trying not to think about Mickey's body a few yards away. Briefly, I consider covering him with a blanket, but I knew enough about suspicious deaths not to tamper with evidence.

There was that word again—*evidence*. Which implied murder. Why couldn't I put that out of my mind? There was nothing to suggest Mickey's death was anything other than natural. It could have been a heart attack, or an aneurysm, or even—I shivered and turned up the heat—hypothermia.

Jeff arrived, parking his cruiser beside my truck. By the time I opened my door and got out, another cruiser had pulled into the parking lot beside him. Jeff made his way over to the constable, and they talked briefly. The only word I heard was "perimeter." The constable opened his trunk.

When he closed it, there was a roll of yellow caution tape in his hand.

He began stringing tape between the fence posts on either side of the parking lot entrance.

When Jeff reached me, he gave me a hug. Then he held me at arm's length, with his hands on my shoulders and a mock-serious expression on his face. "You've got to stop finding bodies, Verity."

I grimaced. "Not funny."

"Sorry. Just trying to cheer you up. Why don't you go home? We can get your statement later." Jeff pointed to the truck, where a squirming Boomer was pressing his nose against the window, watching us intently. "Both of you."

"No. I want to stay."

"There's no need," Jeff said firmly. "Go home." With that, he strode over to Mickey's van and bent over the body leaning precariously out the open door. Jeff placed a practiced finger against Mickey's neck, checking his pulse. He straightened up with a slight shake of his head.

Silently approaching him, I said, "He's dead, isn't he?"

Jeff, startled, whirled around. "Are you still here?"

"Obviously."

"Verity, go home. Please. Let us deal with this. Don't interfere."

"I'm not interfering," I said indignantly. "I'm just standing here."

"Well, stand farther back."

I took a few steps to the rear.

"Thank you." After going over to his cruiser, he raised his handheld radio to his lips and mumbled something into it.

When he was done, I retraced my steps. "What do you think happened to him?"

Jeff narrowed one eye. "Is this your idea of not interfering?"

"I'm only asking a question. I did find the body, after all." Crossing my arms and trying not to look at said corpse, I repeated my question. "What do you think happened?"

"The van smells of dope. Mickey probably fell asleep."

"Mickey? You know him?"

"Let's just say Mickey Doig and the local force are not strangers."

"I don't understand. Did he freeze to death?"

"Possibly. His skin is bright pink, which could be from hypothermia. But it's more likely a symptom of carbon-monoxide poisoning."

"People sit in their cars all the time with the engine running. They don't die."

"Mickey's van is old, and the floor in the back is bare. It's possible rust holes in the exhaust and the floor funneled carbon monoxide inside, particularly since snow is blocking the space under the car. The forensics crew will test the vehicle to determine if that's what happened. But keep this to yourself, Verity. It's equally possible he had an undetected health problem, which—" He stopped talking. "What are you doing? Don't touch the van."

I was bending over the tailpipe, where a tiny fragment of navy blue cloth poked out of the opening. Only a few strands, but— "That's unusual, isn't it?"

Jeff crouched beside me to take a closer look. He pulled a plastic evidence bag and a pair of tweezers from his pocket.

Carefully, he removed the threads and placed them in the bag before standing up. "It's probably nothing."

"Someone could have stuffed the tailpipe with cloth while Mickey was asleep, then removed it after he was dead."

Jeff rubbed a hand across the back of his neck. "You do have murder on the brain."

"I didn't say anything about murder."

"The forensics crew would have found those strands when they went over the vehicle."

"I'm not implying they wouldn't. They'll be extremely thorough, as always. It's just that—"

A shout from the parking lot entrance caused us both to look up.

"You can't stop me," a familiar woman in a sheepskin coat shrieked as she raced past the officer on duty, then broke through the yellow tape. "*Cranberry!* Cranberry, where are you?" She sprinted off across the field.

"Oh, great," Jeff said. "How did they find out?"

Two other women and a man halted in front of Jeff, wheezing for breath. "We have to"—*gasp*—"find our"—*gasp* —"dogs. Anything could have happened to them."

Jeff held out a warning hand. "I'm sorry, but you can't come through here."

All three ignored his attempt to block them. They ducked around him and headed for the path that led to the lookout, jogging after Cranberry's owner.

Alarmed, I clutched Jeff's sleeve. "If the dogs went that way, they could fall off the Escarpment. It's three hundred feet straight down."

The dogs' owners were yelling at the top of their lungs.

"*Cranberry*, where are you?"

"*Pixi*, get out here!"

"*Ranger,* co-m-e."

"Those animals are not obedient," I said, frowning.

Amused, Jeff only shook his head, fighting back a smile.

"Mickey used to walk Boomer, so he's part of their pack," I said. "I bet he can find them."

"Yeah. That dog's a regular bloodhound. Maybe we can conscript him into the force."

I harrumphed. "Maybe you can."

Jeff didn't hear me. He was bending over Mickey's body, conferring with the coroner who had just arrived.

Boomer eyed me intently from the truck's back window. After a moment's thought, I let him out. He sat obediently in front of me, but his front legs beat a staccato rhythm on the ground until his whole body shook. He was raring to go.

"Okay, boy." I pointed to the field beside the parking lot. "Find your buddies."

He took off like a shot.

CHAPTER NINETEEN

BOOMER CHARGED ALONG THE TRAIL, and I did my best to keep up. Four legs were better than two for jogging over rough terrain. It didn't help when the storm that had been threatening all morning finally blew in. Sleet pelted down, digging tiny holes in the snow, making the footing even more treacherous.

We slogged on—Boomer oblivious to the fog rolling in, and me struggling and grumbling yards behind.

Up ahead, the dog owners continued to call, but their pleas were less frequent. Perhaps they were running out of breath. As we plunged into the woods, I turned for a last look at the parking lot, barely visible through the thickening mist. The vehicle that would take Mickey's body to the morgue had arrived. I turned my attention back to the trail as Boomer raced ahead of me. Did this dog ever slow down?

The answer to that turned out to be yes, but only after a half hour of nonstop running. Gratefully, I staggered to a halt. Bent over with my hands on my knees, I gasped for breath. Maybe Aunt Adeline was right when she said I should step up my workouts.

The dog owners plodded past on their return to the parking lot, talking dejectedly among themselves.

"Did you see the dogs?" I asked.

Cranberry's owner stopped beside me, close to tears. "They've disappeared. We're going to get help." She scurried to catch up to the others plodding along the path.

I looked down at Boomer. *So much for your bloodhound ancestry*, I thought as we followed the dog owners.

When Boomer and I reached the parking lot, the coroner was packing up his medical bag while the dog owners argued with Jeff. As I drew closer, I realized they expected the police to mount a search-and-rescue mission for their missing pets.

"We'll keep an eye out. If they're in the vicinity, someone will spot them," Jeff said in the soothing tone that always calmed me down.

It didn't work.

"Keep an eye out?" the man asked indignantly. "Keep an eye out? What good will that do? What about the coyotes? We can't leave our dogs outside all night. We have to find them."

The others muttered in agreement, pressing in on Jeff.

He held his hands up. "I'm sorry. There's not much I can do. We've radioed the dogs' descriptions to the rest of the force. They'll turn up. Or someone will find them."

The man turned to the other owners, pulling a cell phone from his pocket. "Let's ask for help. Get as many people up here as we can."

"No. Don't do that," Jeff implored. "We can't have lost-pet seekers swarming the area. This is a police scene—it's a suspicious death."

I raised an eyebrow. A *suspicious* death? *A-ha.*

Jeff watched forlornly as the dog owners huddled over their phones. "Don't do that."

No one listened.

"The lost-pet sites have picked it up," a woman said. "Post more pictures. We'll have hundreds of people out here before long."

Jeff clapped a hand to his forehead, gazing over the abandoned field. His sigh was inaudible, but I heard it nonetheless. "Those dogs are not here," he said, lowering his hand to make another attempt. "Your helpers should check elsewhere. Meanwhile—"

At my feet, Boomer started barking. *Arf-arf-arf-arf-arf-arf...*

"Stop it," I hissed.

Jeff turned around, his irritation easy to see. "—can we at least get everybody out of the parking lot?"

"Stop it," I repeated, grabbing for Boomer's leash. Too late, I remembered he didn't have one.

This time, he darted in the opposite direction, through the parking lot and across the road, headed for a farmer's field.

Exasperated, Jeff pointed at the dog. "He's trespassing."

I knew what that meant. Farmers were allowed to shoot animals that harassed their livestock. I doubted somebody would shoot Boomer, but if, say, there was a prize bull in that field, I didn't want to take any chances. Tightening the cord on my parka hood, I ran after him.

Navigating the conservation trail was nothing compared to traversing a snow-covered field. Frozen furrows threatened to trip me on every step. Melted ice trickled under the edges of my hood. I was damp, inside and out.

Boomer raced on.

Finally, I halted, exhausted, wiping sleet off my face with a sodden glove. It did not help. If anything, my face was wetter than before. And if my nose got any colder, it was definitely going to fall off.

Worst of all, I couldn't see Boomer through the thickening snowflakes.

Then I heard him bark.

Arf-arf-arf-arf-arf-arf...

I headed in the direction of the sound. Before long, his little form loomed out of the fog. He sat placidly, regarding me with his head tilted.

"Don't *ever* do that again."

Boomer whirled around and trotted off again.

"Oh, come on," I groaned. "Are you kidding me?"

This time, he went only a few feet before stopping to glance back. I followed.

I caught up to find him perched on the edge of a ravine, his tail wagging despite the miserable weather. Drops of water flew off his muzzle as he pawed at the ground.

Behind him, huddled on the floor of the windswept gully, were four dogs—a beagle, a silver-gray poodle with a scrap of patterned wool in its jaws, a black lab, and a border collie nuzzling them all to stay together.

On our way back to the parking lot, I retrieved the torn fabric from the poodle's mouth. It looked like the remains of a hat. I tucked it into the pocket of my parka.

"Cranberry!" shrieked a woman's voice.

The dog owners—who had been joined by two dozen other people in the fifteen minutes we'd been gone—were ecstatic when they saw our group scampering across the field. People whipped out their cell phones. Before long, Boomer and I were social media heroes.

After a round of high-fives, human-canine reunions, and heartfelt thank-you's, I packed Boomer into the truck and promised him meatloaf.

Jeff had been leaning against his cruiser, legs crossed, watching the scene with bemusement. "Thanks," he said after I closed the door on the terrier and walked toward him. "You saved the day. You saved me a lot of aggravation, too."

"Oh, come on. I know you were worried about those dogs."

"They're back. So that's good."

"And Mickey?"

"Headed for the morgue." Jeff frowned. "Coroner's doing a full autopsy."

"Does that mean he's suspicious, too?"

Jeff gave me an enigmatic look. "You and Boomer must be worn out. And your clothes are sopping wet. Better head home. I'm afraid couples' curling is off for tonight." He straightened up, pushing off from the cruiser.

"Before I do that," I said, pulling the gnawed wool fabric from my pocket and holding it out to him. "Look at this."

Jeff gave it a curious look. "What's that?"

"It's a hat, I think. The poodle had it. Must have found it in the field."

"So?"

"Don't you think that's suspicious? It could be Mickey's."

"It could be anybody's."

"Yes, but if it is Mickey's—why would he let a dog run off with his hat?"

I could tell Jeff was trying not to laugh. "Are you suggesting that poodle is the killer?"

Maybe because I was tired and wet, and cold to the bone, his joke didn't strike me as funny. Sudden tears stung the back of my eyes. Twisting the fabric between my fingers and staring at the ground, I said, "That's ridiculous."

"Verity." Jeff drew me toward him. "I was only kidding." He tucked a finger under my chin, gently raising my face to his. "I shouldn't make jokes. Finding Mickey's body was a shock for you. I'm sorry."

"It's okay." Sniffing, I rubbed a damp glove across my nose. "Besides, I'm pretty sure it was the beagle that did it."

Jeff smiled. Then he motioned toward the constable by the entrance. "Leave that thing with Fred on your way home. I doubt it has anything to do with Mickey Doig, but the forensics guys can take a look at it later."

At Rose Cottage, I peeled off my boots, parka, and gloves, then dropped them on the floor, too tired to hang them up.

"Shower," I said to Boomer, pointing to the bathroom. That filthy little animal was way past his best-before date.

The fact he was soaking wet made for a smell in the cottage that was truly overwhelming. Whatever it took, Boomer was having a bath.

Surprisingly, he didn't complain when I carried him into the bathroom. He was too tired.

Once I'd stripped off my clothes, I soaped the little dog and held him under a blast of warm water. When we emerged from the shower—red-faced, squeaky clean, and smelling of lavender—the bathroom mirror was steamed up and the floor soon ankle-deep in damp towels.

Boomer shook himself, drenching any portion of the room that wasn't already soaked.

Later, padding about the kitchen in my favorite drop-drawered flannel sleepsuit, I heated up leftover pizza. "I hope you like pepperoni, Boomer. I'm too exhausted to make meatloaf."

We polished it off in front of a roaring fire. Then Boomer curled up on the sofa, nestled in the last remaining dry towel. I huddled under a fleece throw, mulling things over. Two suspicious deaths in the same week, in the same village? *There had to be a connection*, I thought, munching on stale chocolate biscuits I'd found in the back of a cupboard.

After the cookies were gone, I got to my feet, remembering my parka, still lying on the floor. While I was hanging it up, I gasped as a sudden recollection hit me. I'd forgotten to drop off the battered hat on my way out of the conservation area. I bit my lip. *Well.* Since it was here...

Retrieving it from my parka pocket, I took it to the sofa for a closer look. It did look a bit like Mickey's. His hat had been in one piece when I last saw it, so it was hard to tell.

This one was nearly torn in two and missing its earflaps. Given Jeff's lack of interest, I didn't think it was worth getting dressed again to take it down to the station. I could give it to him later.

Parts of the hat felt strangely thick under my fingers. Turning it inside out, I found a hand-stitched felt pocket with a sheet of paper in it. Like the hat, the paper was ripped and torn.

Smoothing the pieces out on the coffee table revealed them as parts of a crossword puzzle. I noted with surprise that the clues resembled the ones posted on Shanice's bulletin board at the bakery. There was a major difference, though.

On this puzzle, all the clues were filled in, including the ones that hadn't been found yet.

CHAPTER TWENTY

AFRAID THE SODDEN scraps of paper would tear if I kept handling them, I spread them out on the ottoman to dry in front of the fire. Then I retrieved the red shoebox from the bookcase for a closer look. My curiosity was kindled, but I'd promised not to interfere with Jeff's probe into Mickey's death and I didn't intend to go back on my word. The hat and its mysterious puzzle could wait.

Looking over Mickey's photos couldn't hurt, though. Perhaps they would interest Henri after all. Mickey's next of kin—if there was one—might welcome a small payment. I also wanted to confirm my hazy recollection of a photo that matched the one I took from Oskar's house.

It didn't take long to find it. A much younger, and thinner, Oskar York stood in front of the same—school? Hospital? Or was it just a random building? The possibilities were endless.

I flipped it over. Handwritten names on the back identified each person. None of the names, aside from Oskar's, were familiar.

Staring at the picture, I had to admit nothing tied it to Oskar's death. It was just one among dozens of old photos. Jeff believed Oskar's death was an accident and I was wasting my time looking into it. I had no reason to disagree. Tucking the photo back into the shoebox, I set it aside.

But I had promised to investigate Henri's mysterious wallet and those new crossword clues might help. They were here. Seemed a shame to ignore them.

The scraps of paper had curled up while drying before the fire. Carefully, I slid them together until the full crossword was visible. I wrested one scrap away from the General, who had decided that batting crispy paper about was the most fun he'd had in weeks.

"And yet, you've never managed to catch a single mouse, even though the basement is full of them," I scolded, getting down on my hands and knees to retrieve another piece from under the ottoman. "Why is that?"

The General meticulously licked his paw, ignoring me.

I studied the completed puzzle. If that hat *was* Mickey's —and I had no way to tell—how did he find all the clues when the rest of the village was searching every snowbank and trash bin without success? What did he plan to do with them? Wait until the puzzle was nearly solved, and then swoop in with the last answer to claim the prize?

Assuming there was a prize. I had my doubts about that.

My next thought gave me a chill. What if this puzzle was the reason Mickey died? What if someone knew he had the answers, and killed him to get them?

Wow. Like Mickey would say—so harsh.

And now, those clues were mine. I rubbed my throat as a wave of anxiety swept over me. Was I in danger, too, since I had this list? I reached for my cell phone, intending to call Jeff.

By my side, Boomer stretched in his towel, eyes closed, and settled back in with a muffled *woof*. Outside, the low moan of the wind was the only sound. A log snapped in the fireplace, splintering in a shower of sparks.

I drew back my hand from the phone, realizing I was letting my anxiety get the better of me. Even if this was Mickey's hat, no one knew I had it. Or about the list inside.

Besides, these clues proved the puzzle contest was a fraud. The thing to do was to go public so nobody else would be drawn into this ridiculous quest for riches. *Safety in numbers*, isn't that what Sherlock Holmes always said? Or was that Harry Potter?

I pulled over my laptop and typed a group email to everyone whose name I'd copied from the bulletin board in the library.

MEET ME AT THE 5X BAKERY AT TEN AM FOR AN IMPORTANT UPDATE ABOUT THE CROSSWORD PUZZLE CONTEST. I paused, reviewing my note, then added, IT WILL BE WORTH YOUR WHILE. Hands hovering over the keys, I pondered ways to make the invitation more enticing. Finally I decided to add, FREE COOKIES.

After copying it to Emy with a plea to provide the "free cookies," I hit *send*.

Then I went to bed, confident the next day would bring answers.

Shanice, almost beside herself with excitement, had lined up the bakery's new chairs to form rows facing the easel, which sported a fresh piece of construction paper. Shiny new felt-tip pens waited nearby. The bakery's tiny coat rack was overflowing, condensation misted the windows, and a low hum of conversation filled the room.

From behind the glass counter, Emy tilted her head, mouthing at me to, *Start already.*

Normally, I'd be too anxious to address a roomful of people, but today I felt up to the challenge. Maybe it was the laser pointer I held in my hand that gave me an air of unexpected authority. Boldly, I strode to the front. After taking a deep breath, I began.

"I have news about the contest. But first, let's review. We have six answers so far—Us, Field, Ten, April, Amongst, and Park."

I motioned to Shanice, who flipped over the board to display an enlarged crossword. It was several times bigger than the puzzle in the library. Which made it fully visible even in the back row, where Rebecca Butterfield sat beside an empty chair. I assumed her husband, Noah, was still out of town—until reclusive artist Irma O'Kay tried to sit there.

"Saved," Rebecca blurted, plunking her designer tote bag onto the empty seat. Irma tossed her an irritated glance before moving up one row to sit beside fellow artists Zuly and Henri.

Henri was slumped over, holding his head. "Can we get on with it?" he muttered.

"We will. But before we start..." I glanced around at the assembled group. "Did all of you find a discarded wallet?"

Everyone in the room nodded.

"Did any of you try to find the original owner? Other than Henri, I mean?"

Several in the group exchanged puzzled glances.

"How would we do that, exactly?" Rebecca asked.

"Social media. Obviously," gushed a young woman with dyed green hair, multiple piercings, and heavy black eyeliner. This must be Gloria, the part-time clerk from Lucky Lentil. "You can find anybody that way. I use it all the time."

"Seriously?" Rebecca leaned back with a puff of exasperation. "You'd look a stranger up on the Internet? How would you know if it was the right 'John Smith,' or just somebody with the same name? Listen, don't get me wrong—I'm perfectly willing to take a lost wallet to the owner's home." She paused, frowning. "Depending how far away it was. I mean, I'm not driving all the way to Strathcona just because somebody can't keep track of their belongings. Okay. Fine. But what if there's no money in the wallet? You're setting yourself as the obvious suspect. What's to stop the owner from accusing you of taking the cash?"

There was a general murmur of agreement.

"That could happen," offered a young man in the second row—Willy Wilkes, who had introduced himself before the meeting as a friend of Mickey's. He tossed his long, stringy hair in a gesture reminiscent of a heavy-metal rocker. Or *My Little Pony*.

Gloria's snort of laughter cut through the gray mood.

"Don't be silly. Nobody would do that. You're looking at it entirely wrong, Rebecca."

Rebecca tossed her a look of disdain. "Really?"

"Here's what I'd do. First, check the guy's ID photo to see if he's cute. If he is, call the 1-800 number on his credit card, tell them you've found his wallet and want to make arrangements for him to pick it up."

The way her eyebrows arched, I knew there was more. It was dumb to ask, but I couldn't help myself. "And then?"

"Shower, spritz a little scent, put on your slinkiest clothes —and wait by the door." Gloria flopped back against her chair with a wide grin. "Par-tay!"

Rebecca stared at her, mouth agape. Beside the easel, Shanice frowned.

Willy's wrinkled brow indicated he was having trouble with this. Finally, he raised his hand. "What if it's not a dude?"

The young man sitting beside Willy guffawed so loudly Emy dropped one of the shortbreads she was arranging on a platter.

He leaned in and whispered to Willy, who flushed red.

Then they both burst into laughter. "Cool," Willy chortled. "Didn't think of that."

I placed both hands on my hips. "Could we please get back on track?"

"What about this?" blurted Willy's friend. "Wait till no one is home at the dude's place, then break in and leave it on his nightstand. Won't he be surprised when he wakes up?"

High-fives between Willy and his friend. "Cool," Willy said.

Incredulously, I stared at them. "That could backfire in many ways."

Willy lowered his arm. "Yeah. Verity's right," he said in a rare burst of tactical thinking. "Mickey's policy when finding a wallet was always 'pay yourself first.' Then decide if you want to keep the credit cards, too. After that, you have two choices. Either, like, put the wallet back so the owner can find it—which Mickey said was a public service."

His friend nodded woefully. "Mickey was a great guy." They high-fived again.

Eying Willy suspiciously, I said, "What was the second choice?"

"Call the owner and negotiate a finder's fee."

The room fell silent, except for the tick-tocking of the black-cat clock on the wall, and munching noises from those lucky enough to have snared a shortbread before they sat down.

"Moving on," I said. "The rest of the clues—"

"Verity?" Hannah, our resident librarian, shyly raised one tattooed arm. "Before we return to the crossword, may I add something to the current discussion?"

"Go ahead," I said, albeit reluctantly.

"I think you're approaching this in the wrong way. For instance, I found a wallet last year in the trash bin outside the library. When I phoned the owner, guess what?" Hannah swiveled her gaze around, but no one appeared willing to speculate, so she continued. "He came down to the library the next day to bring us a big box of doughnuts from Tim Horton's." She sat back, crossing her arms with a self-satisfied air. "Karma."

Rebecca raised her hand in the air. "Why were you digging around in the trash?"

"That's not the point," the librarian said huffily.

"I think it is the point. Did you handle any library books after that?" Rebecca glanced around the room, seeking support. "It could be a public health issue."

Hannah flipped an arm over the back of her chair, twisting around to scowl at Rebecca. "People throw away perfectly good stuff. It's bad for the environment to send it all to landfill."

"I think you should be more worried about the patrons of the—"

"That's an interesting subject," I broke in. "But can we get back to—"

Henri straightened up, making his overloaded chair creak. "You're all missing the point. How do you know someone didn't drop the wallet deliberately?"

Heads turned to face him. Willy frowned, obviously trying to puzzle out why anyone would give away money.

Henri poked a finger in the air for emphasis. "They put a little cash in the wallet, and a fake ID, and wait for you to call. Then, once they're at your door—bang!" He clapped his hand on the chair in front of him, making Gloria jump. "They whack you over the head and take everything you've got." Henri bit his lip. He was becoming teary. "And if you make it out alive, count yourself lucky." The last word came out as a strangled sob. He bent over with his arms on his knees, staring at the floor.

Tossing her black hair over her shoulder, Zuly gave his back a consoling pat.

For several moments, no one spoke.

Then, "Shortbread?" Emy asked, bending beside Henri with a plate of his favorite bacon-toffees.

Henri raised his head, sniffed, and reached for a cookie. "Maybe just one."

At the front of the room, I cleared my throat. "Let's get back to the clues—" I switched on the laser pointer. Nothing happened. Shanice took it from me, fiddled a bit, and handed it back in working order. "Thank you." I aimed the pointer. "Let's review the ones we already know—or think we know. First, eight down. 'Violent individuals.' Any ideas?"

Rebecca's hand shot up. "Killers."

Shanice uncapped her felt pen, then wrote KILLERS on the puzzle in bold black letters.

I pointed to eleven across. "'Betwixt and between.' The answer, as we know, is..."

Rebecca again. "Amongst."

I pointed to three across—'Like-minded persons?'"

"Us," blurted Rebecca, not bothering to raise her hand this time. Hannah shot her a furious glance.

I flicked the pointer from word to word, until the written phrase sank in.

Killers Amongst Us.

"Cool," Willy said.

"Indeed. There are three other answers we knew. One down: 'Month of showers.'"

"April," said several voices at once.

"Nine across—'Ruminants' home'."

"Field."

"And seven down—'How many toes?' Obviously, the answer is Ten."

Shanice pointed to TEN, APRIL, and FIELD on the puzzle.

"But two more clues were found recently. Two down: 'Prepare for battle?'"

"Arm," Rebecca called out in a singsong voice.

Shanice wrote it on the puzzle.

"And four down—'Opposite of weak.'"

This time, the librarian beat Rebecca to the punch. "Strong," she called, flashing a look of triumph at the investment adviser's wife.

Henri tilted his head to one side as if he was puzzled by the two most recent clues written on the puzzle, ARM and STRONG.

"Questions?" I asked, looking directly at him.

After a glance at Irma, whose gaze was riveted to the board, Henri shook his head.

I circled the board rapidly with the pointer, enjoying the gadget. Maybe I should pick one up for home use. "I've been suspicious of this contest from the start. To put it bluntly, I think it's a fraud."

Loud murmurs from the participants.

"Verity, you're such a cynic," Hannah said.

I rolled my eyes. Again with the cynic. I preferred to think of myself as a pragmatist.

Zuly puffed out a breath. "That's ridiculous. What makes you think it's a fraud?"

"Because I have all the answers. Right here." From my

pocket, I pulled out a copy of Mickey's tattered paper—I'd given Jeff the original that morning—and held it up.

Mouths dropped open.

"Where did you get that?" Irma asked.

Willy added helpfully, "Yeah. What she said."

"You all know that Mickey Doig is dead. This list"—I brandished the paper—"was in his possession when he died."

Technically, it was in the possession of a silver-gray poodle, but—basically true.

"Cool," Willy said. "Mickey was onto something after all."

"What do you mean?"

"He said he was coming into money."

"Did he tell you how?"

Willy shook his head with a hangdog expression. "Wish he'd given *me* that list."

"The point is, Willy, if Mickey knew all the answers to the puzzle, other people did, too. Which is why I'm convinced it's a hoax." When no one replied, I added, "A fraud."

Hannah raised her hand, her brows knitted. "But that can't be. What about the prize? The million dollars?"

"There is no prize," I said.

My pronouncement was greeted with stunned silence.

"Hang on," Gloria said, her multiple lip rings quivering in indignation. "What do you mean—no prize? We have all the answers. We can claim the million bucks."

"No. That's Mickey's money," Willy said.

"Mickey's dead," Rebecca pointed out from the back row.

Willy leapt to his feet, gesturing at the puzzle and shouting. "Then it should go to his friends."

Gloria sprang up to argue with him.

Irma and Zuly exchanged glances, then scooted their chairs out of the way.

Everyone began talking at once, their voices getting louder until the hum reverberated off the windows. Behind the counter, Emy covered her ears.

"Stop," I shouted, stepping on to a chair. "*Stop.*"

The room fell silent.

I took a deep breath. "There. Is. No. Prize."

The combatants slumped into their seats, scowling.

"Are you... certain?" Gloria asked with a petulant air.

I climbed down before answering. "Yes."

Muttering broke out.

"Does anyone have proof this rumored prize exists?" I asked.

"We've all heard about it," Hannah said, searching the onlookers' faces for support.

"That's right," Gloria added.

"Who told you about it?" I asked.

Hannah tilted her head as if deep in thought. "I heard it from a library patron. I don't remember who, exactly."

"I heard it at the Lentil," Gloria said. "One of the customers. It was... it was..." She shrugged. "I don't remember their name."

"Henri, where did you hear about it?" I asked.

He and Irma huddled together for a moment, then Henri said triumphantly, "At the Leafy Hollow Farmers' Market. From the guy who sells designer turnips."

"Designer turnips?"

"Yes. They're different colors."

"Oh, I've seen those," Hannah said, raising her hand. "Does he have the carrots, too?"

During this discussion, Willy had shuffled to the front, running shoes flapping. He pointed to the board, looking bereft. "There's no million dollars?"

"No," I said firmly.

"Really?"

I sighed.

Not bothering to raise her hand, Rebecca snapped, "So far, Verity, you've told us about these new clues, but you haven't shown them to us. I'd like proof."

There was a general murmur of agreement.

Willy brightened. "Cool."

I circled the crossword with my pointer. "Shanice, would you do the honors?"

"Ready." She stood by, pen poised, to fill in the remaining questions and answers.

"Ten across," I said. "Picture museum? Answer: GALLERY."

The felt pen squeaked across the cardboard.

"And the last clue, six across. Shortbread ingredient? Answer—"

Shanice was already writing it in. BUTTER.

Henri pointed to the board. "No. That's wrong."

"Butter? No, that's correct," Emy said from behind the counter, with a wry smile that might have been a wince.

"Which gives us the completed puzzle." I flourished the pointer again.

All eyes faced front.

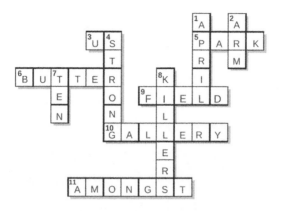

ACROSS
3 Like-minded persons
5 Green space
6 Shortbread ingredient
9 Ruminants' home
10 Picture museum
11 Betwixt and between

DOWN
1 Month of showers
2 Prepare for battle
4 Opposite of weak
7 How many toes
8 Violent individuals

Irma poked Zuly with her elbow, giving her a quizzical glance, but Zuly merely shrugged.

Hannah peered at the board, her eyebrows knitted once more. "But some of those clues are names. Of people who live right here in the village."

Gloria narrowed her eyes at the puzzle. "What do you mean?"

"Look." Hannah strode up to the puzzle to poke at it with her finger. "Two down and eleven across spell ARM-STRONG. And six and nine across spell BUTTER-FIELD." She turned to face the room. "Rick Armstrong. And Noah Butterfield."

Then, in case anyone had missed it, Hannah pointed in

turn to three other words on the puzzle: *KILLERS.*
AMONGST. US.

The ensuing collective intake of breath sucked most of
the air out of the room. Followed seconds later by an explosion of voices all speaking at once.

"Whoa, that's—"

"Holy cow."

"No, it can't be—"

"Cool."

The front door swung open with a sudden jangle of the
overhead bell.

The chattering ceased as wide-eyed faces turned to the
entrance.

A trim man in a tailored suit and camel overcoat, his
brown hair combed back under a fedora, tugged the door shut
against the whistling wind. Noah Butterfield turned,
stamping his feet on the mat. "Am I too late?" he asked,
doffing his hat to shake off snowflakes.

No one said a word.

Until Rebecca rose to her feet, jabbing a finger in the air.
"Where the devil have you been?"

CHAPTER TWENTY-ONE

ONCE REBECCA and Noah started their shouting match, Emy and I tried to clear the bakery. It wasn't easy. After pushing a few people out the front door myself, I turned back to find Gloria filming the battling Butterfields on her cell phone.

Stepping between her and the combatants, I signaled desperately to Emy, who threw up her arms in the universally accepted motion for, "I give up," and flounced back behind the counter.

"Do you think I don't know what you've been up to?" Rebecca screamed at her husband.

"Now wait," I said as calmly as I could. "This isn't the place to—"

"How dare you lecture me?" Noah shouted. "What about Paris?"

"What about Paris? I was there with my girlfriends. We saw the Louvre."

"Liar."

"Ooh, this is good," Gloria muttered, ducking back around me with her phone raised.

I snatched it away from her, held it over my head, and warded her off with my other hand. "Stop that. You're not helping."

"Give that back." She hopped up and down, trying to reach it. "This video's bound to go viral."

Out of the corner of my eye, I saw Rebecca jam one arm into her coat and sweep out the door with the rest of the coat flapping behind her.

"Wait," Noah called, grabbing his fedora off the floor and following her.

Holding the cell phone above Gloria's head, I hit the DELETE button and waited until it was finished before handing the phone back to Lucky Lentil's Employee of the Month.

"Oh, come on," Gloria cried in frustration, checking the screen. "What did you do that for?"

"You'll thank me later."

Gloria gave a snort of disapproval before storming out.

Emy, Shanice, and I surveyed the toppled chairs and scattered shortbreads.

"Do you still think Hawkes Investigation Agency is a good idea?" I asked Emy.

She pursed her lips. "It might need a little fine-tuning."

––––––––

With the revelation that the "million-dollar" crossword

puzzle implicated two villagers in murder, my next interrogation subject was obvious. But first, I had pets to placate.

Back at Rose Cottage, I took Boomer for a quick walk and then shut him in the kitchen, double-checking the latch to make sure he couldn't get out. Then I carried General Chang's dinner to my bedroom. I'd replaced the usual kibble with a tin of salmon—his favorite. I placed the bowl on my chipped wooden dresser, picked up the General, and plonked him down in front of it.

The ornery old tom was not impressed. *"Mrack."* The indifference in his tone was unmistakable. He sat with his nose in the air, intently interested in the play of light on the opposite wall.

"Fine," I said evenly. Hiding a smile, I headed out. After six months with the one-eyed warrior, I'd learned not to feel guilty. I knew he'd have his nose into that salmon the moment the door closed behind me.

A fleeting flashback and a stab of anxiety halted me in my tracks as I walked up to Henri's front door. I stepped over to the side—out of the path of any crazed attackers who might burst out that door—before continuing.

After my raps with the dachshund knocker, the door swept open to be held at arm's length by Zuly Sundae. She gave me a cool and appraising glance. Apparently, I had not been forgiven for dashing the villagers' million-dollar hopes.

"Visitor," Zuly yelled over her shoulder. With a toss of

her jet-black hair, she stalked off, leaving the door gaping open to the blustery weather.

I stepped over the threshold, then quietly closed the door. After slipping off my parka, I hung it from the newel post in the hall. Turning, I saw Henri in the doorway to the living room—more properly called 'The Gallery' now, I reminded myself. The torn plastic strips were gone.

Matisse stood beside him, quivering slightly on his mini-dachshund legs.

"Hello, Verity," Henri said with a dispirited air. "The girls are helping me clean up. Come on in." I followed him into the gallery, where he settled into an armchair.

Irma O'Kay looked up from the floor, where she knelt over one of her paintings. Thin strands of mousy hair drooped over her pallid face and pale blue eyes. Whatever colors nature had neglected to bestow on Irma's person, she'd made up for in her art. The rich blues and reds and oranges of the canvas seemed to vibrate in the pale winter light coming through the windows.

"Verity. Hi. We're taking the opportunity to re-organize." She held out a hand stained with residues of dried paint, and I bent over to shake it. "Thanks for helping Henri when he was attacked. What a horror." She grimaced, then glanced at Zuly, who was studying canvases stacked against the wall, flipping them over one by one, pointedly ignoring us.

"It was a shock for everybody," I said, trying to dissipate the tension in the room. "How are you feeling, Henri?"

Shrugging, he averted his gaze. Irma tossed him a glance, smiling wanly before returning her gaze to the artwork.

"But that's not why I'm here." I took a deep breath,

wondering how to best word my concerns. I could be wrong, after all. "I noticed at the bakery that you didn't seem as surprised as the others that the contest was a hoax."

All three exchanged quick glances. *Noted*, I thought.

"I didn't want to mention it during the meeting, but the police believe Mickey was murdered. It wasn't an accident. Henri—you didn't really like Mickey, did you?"

Zuly straightened up, letting the artwork slap back against the wall, and stared at me, openmouthed. Irma rose to her feet, brushing hair from her eyes and nervously smoothing her paint-splotched smock.

"What do you mean?" Henri blustered. "I hardly knew the man."

"You told me he was a two-bit crook and a scoundrel."

Henri clasped a hand against his chest in shock. "Did I? That doesn't sound like me." He turned to "the girls" for confirmation. They shook their heads, eyes wide.

"Yes, you did. The day of your attack."

"That's easily explained," Zuly said. "Henri was delirious after that blow to his head. He wasn't talking sense."

"I think there's more to it than that. And I'm glad you're all here, because I have something to show you. It has a bearing on your case, Henri."

He fluttered his hands. "I think we should forget about that, Verity."

"Forget about the wallet? You asked me to investigate it."

"It was only a silly contest. And now that we know there's no prize..." He absently pinched the fabric on the arm of the chair. "We should drop it."

"I think there's a connection between the contest and Mickey's murder."

One of the women drew in a sharp breath. When I turned to them, they were both studying the floor. I pulled out my copy of the tattered list of clues. "Let's start with this." I handed it to Irma, who was closest.

She took it hesitantly, scanning the contents. With a puzzled look, she passed it to Zuly.

After a quick glance, and a tightening of her lips, Zuly passed it to Henri.

"You already told us Mickey had all the clues. Why are you showing us this?"

"I was hoping to jog your memory. Mickey was determined to solve that crossword. Obviously, he was successful. But he didn't do it alone. The question is—who gave him those final clues and answers?"

Irma worried a cuticle between her teeth. Zuly bit her lip.

"I think those clues are the reason he's dead," I said.

The room went silent.

Matisse flopped onto the floor. Outside, a car whooshed past on the street, spraying melted ice from its hubcaps. An avalanche of waterlogged snow slid off the roof, landing with a thud that made us all jump.

"You know something—what is it?" I asked.

Irma gnawed at her finger. Zuly glared. Henri leaned over with his bandaged head in his hands, the rumpled crossword sticking out from between his fingers.

I bent over to slide it from his grasp.

"We didn't mean anything by it," Irma said, her voice tremulous.

"Irma," Zuly warned.

"It's too late, Zuly. It's all going to come out. Verity's right. There's a connection."

"You don't know that," Zuly said.

"How do you explain that, then?" Irma pointed a wavering finger at the crossword puzzle in my hand.

From his chair, Henri groaned. He flopped back, sighing heavily. "It's true, Zuly. We have to admit it. There's no choice."

With my brow furrowed, I glanced from one to the other. I was confused. My accusation of "a connection" between the contest and Mickey's death had been a bluff. I didn't expect a response like this. It appeared my attempt to shake loose information was about to be spectacularly successful. I drew up to my full height, waving the paper. "Will one of you please tell me what's going on?"

Both women eyed Henri.

He straightened in the chair, his hands gripping the upholstered arms. "It was a guerrilla marketing campaign."

I stared, trying to take this in. "It was—what?"

"Guerrilla marketing." He rattled out the definition in a singsong tone. "Unconventional but low-cost marketing techniques designed to obtain maximum exposure for a new product."

"For what purpose?"

"The contest was supposed to stir up interest in our gallery opening. It was meant to get people curious, and talking, and trying to solve the clues, and then—" He shrugged. "We planned to reveal our opening show."

"It was a publicity stunt?" I asked, aghast.

"That's putting it a little coarsely. It was clever, we thought. Ingenious, really. Zuly, show Verity the poster."

Zuly plucked a roll of paper from the floor, held it at arm's length, and let it unfurl. The crossword puzzle—with all the answers filled in—ran at an angle across the top of the bright blue sheet. Seven answers were circled in red:

Us. Park. April. Ten. Killers. Gallery. Amongst.

Across the bottom, those circled words were repeated, but in a different order.

Killers Amongst Us

Park Gallery

April 10

My jaw dropped. The crossword was nothing more than an advertisement for the gallery's opening show.

I sank into the nearest chair, staring at the poster in Zuly's hands, trying to understand the connection between this guerrilla marketing campaign and a dead dog walker.

I cleared my throat. "How was Mickey involved?"

"He wasn't, really," Henri said. "We came up with this idea to plant clues in discarded wallets, because who can resist picking up a lost wallet? And that meant we needed a lot of wallets. Since Mickey's always been good at sourcing stuff, we decided—"

"You asked Mickey Doig to steal wallets for you?" The note of surprise in my voice was genuine. "That's outrageous."

"No," Zuly said, rolling up the poster and dropping it on the floor beside her chair. "We didn't ask him to steal anything. How were we to know—"

"Your fearless leader here"—I pointed to Henri, my voice rising—"told me Mickey was a thief. You must have suspected what he was up to."

"We paid him for the wallets," Irma added helpfully.

I had no answer to that. While swiveling my gaze between them, the penny dropped. "You started the million-dollar prize rumor, didn't you?"

Miserably, Henri twisted his hands together. "It seemed like a good move. We didn't know people would take it so... seriously."

"What was the theme of this show?"

"Famous murderers in history," Irma said, looking pleased. "We did paintings and mixed media depicting notorious killers."

I pointed to a covered canvas on a nearby pedestal. "Is that one of them?"

Irma perked up. "It's mine. Would you like to see it?"

"Please."

Irma rose to flick a cloth off the painting. A horrific, distended face with reddened, staring eyes and disheveled hair glared from the black background. Six women's faces—several wearing ringlets and bonnets common to the Victorian era—were arranged in a semi-circle at the bottom.

"Is that Jack the Ripper and his victims?"

"Yes." Irma's delight that I'd readily identified her subject lit up her face. "Is it creepy enough, do you think?"

I regarded the crusty bloodstains, where it looked as if the paint had been applied with a putty knife. "It's creepy, all right. Could you—cover it, please?"

"Sure. We have to keep it under wraps until the show,

anyway." Irma whisked the cloth back over her picture. "You won't tell anyone, will you? About the paintings, I mean?"

Shivering briefly, I turned away from the canvas. "You can count on me to keep that under wraps. But why did you pick famous murderers as your theme? It's so gruesome."

"Verity, you're behind the times," Zuly said. "Horror movies and true-crime shows are all the rage. Don't you ever watch Netflix?"

"Or go to the theater, for that matter," Irma mused. "And there are books. Best sellers."

"That's right," Zuly said. "Gore is everywhere. We simply took advantage of the zeitgeist."

"The zeitgeist? Really?" I think I could be forgiven for once if my tone was cynical. The top-selling paintings at local galleries up to then had been muted street scenes and pastel watercolors. *Killers Amongst Us* seemed a radical departure.

A horrible notion hit me. "By zeitgeist, do you mean Leafy Hollow's own history? Like the Black Widow case? She's not one of your portraits, is she?"

Henri and Irma exchanged glances, then Henri gave an apologetic shrug. "It did seem too good to pass up."

Slumping back into the chair, I lowered my head into my hands.

"We didn't mean any harm, Verity. We were only trying to scare up publicity for the show—and the gallery," Irma said.

I peeked out from under my hands. "But didn't you realize people might take this the wrong way?

Her eyes were wide. "It never occurred to us people

would think it was real. That they'd actually believe there were killers loose in the village."

Given Leafy Hollow's recent past, I thought this was disingenuous, but decided to let it pass.

"And since there *is* a killer..." Irma swallowed, glancing nervously around. "We hope our little contest didn't make matters worse. What if we gave him ideas?"

She looked so contrite I couldn't help lowering my hands to blurt out, "I'm sure that's not the case." I wasn't sure, not at all, but it seemed much too late to mention my misgivings. "Shouldn't you take this to the police?"

"Oh, no," Zuly said. "We can't do that."

"Why not?"

"They might think we know something about Oskar York's murder. If it is murder."

Irma gave Zuly's arm a reassuring pat. "Verity, if you think it will help, we'll go public about our marketing campaign."

"I think you should. But there's something I don't understand. Why did you include the names of two village residents among the crossword answers? Didn't you stop to think that might make them objects of suspicion? And even without Mickey's death, it seems odd to include clues pointing to Noah Butterfield and Rick Armstrong."

Zuly sucked in a breath. Irma nibbled her cuticle again. Henri sat dully, his mouth hanging open. Matisse rolled over onto his back, hoping for a tummy rub.

"Well?" I asked.

They shook their heads in unison.

"We have no idea where those clues came from," Henri said. "We didn't write them."

"What do you mean?"

"Someone else added those clues to our puzzle. It wasn't us."

CHAPTER TWENTY-TWO

"JUST EXPLAIN IT TO ME," I said. "How could a stranger change the answers on your puzzle?"

Zuly retrieved the rolled-up poster, then spread it out on the floor. "They didn't. This poster shows our original answers. See?" She pointed to four down. "The original clue was, 'When winter is dead,' and the answer was supposed to be 'SPRING.' Not 'STRONG.'"

"And the clue for two down," Zuly continued, "was supposed to be, 'It enriches our lives.' The answer was ART. Not ARM."

I studied the artists' poster. "How could that happen?"

"I told you. We have no idea."

"And 'BUTTER?'"

"Should have been 'BITTER.' We only added those extra clues as filler. That way, the players wouldn't figure out our real message right away."

"That message being the name and date of your show?"

Zuly and Irma nodded miserably.

"We wanted to keep the contest going until everyone was talking about it," Irma said. "You have to understand, Verity, it's not easy to make a living as an artist. We're always struggling. Especially Zuly. Her work deserves a wider audience."

"Your artworks are striking," I said. "I hope you sell lots of them. But you misled the entire village. I don't think this guerrilla marketing campaign of yours will have the hoped-for result."

That was putting it mildly, but as I took in their miserable expressions, I didn't have the heart to detail the shortcomings of their "ingenious" marketing plan.

"We know," Zuly said, sinking into a chair. Her face crumpled, tears threatening. Again.

Puffing air through my lips, I studied the original poster. No wonder Henri seemed confused at our bakery meeting when I filled in the answers from Mickey's tattered page. *That's wrong*, he'd insisted.

"So, you never intended to point suspicion at Noah Butterfield or Rick Armstrong?"

"Never. Verity, we prepared this long before Mickey died," Irma said. "We can prove it, too. You can ask the company that printed the posters for us." She pointed to a printer's cardboard box in a corner of the room. "We have several hundred, right there. All useless, now."

"And not paid for, either," Henri morosely added, wringing his hands. "Verity, could you talk to Jeff for us? Explain we didn't mean any harm?"

Why did everyone in the village think I had special influence with the police? Jeff was already touchy about the possibility of anyone suspecting he gave his girlfriend favorable treatment. I could only imagine the speeding ticket I'd get if I ever relaxed my guard and actually drove a little too quickly through the village. He'd probably ask the traffic cop to bump it *up* a few notches.

"You'll have to talk to Jeff yourself. But there is a way to mitigate the damage."

All three clustered around, their stares drilling in to me.

"Mickey was given the list before he died, so I think whoever added those alternative clues wanted to shed light on an earlier death—Oskar's."

"But Oskar's death was an accident," Irma said.

"I'm not so sure. Those magazines had been stacked in his kitchen for decades. What made them suddenly topple over?"

"Maybe Oskar tripped and fell against them," Henri said.

"If he'd done that, he would have landed on top of the magazines, not under them."

Henri winced. "I take your point."

"I think somebody pushed them over on purpose."

"Why would someone kill Oskar?" Zuly asked. "He was harmless."

"Maybe not to everyone. We simply don't know enough about him."

"But if someone suspected Rick or Noah was a killer, why didn't they go to the police?"

"They might have feared what would happen if they turned in a potential killer. Don't forget—there's no evidence Oskar's death was murder. Going to the police with a vague accusation wouldn't have led to an arrest. But the police might have dragged the accused down to the station for questioning. I wouldn't want to be the person who caused that, would you?"

Zuly shuddered. "No."

"So, they reported it anonymously by taking advantage of your marketing scheme. It's a roundabout method, but feasible. With everybody talking about your crossword puzzle, it would guarantee attention for their claim."

"See!" Zuly said triumphantly, bumping a fist into Henri's shoulder. "I told you the contest was a good idea."

At the look on my face, she winced. "Sorry."

"But how would they know about it?" Henri asked.

"That's the question. Who knew about your marketing campaign? Did you tell anyone?"

"We knew, naturally. So, there's the three of us," Irma said, counting on her fingers. "And Mickey—we had to take him into our confidence to get the wallets, but we never showed him the puzzle."

"Or the posters," Henri added.

"Did Mickey ask why you needed the wallets?"

"Several times. He was very curious. But we were adamant."

"What about the printers?" I asked. "How many people there handled your poster?"

"Oh, we asked them not to tell anybody. We were quite firm about that. I'm sure they wouldn't betray our confidence."

"Yes, but—how many people knew? They didn't print your posters in the dead of night, did they? Couldn't someone else have seen it?"

Irma grimaced. "It's a tiny company. Three people at best. And the receptionist. Four in all."

For a hush-hush marketing campaign, these guerrillas had been anything but discreet. The field of potential wrongdoers was widening, which was not a good thing.

"That means at least eight people knew about your secret contest. Not to mention customers who might have wandered into the printer's and potentially caught a glimpse of those posters. Any one of those people could have devised alternative clues and answers."

Scanning the circle of faces, I said, "Which brings me back to my original question—why those two names in particular? Let's start with the Butterfields—Noah and Rebecca. What was their connection to Oskar York?"

Henri grimaced. "Ah. Noah Butterfield. *There's* a suspicious character. Something is definitely fishy with him."

"It was Noah who suggested you approach Oskar for the funds you needed for the opening show, wasn't it?"

Zuly looked surprised. "He did? Why didn't you tell us, Henri?"

"Because there was no point. I didn't have a chance to ask him before—Oskar-gate," he said, muttering the last words.

Irma dug a finger into his shoulder. "Why did we need more money? You said everything was fine. What about that government grant you told us about?"

He winced. "We didn't qualify."

"Are you saying we can't afford it? That the show is off?" Zuly took a step toward Henri.

"Can we get back to the topic at hand?" I asked, holding up my palm to stop her. "I know you're concerned about the show, and I don't blame you—but two people are dead."

"Sorry, Verity. Continue."

"Henri, why do you think something's up with Noah?"

"He knew Oskar had money, for one thing."

"And?"

"Isn't that suspicious enough?"

"No. Noah's an investment manager. He might have advised Oskar on his portfolio."

Irma snorted. "What portfolio? That old man lived in a pigsty. Surely, if he had money, he would have cleaned up that house."

"Not necessarily," I said. "Hoarding is a mental health issue. He may not have been able to stop." I regarded Irma intently. "You delivered meals to him. Did you see him often?"

"No. Only the once. He wasn't one of my regulars. I filled in that day for someone else."

"Who?"

"Sorry, can't remember. It was months ago." She wrinkled her brow, trying to think. "I can't even recall what was on the menu."

"Something easy to chew, no doubt," Henri offered drily.

Zuly snickered.

"But—" Irma wagged a finger at me. "You'll never guess who I saw coming out of Oskar's house that day."

"Noah Butterfield?"

"Right in one."

"Did you talk to him?"

"No. I don't think he even saw me. He walked out of the

house carrying a briefcase, got into his car, and drove away before I had time to undo my seatbelt." She shrugged. "I didn't think anything of it, back then. It wasn't any of my business."

"Did you see any photos while you were in Oskar's home?"

"There was a lot of stuff on the walls. Is that what you mean?"

"I'm thinking more, like, shoeboxes full of pictures. Or photo albums? Anything like that?"

Irma shrugged. "Honestly, I just delivered the food and left. Many of our clients love to talk—they're lonely, and it's the highlight of their day. But Oskar wasn't like that. He wouldn't let me come in the house at all, really. Not any farther than the front hall. And that had so much junk in it, you couldn't see much else."

I turned to Zuly. "Did you have any contact with Oskar?"

"Never met the man. Sorry."

Henri stood up, stretching his back. "We have to finish cleaning up, Verity. Is there anything else?"

"No. Except—you'll tell Jeff about your marketing campaign, right?"

"Definitely."

At the door, I turned around. "I do have one other question. Have any of you ever heard rumors that Oskar kept a lot of cash hidden in his house?"

Henri chuckled. "That's a story the kids liked to tell. Like a local haunted house. That tale was especially popular at Halloween. Nobody actually believed it."

Henri's home—sorry, The Park Gallery—was only a few blocks from Noah Butterfield's investment office, so I made that my next visit. Even though Rebecca refused to confirm Oskar was a client, if Noah had visited him with a briefcase, it seemed likely. And I still wanted to know who gave the order to clear out Oskar's house and put his belongings in storage. In my horror at finding Mickey's body, I'd completely forgotten to call Wilf Mullins, the lawyer. Noah was the next best thing. Particularly since I was more convinced than ever that he was involved.

I circled the block twice before a parking space opened. Main Street had been cleared, but piles of grimy snow clogged the end of each block. Turning off the engine, I glanced up to see the Butterfield's office door open and Rebecca step out. *Perfect.* I wouldn't need an excuse to talk to Noah. I could walk right into his office without interference from his wife.

Rebecca glanced up both sides of the street before running a hand down her throat and smiling. Either she enjoyed a hard, sleeting rain or she was looking forward to her next appointment. She shot a furtive glance over her shoulder at the office door before setting off down the block.

At least, her glance seemed furtive to me. But then, I was notorious for cynicism, apparently.

Once Rebecca was far enough away, I got out of the truck. I'd no sooner flipped up my parka hood and made it to the sidewalk than the office door opened again. This time, Noah Butterfield stepped out. He was bareheaded, and the edges of his unbuttoned camel coat flapped in the wind. Not only that, but despite the slush underfoot, he wore no galoshes. His Italian leather loafers were in for a surprise.

I watched in astonishment as Noah scurried from one doorway to another, headed in the same direction as his wife, tucking into storefronts from time to time. He was following her.

I didn't need Lorne on hand to identify this as a clandestine maneuver. Longingly, I thought of the cell phone in my pocket. Too bad I hadn't enlisted Lorne's help. As an enthusiastic reconnaissance operative, he'd be disappointed he missed this opportunity to hone his skills.

But I knew what he'd say. If Noah was following Rebecca, then I should follow Noah. Flipping my hood back down to ensure visibility, I set off in pursuit.

Rebecca turned right at the end of the block, crossed over at the banking district—which was how Leafy Hollow villagers referred to the intersection with a bank branch on each corner—and continued down a side street.

Noah followed, taking care not to be seen.

I followed him, but without worrying about being spotted myself. No one in this strange procession was paying any attention to me.

At the next corner, Rebecca turned right again. She was heading back toward the Butterfields' office, but one block south. Mid-block, she paused, glanced around again—Noah hastily ducked behind a cedar hedge—and then walked up the alley that led to a parking lot behind the storefronts.

The offices and stores on this block of Main Street had

back entrances accessible from the side street. It looked like Rebecca was headed for the back entrance to Lucky Lentil.

If my gloves hadn't been sopping wet, I would have slapped my forehead. I'd assumed that 'Butter' and 'Field' in the crossword puzzle referred to Noah Butterfield. It could just as easily have meant *Rebecca* Butterfield. And if Rebecca was linked to Rick Armstrong, that might be why he was named in the puzzle, too.

Further, if Oskar really was a client of Noah's, then Rebecca, as Noah's office manager and assistant, would know all about Oskar's account, including how much cash he had. And possibly, where he kept it.

If I could figure that out, Noah could, too. Was that why he was following his wife?

Mentally, I added that to the questions I intended to ask him the moment this reconnaissance mission ended.

Rebecca stopped short, staring at something.

Noah jerked back out of the way—splashing into a three-inch-deep puddle of slush. I winced at the state of his shoes.

Mimicking their movements, I also stopped. As wind whipped through my hair, I flipped up my hood. Since there was no place for me to hide, I gazed at the sky, feigning an implausible search for rare birds.

The back door to the restaurant popped open. Rick Armstrong—wearing an apron over his sweater and khakis, his vivid blue eyes discernible even at this distance—stepped out.

Rebecca waved, but he wasn't looking in her direction. Before she could call out to him, the driver's door opened on a car parked in the lot behind the restaurant. A woman emerged.

For the second time that day, I gawked.

Shanice's afro puff bobbed as she waved merrily at Rick. He hurried over to her. Grinning broadly, he threw his arms around her in an affable embrace. Then he delivered the coup de grâce—an even more affable squeeze of her bum.

Even over the wind, I heard Rebecca's muttered curse.

This was not going to end well. I moved closer, angling for a better vantage point.

For a moment, Rebecca stood, dumbstruck. Then, "You son of a—," she screamed, running straight at Rick with her handbag swinging.

He released Shanice, stepped back in alarm, and put up his hands.

Rebecca got in multiple whacks with that bag. It was a heavy tote, one of those leather carryalls popular with celebrities the previous season.

Rick tried ineffectively to shield his head. "No, no. I can explain," he gasped between blows.

I can explain? When had that ever worked?

I bit my lip, wincing, as Rebecca's tote bag connected with Rick's face. That had to hurt. Should I step in before the village's new restaurateur had to be taken to the hospital?

Fortunately, I didn't have to decide, because Shanice took that as a perfect opportunity to step in herself. Possibly she felt guilty. I promised myself to find out later, when I grilled her about her fondness for her boss's competitor. My heart burned for Emy over the injustice of this betrayal. To think

I'd believed Shanice's completely implausible story about butter sculptures.

"Stop—Rebecca, stop," she shrieked, grabbing for the tote bag.

The two women tugged on the bag, one at either end.

Then Rebecca raised a foot, driving the sole straight into Shanice's stomach. Shanice toppled backward, into the nearest snowbank, where she sat—stuck, struggling, and shrieking.

I slapped a hand against my cheek in admiration at Rebecca's move. Then I made a mental note to tell Adeline I'd found a new sparring partner.

Rebecca renewed her attack on Rick, who was struggling to escape through the restaurant's back door. "Ow, ow," he cried, trying to block the smacks. "Rebecca, stop it, for pity's sake."

In all the excitement, I'd forgotten about Noah. He picked that moment to barrel into the fray.

"What the hell is going on?" he roared as he ran toward the combatants.

Horrified, Rebecca froze, her tote bag arrested in mid-thwack.

Rick stood motionless, his mouth hanging open.

"Help," Shanice called feebly from the snowbank.

Noah surged forward. "I said, what the—"

It was unclear to me whether he intended to rescue Shanice, argue with his wife, or punch Rick. And I never found out, because that was the precise moment when Noah's Italian leather gave up its one-sided battle with the elements.

His feet slid out from under him, and he toppled head-first into Shanice's snowbank.

―――――――

By the time we'd freed Noah and Shanice and I'd corralled everybody into the restaurant, the worst of their collective rage had cooled. Shaking my head, I took in the pitiful scene.

Rick, wincing, held an ice pack to one cheek. Shanice brushed snow off her jacket while darting guilty glances at me. Noah scowled and paced, ignoring the wet footprints he was leaving on the floor. As far away from him as possible, Rebecca sullenly assessed the damage to her tote bag.

It was hard to know where to start.

Turning to Shanice, I said, "I think you owe Emy an apology."

"What do you mean?" Her stricken gaze implored me to explain.

I flexed my eyebrows. "About the reviews?"

"No, no. You're wrong, Verity. The only reason I put up with his—" she flailed her arms to indicate the bruised restaurateur, "ridiculous advances was to find out if he was behind those reviews. I'd never betray Emy."

From behind his ice bag, Rick shot her an incredulous look. "Ridiculous?" he asked. "Ridiculous? Is that what you think of me? And what reviews are you talking about?"

Rebecca slammed her tote bag on to the nearest table. "You *are* ridiculous," she said loudly, crossing her arms and glaring at Rick. "This woman is young enough to be your daughter. It's all so embarrassing. You're embarrassing."

"Oh, really, Rebecca? That's not what you said last—"

Noah cleared his throat, and we turned in his direction.

He was staring out the front window, not looking at anyone in the room. "He's not the only one who's ridiculous," Noah said. Then he pushed open the front door and stepped out, his shoes squelching. The door swung shut behind him.

I waggled a finger at Shanice. "Later," I said. "You better get back to the bakery." Then I hurried to follow Noah. From experience, I knew that when people were in shock, they were much more likely to answer impertinent questions.

CHAPTER TWENTY-THREE

WHEN I PUSHED OPEN the door to Noah's office, his dripping overcoat was hanging from the coat rack and he was slipping off his ruined shoes.

He raised his head, his expression blank. "Verity. I'm sorry you had to see that."

"I'm sorry you had to go through it."

"Yeah. It's possible I deserved it." He picked up his shoes and tossed them, one after the other, into the trash bin behind Rebecca's desk on the other side of the room. They landed with a *thunk* against the metal sides.

"Nice shots," I said.

Noah chuckled weakly, holding out his hand for my coat. "At least I can do one thing right. Come on back to my office, and I'll make us some coffee." After adding my parka to the coat rack, he glanced at the front door. "I think we'll be alone for a while."

He padded on his stocking feet down the hallway, leaving damp footprints on the Berber carpet. I followed.

Noah settled himself into the executive chair behind his desk. "High school basketball," he said.

"Excuse me?" I sat in a leather armchair facing his desk.

"I played forward on our team. Slam dunks were my specialty."

"Oh. Right."

"In fact, that's where I met Rebecca." He swiveled his chair to face the opposite wall, then lifted one leg onto the opposite knee to massage his wet foot. "She was a cheerleader —did you know that?"

Shaking my head, I said, "No, but I'm not surprised."

He shot me a sharp look, switching legs to knead the other foot.

"I meant because she's so attractive and so—" A vision of Rebecca knocking Shanice into the snowbank came to mind. "Athletic."

A smile flickered on his face as he lowered his foot to the floor and stared at the wall. It was obvious he was picturing something other than its STOCK MARKETS OF THE WORLD chart.

"She was the most beautiful thing I'd ever seen. I was smitten." He sighed. "Young love. We assumed it would last forever. And it nearly did. But sometimes... you take your eye off the ball and the whole game goes south."

I wasn't sure why we were talking about sports again, but before I could ask, Noah swiveled back to face me, suddenly all business.

"Rebecca said you came in for investment advice while I was away."

"I did. Yes. But not for financial advice."

He gave me a half-smile. "I figured that."

Ignoring his condescending tone, I rambled on. "Actually, Noah, I was hoping to ask you a few questions about Oskar York. Did you know him?"

"Everybody knew Oskar. He lived in Leafy Hollow for decades."

"Yes, he did. But I don't think everybody knew him. Not well, at least. He rarely left his house. And he had mental health problems, didn't he?" My voice rose in pitch along with my anxiety, but I wasn't able to modulate either one. I shouldn't be asking Noah about Oskar York.

In fact, I fully expected the next words out of his mouth to be, "None of your business."

He surprised me.

"I thought of Oskar as a friend. Whether he considered me as one—I really don't know. I tried to convince him to get help." He picked up a pen, rolling it under his fingers along the desktop. "He wasn't always like that, you know."

"A recluse? Or a hoarder?"

"Either. He was a schoolteacher at one time, but not here in the village. He did write a book about Leafy Hollow, I believe."

"What happened?"

Noah shrugged. "I don't think anybody knows. How can you predict something like that? He must have had... latent tendencies." He picked up the pen and slapped it down on the wooden surface. "I think Oskar regretted a choice he'd made in the past. I never had any idea what it was, though. He made a few vague allusions, and never brought it up again."

"Sounds like you talked to him quite a bit. Was he a client?"

Another sharp look. "A client? Oskar had no money. That house was rented. And he was years behind on his rent." He shook his head. "I really shouldn't tell you that, but since he's dead..." He shrugged.

"Did the owner of the house order the removal of Oskar's possessions? I went by there the other day, and workmen were bundling everything into a van."

"Yes. He was within his rights to clear the house, as long as he didn't destroy anything."

I recalled the indifferent way the workmen treated those objects. "How would you know if anything was damaged? Did Oskar have any relatives to check it over? Heirs, I mean?"

"None that I know of—and nothing to leave them if he had."

"You've been in that house."

"Several times."

"And never saw anything of value?"

At that, he smiled. "I've heard the village stories about hidden riches. But they're just that—stories. If Oskar had anything valuable, he sold it long ago."

"How could he sell it, if he never went out?"

Noah rubbed a hand across his jaw, regarding me as he weighed his next words. He lowered his hand onto the desk to fiddle again with the pen. "There was someone else who visited him fairly often. I suspect that person assisted with those... sales. I don't know for sure."

In the hall, the office's front door opened with a rush of air and noise. Vehicles swooshed past on the sloppy road. The door closed, shutting out the sound.

"Anybody in?" a man's voice called.

Noah rose to his feet. "One minute," he called, then turned to face me. "My next appointment is here, Verity, so —" He extended a hand to the door.

I stood up. "One more question, please. Who was this person who visited Oskar regularly?"

"I can't say."

"Was it Mickey Doig? I believe he walked Oskar's dog occasionally. And now—they're both dead."

Noah stopped short of the door, eyebrows flying up. "*They're both dead?* What does that mean? Seriously, Verity, that's fairly—"

"Cynical?"

"Exactly."

"Do you know of anyone who might have wanted Oskar dead? Or Mickey, for that matter?"

"No," he said sharply. "No one."

"Noah? Are you there?" came the man's voice from the hall. Judging by the rise in volume, Noah's next appointment was getting impatient.

"One minute. Be right there," Noah called. "Verity, I have to go." He turned to the door, then swiveled back to face me. "Look, it's a coincidence, that's all. Mickey knew a lot of people. He even walked our boxer, Axel, from time to time. And he did walk Oskar's dog. But Mickey wasn't reliable.

And there were rumors about his other activities." Noah grimaced. "Whatever happened to Mickey Doig, it was likely self-inflicted. As in—his own fault."

I found that a bit severe, but kept that opinion to myself.

"Noah?" The voice had become downright petulant.

Noah strode down the hall. I followed.

"Why don't you ask Mickey's friend—Willy Wilkes?" he said over his shoulder. "Maybe he knows something. Larry—great to see you. Come on in." Noah slapped the tweed-jacketed back of a burly man wearing a bow tie, whose unzipped snow boots flapped open as he walked.

It wasn't until I was outside on the sidewalk that I remembered the other question I'd meant to ask Noah Butterfield. Where, exactly, did he disappear to for two days?

Willy Wilkes had given me his address at the bakery meeting. During our brief talk, there had been no mention of a job, or school, or anywhere his presence would be required on a daily basis. I figured there was a good chance he'd be home.

A row of precisely pruned yews marched along the driveway of the Wilkes' two-story yellow brick house, in a suburb not far from the village center. Someone had brushed the shrubs free of snow and swept every trace of it from the walkway. I assumed that someone had not been Willy.

"Mrs. Wilkes?" I asked the woman in trim yoga pants and navy sweater who answered the door. Her hair was tied back in a ponytail, her skin clear, and her gray eyes piercing. This was a woman who would not appreciate having her time wasted, I suspected.

At her quick nod, I said, "I'm Verity Hawkes. I was hoping to talk to Willy."

"You're Adeline's niece." She held out her hand for a quick shake.

"Correct."

"Come in." Uma did not offer to take my parka, or show any curiosity about why I was there. She merely pointed to the stairs off the front hall that led to the basement. "He's down there."

"Mrs. Wilkes?" I asked before she walked away. "Did Mickey Doig ever stay here?"

She rolled her eyes to the ceiling, issuing an exasperated puff of air. "What a pain in the backside that kid was."

"You're not sorry he's gone, then?"

"He was a bad influence on Willy." After wrinkling her forehead, she added briskly, "I'm sorry he died." Then she turned back toward the aroma of roasted chicken wafting from the kitchen.

In the unfinished basement, Willy was sprawled on a sofa, his long legs planted on the floor, playing a video game on a big-screen television. *Halo*, it looked like. A lot of gunfire, anyway.

"Willy?"

He grunted. "Verity. Oh, man—look at that!"

"Can we talk?"

He shot me an annoyed glance. "Now?"

"I'm here now, so that would be good."

More gunfire. Followed by an explosion that lit up the screen.

Willy muttered a curse before flinging the controller onto the sofa beside him. "What's up?"

I gestured to the armchair. "Can I sit down?"

"Cool. I go by Viper."

Taking this as an invitation, I settled into the chair. "I'm sorry—what?"

"My name." He grinned. "Viper."

"Oh. Is that new?"

"Nah. Been using it for ages. So?" He shrugged. "What can I do for you?"

"It's about Mickey."

Willy—sorry, Viper—slumped, grin fading. "I'm really bummed about that. He was a good guy."

"He stayed with you, right?"

"Right here in this room, in fact."

After glancing around at the cluttered surroundings, I pointed to a metal bookcase filled with tattered board games, action-movie DVDs, and cardboard boxes stuffed to over-flowing with old clothes.

"Any of Mickey's stuff still here?"

"The cops took it all away."

"That's too bad."

He shrugged. "Mom was happy. Saved her throwing it out, she said."

"I have something that belonged to Mickey. Could you take a look at it?" Pulling the wool hat from my pocket, I handed it over.

"Cool," he said, turning it over in his hands. "Mickey

loved this hat... picked it up during his peyote days." Willy peered closely at it, fingering the tears. "What happened to it?"

"The dogs wrestled over it, I think."

"That's weird. Mickey never let this hat out of his sight." He handed it back.

"Maybe because of this?" Turning the hat inside out, I showed him the secret pocket.

His mouth gaped in astonishment. "Cool. What was in it?" He brightened. "Money?"

"Remember I said at the bakery that those crossword clues belonged to Mickey?"

"Yeah. I was meaning to ask how you knew that."

"This is where I found them. The clues were in this hat." I dangled the torn fabric from one hand, raising my eyebrows.

"Cool."

"Indeed. Cool. Now—Viper. Do you have any idea who gave Mickey those clues?"

He crossed his arms, intently regarding the hat, his brow furrowed. In the opposite corner of the basement, the furnace kicked on. Warm air wafted over us from a vent in the ceiling.

"No," he said finally, uncrossing his arms. "I don't."

I knew it was too good to be true that Mickey might have confided in his friend. To be honest, I was beginning to think Mickey Doig was a one-way acquaintance—with all the information flowing in Mickey's direction.

Perhaps my disappointment was obvious, because Willy added helpfully, "He used to walk Old Man York's dog."

"And that's significant because—?"

Willy glanced around the room, almost as if he were

afraid of being overheard. Then he leaned in. "Mickey was after his money."

"But Oskar didn't have any money."

"Nah. Not true. He was loaded. Just didn't flash it around, that's all."

"I see. Do you have any evidence to back that up?"

"Whoa." Willy jerked back. "Evidence? You're a nice lady, Verity, but I'm not getting involved with any cops."

Restraining the urge to point out that, at not yet thirty, I hardly qualified for the "lady" moniker, I said, "This is between you and me, Viper. I will tell no one. Unless you don't really know anything at all, and you're just making this up."

That had the desired effect.

"I know lots of stuff that goes on in this village." He tossed his stringy hair.

"Then tell me—what did Mickey plan to do?"

"I don't know that. Not exactly. But somebody did something wrong, and he found out about it. It was worth a lot of money, he said." Nodding sagely, Willy sank back against the sofa.

"That's all you know?"

"That's all I know. Keep it to yourself." He flicked a cautionary hand in the air as if he'd just confided a state secret.

Outside, I flipped up the hood of my parka before carefully negotiating the newly slippery walkway. More sleet had fallen while I'd been inside, and the yew trees were starting to bend. The promised ice storm had started.

CHAPTER TWENTY-FOUR

SNOWPLOWS AND SANDERS rumbled past as I drove along Main Street and up the two-lane road that zig-zagged up the Escarpment. Falling sleet spattered the snow and pinged off the truck's roof. Tree branches hung low over the pavement, weighed down with a coating of ice. The power lines were also heavy with ice, sparkling in the muted winter sun. As I drove past, that sun—by now only the barest suggestion of yellow in a groggy gray horizon—dipped even lower.

The truck had reached the top of the Escarpment when my phone rang. Jeff's name flashed on my call display. I flicked on the speaker. "Hi. I tried to call you, but your voice mail is full."

"I know." He groaned. "I'm working my way through it. Where are you? At home?"

"Not yet."

"The storm's getting bad, Verity. You shouldn't be out on the roads."

241

"Stop worrying, Jeff. I'm fine. I'm on my way to Rose Cottage. And I'm in the truck. It's not like I'm driving Emy's Fiat."

"Emy doesn't drive that car in weather like this, does she?"

I paused, carefully considering my answer. "Probably not?"

"Where are you?"

"Five minutes from home. If that."

"Do you have plenty of candles?"

"Yes," I answered, exasperated. Between Emy, Adeline, and Jeff, I had enough candles to light the entire Escarpment. Possibly someone should inform NASA.

"Be careful where you put them. You should be using battery-operated lanterns."

"For heaven's sakes, Jeff—"

"Sorry. It's just—I worry about you."

"I know. And I love that about you."

"Is that all you love?"

I smiled. "Now you're teasing. You get yourself over to Rose Cottage, and I'll show you which parts I love."

"Wish I could, but we'll be working all night."

"Does that mean you're not following up on Mickey's case?"

"Your local police department can do more than one thing at a time, you know."

"Meaning?"

"We found evidence Mickey owed the wrong people money, possibly drug debts. We think he was dealing, in a small way, and may not have paid his supplier on time. Or even double-crossed him by trying to go into business on his own."

I refrained from gloating. "Then it was murder, after all?"

"Not necessarily. But unpaid drug debts could be a motive. We're taking it seriously. Keep that to yourself for now."

"What about the threads from the van's muffler?"

"A wool garment, possibly a scarf. That would be readily at hand if it was a crime of opportunity."

"Woman's or man's scarf?"

"No way to tell. It was navy blue. Could be either. Or not a scarf at all. Could be a sweater."

A vision of Henri's intruder barreling past me on the walkway came to mind. "Henri Vartan's attacker had a scarf wrapped around his face. It was navy, too."

"Probably a coincidence."

"Maybe, but—"

"A lot of people have navy scarves, Verity. I have one."

"Hmmm. Where were you that afternoon?"

"Very funny. Enough about Mickey's case. I've told you too much already."

"Well, I have something to tell you. Those crossword puzzle clues were fakes. The whole thing was a contest started by Henri and the girls."

"I know." He groaned again. "Henri called me. Look, sorry—I don't have time to talk about it now. I'm only calling to make sure you stay off the roads. The Weather Channel is calling this the storm of the century."

"They always say that."

"Still. Are you—"

"Nearly home."

"Stay safe," he said before hanging up.

"You too," I muttered over the dial tone.

The road that meandered along the conservation area was narrow. Even in summer, drivers had to back up to let another vehicle pass on the curves. But today, with snow-banks piled high on either side, it was even worse. I focused on keeping the pickup on the straight and narrow, conscious of the ice-laden branches looming above me.

It was slow going. I had plenty of time to think. Emy's idea that I should investigate the villagers' little mysteries had seemed clever at the time. I no longer believed so. Take Mickey's death, for instance. How would I have found out that he owed money to drug dealers? Did I even want to know something like that? Police officers were backed by the full weight of the law, not to mention automatic weapons. What did I have—besides an ancient pickup truck and a talent for word games? Jeff was right. I should stick to lawn mowing and woodland garden design. Let smarter minds than mine probe the village's secrets.

I had almost convinced myself until I remembered Oskar York's connection to Mickey—and Noah's warning. *Whatever happened to Mickey Doig, it was probably self-inflicted. As in —his own fault.* Given Jeff's recent disclosure, Noah was probably right. Worse, what if Oskar got caught up in Mickey's bad timing?

A branch groaned and dipped overhead, shedding a load of snow that thumped onto the roof of the cab. Instinctively, I slowed the truck before noticing in the rearview mirror that a dark-colored SUV was coming up the road behind me. The

SUV kept plowing forward until it was almost hugging the rear of my truck. I flailed my arm, trying to signal the driver to go around.

Instead, his lights flashed.

What does he want me to do? Drive off the road? Hoping to signal my reluctance to speed up on such a treacherous route, I tapped on the brakes.

The SUV driver ignored my brake lights, moving even closer. If I had to make a sudden stop, he'd hit me.

"All right, all right. I'll move over," I muttered. Gingerly, I edged the truck to the side of the road, steering clear of the snowbanks, to give the SUV room to overtake me.

It accelerated, pulling out to pass on my left.

In the glare of my headlights, a bumper sticker glowed bright orange.

Leafy Hollow Farmers' Market. We like it fresh.

I half expected to see a "Turnips Aboard" sign.

The SUV hadn't pulled all the way back in when a dump truck loaded with snow crested the hill ahead, rumbling toward us. The truck driver would never be able to stop in time. I wrenched the steering wheel over to make more room.

My pickup truck veered off the road toward the nearest snowbank. When I tried to turn back, the rear end fishtailed on the icy road and the truck spun around. With a jolt, the front end slammed into what felt like a solid block of ice.

The airbag exploded, hitting me in the chest and face.

Then, everything went still.

Gradually, I recognized the sound of sleet spattering against the windshield.

I assessed my body parts, one by one. They were all attached. All I had to do was back up the truck and get the heck out of there.

Gunning the engine, I shifted into reverse. Even over the shrieking of the wind, I heard tires spinning against ice. The truck heaved and shuddered, but went nowhere.

With a shiver of misgiving, I got out to check the damage.

I was alone on the road. The dump truck was gone. So, too, was the SUV. The only sounds were those of the wind whistling through the trees and the hiss of sleet hitting the ground.

The front of my truck was stuck in an icy snowbank. But that wasn't the problem. The two front wheels had plunged through the drift and over the edge of the ditch at the side of the road, where they hung uselessly in the air. It would be impossible for me to get the truck back on the road. I'd have to call for a tow.

I climbed back into the cab, shucked off my clammy gloves, and dialed the auto club.

"Is anyone injured?" the female dispatcher asked.

"No. But my truck isn't going anywhere without a tow. Can you send someone?"

"I can add you to the list, hon, but it's a two-hour wait. Or longer. Our drivers are swamped with calls, with more coming in all the time." She sighed. "You'd think people would stay off the roads on a day like today."

I tried to chuckle, but my throat was dry—unlike my parka, which was dripping water into the truck's footwell. "I'll try something else."

"You want me to add you to the list?"

"Might as well. But I can't stay here. It's too cold."

"When someone's free, we'll give you a call." She clicked off.

Glumly, I regarded the phone. Time to call in the cavalry —otherwise known as Jeff Katsuro, Hero Boyfriend. I was reluctant to disturb him, but I knew he'd be annoyed if I didn't. I made the call.

To tell the truth, I only wanted to hear his voice. Jeff's calm demeanor would soothe my growing anxiety. Besides, I loved talking to him. I had been alone a long time. It was comforting to be in a stable relationship again—to have someone who would always take my calls.

His phone rang and then picked up. "You've reached Detective Constable Jeff Katsuro. Leave a message." *Beep.*

"Hi, Jeff. I—"

"The mailbox is full. Please try again later." Click.

Great. No tow truck, no boyfriend riding to the rescue, no —I glanced through the windshield at the sky—sunshine, even. The darkness had closed in.

I decided to try the police station's main number, knowing they could radio Jeff. Even if he wasn't able to come himself, he would know what to do. As I dialed, I reconsidered. There would be casualties on a day like this, and injured people needing ambulances and paramedics. Car crashes could block major intersections, delaying snowplows and emergency responders.

It was wrong to take Jeff away from serious calls to pick up his girlfriend.

Briefly, I considered calling the local fire department. After the arson at Rose Cottage—there had also been that embarrassing cliff rescue, which I hoped they'd forgotten—I was on a first-name basis with Captain Bob Valens and all of his crew. I even knew the fire station's cat, an enormous, cuddly white tom who was no threat whatsoever to the station's vermin. After searching for their number, I started to dial.

But I clicked off that call, too. Winter weather brought fires sparked by candles, blocked chimneys, and overloaded furnaces. Captain Bob and his crew would have their hands full. After all, I wasn't hurt, and home was nearby.

The road I was marooned on followed the border of the conservation land, so there weren't any doors to knock on. But it was barely a fifteen-minute walk to Rose Cottage. And my truck wasn't blocking the road, so I could leave it stuck in the ditch. If I was lucky, I might hitch a ride with a passing motorist.

That faint hope of a lift soon evaporated in a haze of fog and sleet. I struggled through snowdrifts, dodging slippery ice patches. Water dripped from the rim of my hood into my face, which was soon wet and raw. Ten minutes into what normally would be a casual stroll, I was exhausted, wet, and miserable. Sleet hissed into the snow, and branches creaked overhead.

Not a single vehicle came by.

I wondered if I should turn back to the truck. At least it was on the road and visible. Eventually someone would drive past—an emergency vehicle, probably. I could turn on the engine for a while to heat the cab.

That conjured up an image of Mickey slumped over in his van, his face bright pink. I shuddered. The Coming Up

Roses truck had formerly belonged to my aunt. It was nearly two decades old. Did it have venting issues similar to Mickey's van? Mentally, I added that to my to-do list—*check the truck's exhaust system.*

Ahead, a yellow light shone through the haze, a welcome beacon. I had reached the turnoff to Lilac Lane, and the small stone cottage that perched there. If there was a light on, the occupant—Irma O'Kay, the reclusive artist—must be home. I'd never visited her house, but there was no time like the present. It would be warm and dry, at least, and I could wait out the storm there.

I struggled up the slippery drive, sleet driving into my face like needles.

Carefully, I mounted three stone steps to the front door and knocked. No reply. I hammered on the door with both hands, competing with the sound of the keening wind.

The door opened, and I stumbled across the threshold.

CHAPTER TWENTY-FIVE

IRMA SHUT her front door against the wind before turning to face me. Two spots of red glowed on her normally colorless cheeks. "Verity—good grief. What are you doing out in this? Did you drive?" She leaned over to peer through the sidelight by the front door. Swirling mist and sleet obscured the view. Irma's cottage was too far back to see the road, anyway.

"My truck's in a ditch. I tried to walk home, but the storm's getting worse. I could barely see my hands in front of me."

"Give me your coat." Irma helped me off with my parka, shook it out, and hung it up on a hook in the hall. She pointed to an antique grill plate in the floor. "Turn your boots upside down over that vent so they'll dry. And go into the living room—you must be freezing. I have a fire going." After pointing me in the right direction, she disappeared down the hall. "Back in a sec with tea," she called over her shoulder.

I stopped in the doorway, awed. Color overwhelmed the

living room. A brilliant yellow fire snapped and crackled in a fireplace edged with vivid blue tiles. Antique lamps with multicolored glass shades glowed green and pink and orange. But the real display was on the ten-foot-high walls, every inch covered with framed prints, oils, and drawings. I recognized Irma's distinct swirling style in many. Most were abstracts, but several portraits stood out, especially one of fellow artist Zuly Sundae. In the picture, the normally assertive Zuly gazed shyly out at the viewer, one hand resting lightly on the back of her head.

Drawing an ottoman up to the fire, I glanced around to admire the artwork while rubbing my chilled hands in front of the flames. Then I took out my phone to call Jeff.

"The mailbox is full. Please try again later."

Hanging up, I mulled my options. There was no point in calling Lorne. He'd be more than willing to rescue me, but he'd have to use Emy's tiny Fiat 500. Jeff was right. That Fiat wasn't a suitable vehicle to take out in any ice storm, never mind the "storm of the century."

I couldn't call my next-door neighbors, Adeline and Gideon, because they weren't home. *We're taking a vacation*, my aunt had said. Their destination had not been mentioned. I didn't even know what country they were in.

Typical.

Aunt Adeline constantly worried about me, yet my concerns about her welfare were routinely met with a chuckle and, "I can take care of myself." I'd never been able to adequately explain to her the feeling of dread caused by the phone call that began, "Your aunt is missing and presumed dead." I finally understood the sleepless nights my mother—Adeline's sister—suffered all those years ago. Poor Mom. With no husband at home to support her, and a precocious child who worshiped her risk-taking aunt, it must have been tough. At the time, I never gave it a thought.

And then—Mom was gone. The familiar sense of loss opened like a chasm in my chest. For a moment, I let myself fall into it.

But only for a moment.

With a sigh, I dropped the phone beside me on the ottoman. Everyone should stay home. The storm would pass.

Irma reappeared, carrying a varnished wooden tray hand-painted with more swirling designs. I moved to a high-back armchair, so Irma could set the tray on the ottoman.

"There," she said, patting its edge with satisfaction. "You'll feel better with a hot drink in you." She pointed to the plate. "Ginger cookies. Not as good as Emy's, but almost. Try one."

Irma lifted the teapot to fill our cups.

"Thanks," I said, accepting a cup and clearing a space on the table beside me to set it down. "I really appreciate you taking me in. It's deathly out there."

"Any time. I'm sorry it took bad weather to convince you to visit." Irma sat opposite me, in an armchair swathed in colorful knitted afghans, to sip her tea. "It's comforting to have company to wait out the storm with." She glanced at the ceiling, puffing out air as she studied it. Smiling weakly, she picked up her teacup again.

Something in her tone set off alarm bells in my head. "We're safe here, aren't we?"

"Yeees." She bit her lip again.

"Is there something you're not telling me?"

Irma set her cup down decisively, then leaned in. "It's that tree. You probably saw it when you came up the driveway. The huge black walnut that shades the cottage?"

When I was struggling up the drive, I hadn't noticed any one tree in particular. Irma's cottage faced the Pine Hill conservation area. There were trees everywhere, groaning in the wind and laden with ice. They all seemed menacing to me. Nevertheless, I nodded. "What about it?"

"Last summer, I called a tree service to take a look at it. They warned me that big branch overhanging the roof should come off. In a wind storm, they said, it could snap and take out half the house." She leaned back, groaning. "You wouldn't believe the estimate they gave me. It was impossible."

"That doesn't sound good. Did you get a second opinion?"

"Yes. The second arborist wanted even more money." She waved a listless hand. "They have to tie off the limb to make sure it doesn't fall on the cottage before lifting it away and then—"

"It's a dangerous job."

"Yes." Irma gave me a sharp look. "I understand that. I don't want anyone to put themselves at risk for me. But artists in this country aren't exactly rolling in cash, Verity."

I decided not to point out she'd already told me that.

Glumly, Irma sipped her tea.

"Maybe your insurance would foot the bill," I said. "If you do nothing and that branch comes down on the house, they'll have to repair the damage. They might decide to deal with it before that happens."

Irma scowled. "That won't work. The cost of my home insurance was so high, I opted for a ten-thousand-dollar deductible." She twisted the teacup around in her hand, watching the liquid swirl. "It's never over," she muttered.

"Oh." I sipped my tea, wondering what to say to that.

"I was hoping to sell enough paintings at the gallery opening to pay for the work. But that's not going to happen now." She reached for a cookie, then munched on it morosely.

"I'm sorry, Irma. Your paintings are lovely. Couldn't you sell them elsewhere?"

"Not without paying commission. It wouldn't be nearly as profitable. Most of the time, it's all I can do to break even. If my parents hadn't left me this house..." She glanced around, pursing her lips, then resumed munching.

"And the bank..." she mumbled.

"Pardon?"

"The bank. They sent me a foreclosure notice." Irma bit down so hard on the biscuit that a piece flew off and hit the carpet. I pretended not to notice. Rising, I picked up the teapot to top up our cups.

We finished the tea in near-silence, listening to the crackling fire, the keening wind, and the sleet tapping the windows.

With a sudden movement, Irma set down her cup. "Verity—your phone! I didn't notice it before." She pointed to my cell lying on the ottoman next to the tray. "I'll plug it in for you. If the power goes out, you won't have a chance to top it up later."

I handed it to her with a dull sense of dread. "Is that likely? For the power to go out, I mean?"

"I'm surprised it's stayed on this long." Clutching my phone, Irma hurried out of the room. "I'll plug it in on the kitchen counter," she called over her shoulder.

Since the teapot was empty, I picked up the tray and followed her into the kitchen at the back of the cottage. Six wooden chairs—each a different color—surrounded a harvest table. The light fixture hanging over the table was made of jam jars with tiny, glowing bulbs.

I set the tray on the counter.

Irma reached for the tea kettle. "Should I add more hot water?"

"Sure. And I wouldn't say no to another cookie."

While she was prying open the tin, I wandered over to look at a collection of framed photos on an antique sideboard. "Are these your parents?" I asked, picking up a picture of Irma as a young girl with a man and woman standing behind her. The woman's hand rested on Irma's shoulder.

She glanced up. "They've been dead for years."

"I'm sorry. What happened?"

"Father in a car accident, Mom to cancer. I was just a kid."

"Where did you live after that? With relatives?"

"Foster homes, mostly. Both my parents were only children, and I had no aunts or uncles. I was eleven when Mom died. Older kids don't get adopted very often." The kettle boiled, and she picked it up to refill the teapot.

I replaced the photo on the sideboard. "Come to Rose

Cottage and I'll show you the photos Mickey gave me. There's a startling resemblance to a person we both know."

"Is that right?" Irma asked absently, adding more tea leaves to the pot. "I must do that."

I walked over to peer out the back window. "The storm's letting up. There's not as much sleet falling." By the light that spilled from the kitchen across the yard, I could make out a parked vehicle. It was a dark-colored SUV.

I chuckled. "Your SUV looks like the one that ran me off the road." Noticing a flash of orange on the bumper, I peered more closely. LEAFY HOLLOW FARMERS' MARKET. "It *is* the same one." I swiveled to face her. "You ran me off the road. What were you thinking?"

Irma, her back to me, stiffened. Slowly, she turned around. "Was that—your truck?"

My mouth dropped open, wondering how anyone could fail to recognize my bright pink vehicle. "Why didn't you stop?"

Irma grimaced. "I'm so sorry, Verity. I didn't realize you were in trouble. I saw your truck skid, in my rearview mirror, but I didn't see it leave the road. I assumed you were fine." She pointed out the window. "My SUV had no trouble getting through."

Because I got out of your way, I thought sarcastically. "Why were you in such a hurry?"

Irma shuddered. "I hate weather like this. My father's accident happened during an ice storm."

To my mind, that should have made her more concerned, not less, about potential collisions. I kept that to myself.

256

"I wanted to get home," she continued. "I'm sorry, Verity."

"No harm done. My truck's only stuck. A tow truck will get it out eventually." Forcing a smile, I pointed to the restocked plate in her hand. "At least we have cookies."

We sat at the kitchen table, chewing. The ginger cookies had lost their appeal for me.

"Why were you out on the road at all?" I asked finally. "Where were you coming from?"

"Oh." She waved a hand. "Errands. You know—groceries and stuff. You need to stock up for bad weather."

"You left it a little late." *You're one to talk, Verity.* Ruefully, I remembered my casual approach to the impending storm.

Irma shrugged. "I forgot a couple of items."

Swallowing the last of my cookie, I got to my feet. "The wind's dying down, too. I think the storm's blowing over. I can walk home."

Before I could take a step, there was a brief metallic whine overhead.

With a loud *pop*, the lights snapped off.

I swallowed heavily, with a hand to my throat. The pitch blackness was oppressive, like being in a tunnel.

"I'll get the candles," Irma said.

I wasn't afraid of the dark. Really, I wasn't. But the power going off unsettled me. Once the fridge in the corner had shuddered to a halt, it was eerily quiet. Only the groaning of that huge branch overhead broke the silence. Lifting my face to the ceiling, I tried to peer through the dark, envisioning a tree crashing through the roof.

As the blackness pressed in, the vein in my throat started to throb and my chest tightened. Was this claustrophobia? Or an anxiety attack? I closed my eyes momentarily, breathing steadily, determined to stave it off.

"Here we are." Irma entered, holding a hurricane lamp that lit her face from below. It threw a warm glow when she set it on the table, but the corners of the room were in darkness. I sat down, tapping my fingers nervously on the tabletop, staring into the lamp's tiny flickering flame.

"Tea?" Irma asked, heading over to the counter to fill our cups. "It's still warm."

"Thanks." My voice lacked confidence, but I couldn't help it. My breath quickened with every groan of that branch. "Listen to that tree," I said, shuddering. "I didn't notice it before."

"Would you like to sit in the other room?"

"I'd like to go home, to be honest. The sleet has stopped, and it's not far."

"No, don't. It's dark out. What if a snowplow comes up the road while you're walking? It might hit you."

"They have headlights. They'll see me." The more I dwelled on it, the more anxious I was to get away from that darkened kitchen and the ominous creaking overhead. "Besides, the dog will be panicked."

"What dog?"

"Oskar York's. He's staying with me at Rose Cottage until we can find him a home. I left an audiobook on for him, but it will have stopped when the power shut off. He's probably upset."

"It's a dog. He'll be fine. He'll go to sleep."

I rose to my feet. "Maybe, but I'd feel better if I went home. A dog can do a lot of damage in a brief time."

"If it was going to damage anything, it's already done it. Don't go. It's not safe."

"Even so. I should leave."

"Sit down and finish your tea, at least. Why an audiobook, by the way?"

"Huh?"

"Why did you get an audiobook for the dog?"

"I heard they were good for calming them. I read it somewhere." The vein in my neck was pulsing. I was trying to ignore it. The mere act of ignoring it was stressing me out even more.

"Any author in particular?"

"What?"

"The audiobook. Which author was Boomer listening to?"

"I never said his name was Boomer."

"Yes, you did."

"I don't think so."

"Which book was it?"

"Dickens. *Nicholas Nickleby.*"

"Why did you pick that one?"

"It's long. No dogs are harmed. And I don't know, really. Irma, I have to go. I'm sorry."

I bolted for the hall, grabbed my parka, and put it on, followed by my damp and chilly boots. The furnace grate was no longer warm. With the power off, my furnace would be off, too. Not only would Boomer be cold, but General Chang—I'd forgotten all about him, I realized with a pang of guilt—would definitely be out of sorts. Well, *more* out of sorts.

I should get home, light a fire, and crack open another tin of salmon for the General.

Good thing my can opener wasn't electric.

Irma hurried down the hall behind me, holding the hurricane lamp. "Verity, don't leave. It's dangerous."

She placed a hand on my arm, but I shrugged it off.

"I have to go before the sleet starts up again," I said, wrenching open the door. I turned back to face her. "You should come with me. If that branch falls—" I shuddered again, glancing at the ceiling. "You'll be safer at Rose Cottage."

She took a step back. "I can't leave my pictures."

I stared at her, conscious of the wind wailing behind me. "You can't—what?"

She muttered something under her breath, looking down at the floor.

"Okay," I said, anxious to get out of there. "I'm going."

"Wait. If I shovel out the driveway, I can drive you home in the SUV."

"It's not necessary, Irma. Stay indoors, where it's dry." I stepped out, closing the door behind me. With a shiver, I turned up my collar, flipped the parka's hood over my head, and plunged into the storm.

CHAPTER TWENTY-SIX

IT WAS ONLY a quarter mile to Rose Cottage. But that ten-minute walk turned into half an hour of battling snowdrifts, icy surfaces, and frigid wind. Lilac Lane's steady upward slope made the footing even more treacherous. The few houses I passed were all dark.

Overhead, branches groaned and shifted, and power lines sagged under thick coatings of ice. At only a hundred feet from Rose Cottage, I paused, momentarily disoriented by the vista ahead. Then I realized what was different, and drew in a quick breath.

The magnificent chestnut tree was partially uprooted and leaning over the road. If it fell any farther, it would snap the power line beneath its branches, and the severed line would hit the ground. A transformer hummed and whined overhead. This wasn't the feeder line that serviced Lilac Lane. It was a much bigger line, headed for a subdivision over the hill.

I gave the stricken tree a wide berth, detouring onto the opposite shoulder and trudging through the snowbanks, my boots sinking in with every step. It meant wresting my foot out of the snow with each stride, but I remembered Adeline's advice about fallen power lines.

Stay well back. Electricity can travel through the ground.

My spirits lifted when the familiar outline of Rose Cottage loomed in the shadows, its dark fieldstone walls standing out against the white snow. Elated, I tramped up the driveway, picturing a roaring blaze in the fireplace. Both Jeff and Adeline had shown me numerous times how to make a proper Boy Scout fire. It began with twisted scraps of paper, then kindling, and finally logs stacked in a pyramid. I always listened with rapt attention.

Then, I generally unwrapped a preformed starter log from the corner store. They were foolproof—as long as I remembered to buy them.

I was trying to recall my last purchase when I pushed open the front door. As usual, it was unlocked. Like most people in Leafy Hollow, I didn't take security as seriously as maybe I should. According to Jeff and Adeline, anyway. I attributed that caution to their chosen careers. Most of us didn't worry about potential assassins.

Obviously, the power was out here, too. So, I wasn't alarmed to find the interior pitch black. I shucked off my parka and boots, leaving them on the floor, before shuffling into the room on my stocking feet.

But the chill in the air did concern me. It was surprising how quickly the cottage cooled once the furnace was off.

Remembering the fleece blankets and heavy-duty cardigans stored in my bedroom closet, I headed that way.

In the darkness, the kitchen door rattled, as if someone was trying to force it open.

I froze, unable to breathe. Until—

Arf-arf-arf-arf-arf-arf...

Sighing in relief, I realized it was only Boomer.

Arf-arf-arf-arf-arf-arf...

"Be right there," I yelled, padding through the living room. "*Ow!*" Pausing, I rubbed my shin where it had struck the coffee table.

Arf-arf-arf-arf-arf-arf...

"I'm coming."

I took two more steps, rebounded off the wall, and paused again—this time to rub my forehead.

"Ow, ow, ow," I muttered.

Arf-arf-arf-arf-arf-arf...

"Okay! Coming." I waited a few seconds, hoping my eyes would adjust to the dark. That didn't work. If I didn't find a light source soon, I'd be unconscious.

I had bought candles, but where did I put them? With an uneasy feeling, I recalled storing them in the basement the previous summer, intending to bring them upstairs before the winter. Not a good plan, as it turned out. The thought of trying to negotiate the narrow basement stairs in darkness was not encouraging. Mulling over my options, I decided that a fire would give off enough light for me to reach the kitchen. But a fumbling search for the matches that should have been on the mantelpiece was also fruitless.

Wait—my phone's flashlight app would work. I

attempted the short trip back to the foyer. One step. Two steps. Three—

I tripped over the ottoman, pitching face-first onto the sofa.

Arf-arf-arf-arf-arf-arf...

With my mouth muffled by fabric, I couldn't respond. Not that it would have made any difference. I didn't blame Boomer for his distress. He was in a strange place, it was dark, and his escape route was barred. But I really wished he'd pipe down.

A series of *whomps* on the door, followed by furious scrabbling, got me to my feet again. At this rate, Rose Cottage would soon be an open-concept loft.

Carefully, I made my way back to the foyer and my phone. After getting down on my hands and knees and feeling along the floor, I finally found my parka. I plunged my hand into the pockets, one after the other. All of them, interior and exterior, were empty.

No phone.

I settled back on my haunches, trying to think. Where had I seen it last? Oh. Right—plugged into an outlet in Irma's kitchen. After all the advice I'd received, ad nauseam, from Adeline and Jeff—I'd forgotten my phone. If Adeline discovered I couldn't hear those irritating national emergency alerts, she'd secure my phone to my body with duct tape the next time she saw me.

I sagged to the floor with my back against the front door, suddenly cheerful despite my predicament. Considering the dangers that came with the clandestine jobs my aunt had performed over the years, it was amazing how risk-averse she was for her only niece. With a smile, I remembered photos of me as a toddler at Rose Cottage, negotiating furniture corners duct-taped with squares of foam rubber.

It was a good thing I was temporarily lost in thought, because otherwise the sudden hammering on the door would have startled me right into another piece of furniture. As it was, I reacted so abruptly I pulled two coats off their hooks trying to leap to my feet.

Bang, bang, bang.

With my heart in my throat, I scrambled from under the coats to wrench open the door. Pale moonlight had broken through the clouds. Its reflection off the snowy landscape provided just enough illumination to see a figure standing on my front porch.

"Verity?" came an anguished cry.

"Irma? Good heavens, what happened?" I clutched her arm. "Get in here."

From the doorstep, I saw her SUV parked in the driveway.

She took a step over the threshold, but halted abruptly. "It's pitch black in here. I can't see anything." Her voice rose. "Oh, Verity, you'll never believe what happened."

The wind had picked up, and I had to use my full strength to shut the door. I turned in Irma's approximate direction, straining to hear her over the water dripping from her coat onto the tiled floor, the keening wind outside, and the sudden *crack* of a branch across the street.

Then the dog started up again.

Arf-arf-arf-arf-arf-arf...

"Boomer—stop it," I yelled, hoping he would comply

265

before my eardrums ruptured. I lowered my voice. "Irma, tell me what happened."

"It's the tree—the tree. It came down. On my roof. It was *horrible*." Then she burst into tears.

I couldn't see her face in the dark, but I assumed she'd need tissues soon. Given current conditions, I had no chance of finding any. Irma would have to use her sleeve.

I flailed about in the dark until I connected with her shoulder. "Wait here. If I open the curtains, maybe that will let in a little moonlight so I can find my way to the kitchen—"

Arf-arf-arf-arf-arf-arf...

"—let Boomer out, and look for my candles."

"No!" Irma shrieked, inflicting a Vulcan death grip on my arm. "It's not safe. What about that tree overhanging Rose Cottage? What if a branch comes off in the wind? It would smash right through your window. Broken glass would be everywhere. You have to keep the drapes closed."

Irma was overwrought. Drapes wouldn't stop a tree. But I had underestimated the ice storm despite warnings from everyone I knew and should have trusted. I didn't think I should start arguing about it now. So, I left the drapes in place.

"Hand me your wet coat, and I'll get you a sweater."

She relinquished her grip on my arm. The sniffling continued while she shed her parka and handed it to me.

Tossing it in the general direction of the coat rack, I said, "Do you remember plugging in my phone at your place?"

"Hm-hmm," she said in a faltering tone.

"Did you bring it with you?"

"Oh, Verity. Your phone. I'm so sorry," she said, punctuating each phrase with a sniffle. Both sleeves were in play by now, I suspected.

"That's okay. I didn't remember it, either. Maybe we can go back and get it," I said.

"No. We can't."

Arf-arf-arf-arf-arf-arf...

"Boomer, for pity's sake—cut it out," I yelled. "What do you mean, we can't? Because of the weather? It's clearing up."

"Because of the branch, Verity. Remember the branch? It crashed onto my roof."

"Oh. Right. You told me that when you came in. I'm sorry. But you're not hurt, are you? I mean, you got out of the house okay, so I guess you're not hurt. If your roof is damaged, we should try to get help. Unless you think—"

"Verity." Irma's sharp voice cut through my reverie.

"Yes?"

"That branch fell on my kitchen roof."

"That's awful, Irma. I know. But we need to call for help."

"That's just it. We can't. When the branch hit, it made a hole in the roof. Water came in and—both our phones are ruined. I'm sorry."

Imagining the scene in Irma's kitchen, I struggled to form an articulate response. "Wow. That's... unfortunate."

A memory of my aunt's cell phone and its waterproof case came to mind. I'd always considered that case as a bit over the top, but I hadn't counted on Leafy Hollow's mysterious ways. Aunt Adeline might have been on to something.

Arf-arf-arf-arf-arf-arf...

I rubbed my hands over my face, trying to think of a workable option. "I have to let Boomer out of the kitchen—I can't think with all that barking. And find the candles. Then maybe we can, I don't know, wave down a passing snowplow."

I brightened, remembering something else about my aunt's emergency preparedness drills—the heavy metal flashlight she had left on my nightstand months earlier. Hopefully it had fresh batteries. It must, if Adeline was involved. She wouldn't forget a thing like that.

"You stay here while I get a flashlight from my bedroom."

Irma clutched at my sleeve. "No, don't leave me."

Hoping to distract her, I added, "While we're waiting for that snowplow, you can take a look at the photo I mentioned. It's with a bunch of other pictures in a shoebox Mickey Doig gave me. You'll be amazed at the resemblance."

Irma released my arm. "Okay," she said calmly. "Go ahead, if you must."

I took a few tentative steps into the blackness until I felt solid plaster under my outstretched fingers, then sidled along with my hands on the wall until I reached the bedroom door. It was closed. After turning the handle, I pushed it open. There was a soft *click*, and then a blinding light shone into my eyes, blotting out my surroundings in a blaze of white.

My hands flew up to cover my eyes. "What the—"

Something soft wrapped around my face, jerking my neck backward. I pawed at it, struggling for air, trying to twist around to confront my attacker. Another set of hands shoved my shoulder, ramming my head into the wall.

My forehead rebounded off the plaster and I fell

heavily to the ground, dazed and unable to stand. With my arms flailing, I tried to strike a blow. Before I could land even the feeblest punch, my assailants forced my arms behind me and bound them with tape, leaving me wriggling helplessly.

My heart was pounding, and my lungs were screaming. But when I tried to breathe, fibers from the suffocating fabric were sucked into my mouth, making me choke.

"Stop struggling. You're only making it worse," Irma said.

Sensing no alternative, I stopped moving.

"Hand me the flashlight. Did you bring the lantern?" she asked.

"It's right here," a different voice said. A familiar voice.

I heard the *click* of a switch, and jerked my eyes away from another brilliant light.

A hand tugged down the cloth that covered my lower face, leaving it puddled around my neck. From the light of a battery-powered LED lantern, I saw it was a navy-blue scarf. Heart in my throat, I raised my head.

Zuly Sundae was crouched on the floor directly in front of me.

The lantern's light shone under her chin as she studied me. Lit from below like that, she could have been filming a scene from *Interview with a Vampire*.

I spit out wool fibers. "It was you in that photo, wasn't it?"

Zuly ignored me. "Did you take her phone?"

"Of course."

"Any calls?"

"Just one. I dealt with it." Irma handed a dripping cell phone to Zuly. "Careful. It's wet."

"Hey," I said, struggling to wrench free of the tape holding my wrists. "That's my—"

Irma rapped my head with the metal flashlight.

"*Ow*. Cut that out," I cried.

She rapped me again, harder this time. I winced, but said nothing.

"Let's not take any chances with this phone." Zuly dropped it onto the floor, took the metal flashlight from Irma, and raised her arm to crack the glass face with a brutal blow. Then another, to finish the job. "Ooh," she said with a smirk. "It's definitely broken now."

She got to her feet and kicked it out of the way. Then she handed the flashlight back to Irma, who snickered.

These were not "the girls" I remembered. Another idea struck me.

"Irma—that branch didn't fall on your house, did it?"

"No."

"How did my phone get wet, then?"

"I dropped it in the toilet."

"Accidentally?" I asked hopefully.

"That's sweet. I don't understand why people say you're cynical, Verity."

"Let's get her on her feet," Zuly growled.

Tucking both hands under my armpits, she pulled. I stubbornly refused to move, bracing my body against her tugs.

"You'll have to help me, Irma," she said.

"No problem." Irma raised the flashlight, swinging her arm back to gain traction.

"Okay—stop. I'll get up," I blurted, struggling to my feet. I stood, swaying slightly. I must have hit that wall hard. "What do you want me to do?"

"Step into the living room."

"Tell me why you're here."

"Because—as usual, Verity, you couldn't mind your own business."

That was absurd, but I decided I'd rather hear the rest sitting on my sofa instead of the hard floor. Maybe I could wheedle some ice out of them for my bruised forehead. There was certainly plenty of it outdoors. I shuffled after Zuly, with Irma bringing up the rear.

The lantern's light bounced off the walls, illuminating Zuly's shadowy form a few feet ahead of me. Mentally, I calculated the distance. If I ran at her and knocked her over... But my hands were bound behind my back, and Irma had a mean way with that flashlight. She might have other weapons, too. I should sit tight, find out what this was all about.

As she shoved me onto the sofa, I realized with a chill in my gut that I already knew.

Why had I given up on the case when the key to the mystery was right in front of me all along? Why hadn't I trusted my intuition? I took that photo from Oskar York's house because my subconscious, at least, recognized the much younger Zuly in it. If only—

They sat opposite me, and Zuly placed the lantern on the coffee table. Now we all resembled vampires, the light casting eerie shadows.

"Just tell me what you want," I said loudly.

Boomer was reenergized by the sound of my voice.

Arf-arf-arf-arf-arf-arf...

The kitchen door rattled. The lantern cast just enough light that I could see the door crack open with each *whomp* of the terrier's feet, but the latch held. *Now* it worked?

"Deal with that dog," Zuly said with an irritated tone. Irma rose to comply.

I tried not to look in the direction of the kitchen, or reveal my glimmer of hope. Boomer was a dog. He'd protect his owner. Sure, he hadn't known me long, which meant I wasn't his actual owner, but I knew how to make meatloaf. Once he saw I was in danger—

I didn't need to finish that thought, because Boomer beat me to it. With one final blow of his feet against the door, the faulty latch gave way. The terrier flew through the opening like a caped avenger. His claws scrabbled across the floor as he ran straight at us.

I tensed, ready for action. Once the furious Boomer had provided a distraction, I could take out Zuly—duct tape or no duct tape. A head butt, if that was all I could manage.

That would leave only Irma, and I sensed she was the weaker of the two. Criminal conspiracies always had a leader and a follower. Zuly was clearly the leader in this plot. Confident I could convince Irma to give up this crazy scheme, I took a deep breath.

Boomer's claws skittered and scratched as he raced toward us.

Wait for it...

Leaning forward and pressing the balls of my feet against the floor, I prepared to join the inevitable attack.

Wait for it...

Skidding on his paws, the terrier crashed to a halt by bouncing off the coffee table. Quickly regrouping, he managed a sprawling sit. He stared at us, tail wagging and tongue lolling.

"Hi, sweetie," Zuly said. "Want some cheese?"

Boomer's ears pricked forward at the word *cheese*. He trotted over to Zuly, then sat obediently in front of her. She pulled something from her pocket—it could have been a ball of lint, for all Boomer knew, since he swallowed it before it even left her fingers.

My mouth dropped open in disbelief. "What kind of a dog are you?"

At these words, the terrier—apparently anxious to prove his worth—leapt onto my lap and furiously licked my face. With my hands bound behind my back, I could hardly stop him. He twisted around to perch on my knees, panting happily at Zuly and Irma.

"Thanks," I said. "You're a big help."

Boomer waggled his entire body.

I sighed. *So much for the canine corps.* However, I had one more card to play.

"Jeff will be here soon," I said.

Irma shook her head, displaying that charming half-smile of hers. At least, it would have been charming, had it not been for the lantern light that transformed her face into a gargoyle's.

"No, he won't," she said. "I answered his call on your phone, after you left. I told him you planned to wait out the storm at my place. And you couldn't come to the phone because you were outside brushing snow off your truck."

Sullenly, I watched Zuly and Irma share a high-five.

I tried again. "He'll go to your place and realize I'm not there."

"Nope. Jeff is super busy with accidents and road closures and emergency calls. He'll be out all night. And when he finally does show up at my place, I'll tell him you insisted on slogging through the snow to get back to that poor little dog, and I couldn't convince you to stay."

Zuly added with gusto, "And he'll find you on the road, under a fallen branch—dead." They shared another high-five.

I couldn't believe it. That was my imminent death they were so jazzed about. I had really misjudged this pair. "Could you at least tell me why you want me out of the way?"

They exchanged glances.

"You don't know?" Zuly asked, her lips curling. "I thought you were smarter than that, Verity."

Heaving a sigh, I lifted one knee to dislodge Boomer, who landed on the floor, still wagging his tail. Glaring at Zuly, I said, "I think I can guess. You killed Oskar York."

CHAPTER TWENTY-SEVEN

ZULY SMIRKED, then reached a hand into her pocket to throw another ball of linty goodness at Boomer. He snapped it up.

"It was you in that photograph," I said. "Standing next to Oskar York, when you were a girl. Mickey Doig took it from Oskar's house. And gave it to me."

"And I took it back, when I searched your house just now. Too bad you came home early. Another fifteen minutes and I would have been gone."

"But Oskar had a copy of that photograph." I inclined my head toward the foyer. "It's in the inside pocket of my parka. Take a look."

Zuly picked up the metal flashlight. She jerked her head at Irma, who got to her feet. After hunting around on the floor of the foyer for my parka, she held up the photo. "Got it."

"Bring it here," Zuly said.

Irma showed the picture, wrinkled and damp, to Zuly, who glanced at it without relinquishing her hold on the flashlight.

"So, you see," I said. "The photos in Mickey's shoebox are not the only copies."

Zuly merely glared at me.

"How did you know I had the box in the first place?" I asked.

"We didn't. Irma saw Mickey come out of Oskar's house with it, and we assumed he still had it."

"So why are you here? Who told you I had the shoebox?"

"Mickey. The idiot."

"Why would he do that?"

"None of your business." Zuly started to get up.

"Then what's your connection to Oskar York?"

Scowling, she slumped back onto the sofa. "Might as well tell you. He's my uncle. Sort of."

"Sort of?"

"My mother married his cousin—an absolute bastard who left her when she got pregnant. I have no idea where he is. Mom asked York to help her, and he did—for a while. A little money here and there. Nothing substantial."

She puffed out a breath, clicking the flashlight on and off. "My mother died when I was eleven. Child Services asked Oskar if he'd take me in. Adopt me, I guess. He said no. So, they put me in foster care."

"Where you met Irma."

"That's right." Zuly twisted her head to glare at her. "Did you tell Verity that?"

Irma shook her head. "I told her I was in foster care. I didn't mention you."

"And you became friends," I continued.

"More than friends. Like sisters. We were inseparable."

"Why wouldn't Oskar adopt you? You were family."

"I don't know. No one told me why. But I was in the Child Services building the day he came in. They took Oskar into a closed office, and there was a discussion. An argument, really. Raised voices and so on. I was on a bench outside. He came out, barely glanced at me, put on his hat, and left. Without a word. That was the last I saw of him until I graduated from high school in Strathcona. I took a job at the grocer's in Leafy Hollow. Oskar York was one of their customers, because they were willing to deliver to his home. One day, I filled in for our regular delivery person and took him his order. When Oskar came to the door, he didn't even recognize me."

"But you recognized him?"

"Yeah. I mean, he was a lot fatter and a lot older but I knew who he was."

"Why did he have to die? Because he wouldn't adopt you?"

Zuly thumped the flashlight on the coffee table, and her voice rose. "You don't know what it's like to be a kid and lose your home. I never knew my father, and I'd just lost my mother. That was bad enough. But when they took me from my school, my friends, my home—they took my identity. I wasn't a person anymore. I was nobody."

I knew what it was like to lose a mother, but at least I'd

been an adult when it happened to me. "I'm sorry, Zuly. That must have been—"

"Spare me the fake tears."

From the floor, Boomer whimpered. Zuly switched the flashlight to her other hand and reached down to rub his ear.

"Why did you kill him now, after all this time?"

Zuly tipped her head to the side in surprise. "I didn't kill Oskar York."

"Are you saying it was an accident?"

"I'm saying I wasn't there. I didn't do anything to him. Yeah, I wanted to. I'm not denying that. But I didn't."

Irma cleared her throat. "Verity—"

"Don't," Zuly snapped. "Don't you dare."

Irma pressed her lips together.

I glanced from one to the other—Zuly, defiant as always, and Irma, with her strange half-smile.

"Then tell me this. How did you rig the crossword puzzle?"

"It was easy," Zuly said. "I worked out the new answers, then changed the clues in the wallets we left around the village. I knew that would do the job."

"Which was?"

"Point the finger at the real killer, naturally."

"And that was?"

"Noah Butterfield."

At this, Irma's eyes widened, but she said nothing.

"Then why add Rick Armstrong's name?"

"That was a smokescreen. What do mystery writers call it? A red herring?" Zuly chuckled. "Although, I guess nobody eats herring at Lucky Lentil." She laughed again, then her expression darkened. "Henri didn't know about the changed clues. I never told him."

"Did you attack him?"

Zuly shrugged. "It helped deflect suspicion from the gallery."

"And us," Irma added.

"Anyway, it doesn't matter," Zuly said. "Noah's the killer."

Irma stared at the floor.

"Why would Noah kill Oskar?" I asked.

"Because he wanted Oskar's money."

"Noah said Oskar had no money."

"That's not true. That old man had plenty of cash. And if he'd only agreed to give it to us—"

"Zuly." Irma placed a warning hand on her shoulder. "That's enough."

"I don't believe it," I said flatly. "Isn't the real truth that you two wanted Oskar's money? To pay for the gallery opening? And he refused to hand it over?"

Zuly's eyes flared, and her voice rose. "He could have remortgaged that old house to fund the gallery. And he should have, in return for abandoning me. I deserved that money. But he wouldn't give it to me. And you know why?" Spit flew from her mouth as she yelled, the flashlight swinging wildly. "Because Noah Butterfield told him not to."

She flung the flashlight across the room, and it clattered off the wall. Zuly leaned forward, dropping her head into her hands. "Oskar deserved what happened to him. I'm glad it happened."

"Let me get this straight. Oskar's death *was* an accident?"

She straightened up. "Must have been."

"Then what about Mickey Doig? That wasn't an accident. The police found wool fibers in his exhaust pipe."

Glancing down at the scarf looped around my neck, I saw no need to admit I'd found the fibers. Or that I knew they were navy.

Zuly frowned. "That was a slip-up on somebody's part."

"Are you saying you killed Mickey?"

"I'm not saying anything of the kind."

"You had nothing to do with Oskar's death—or Mickey's?"

"That's right."

"Then why are my hands taped behind my back?"

"She has a point, Zuly," Irma said quietly. "Maybe we should—"

I twisted around to stare at Irma. "Why didn't you refinance your own house to pay for the gallery?"

Irma lips twitched in that half-smile again. "I told you why. I already have a mortgage—and a second mortgage. The bank refused to give me a third, since I can't meet the monthly payments as it is." She clenched her fist, tapping it absently on the sofa cushion beside her. "You don't get it. Zuly's work deserves to be seen, to be praised, to be purchased. But since Henri couldn't get funding for the gallery, our work on the marketing campaign was useless. We had to find another source of funds. So... I went to see Oskar York."

"Stop." Zuly rose to her feet. "Don't say anything else. Please, Irma."

Irma waved a dismissive hand. "It doesn't make any

difference. Verity won't be telling anyone. I knew of Oskar's connection to Zuly. She told me about it years ago, when we shared a room at our foster home. One of them, anyway." Her voice dripped with disgust. "Do you have any idea how many times we were shuffled around, like garbage? How many homes we lived in? Oskar abandoned Zuly without a second thought."

"Oskar York was unwell. Mentally," I said. "I'm not sure his actions were entirely voluntary."

Zuly snorted and turned her head away.

"As for the money," Irma said. "He did have money, but he gave most of it to Mickey Doig."

"Why would he do that?"

"Oh, he didn't do it voluntarily. Mickey was a thief, just like Henri said. He stole quite a lot from that house during his weekly visits to walk Boomer. Not only that, but where do you think most of Oskar's trash came from?"

"What do you mean?"

"Mickey collected junk, absolute garbage, and sold it to Oskar for cash. He convinced the old man he could resell it at a profit. As if." She snorted. "When I went to see Oskar, I took Zuly's shoebox of photos with me. I thought if I reminded him what he'd done to her, I could shake loose some of his cash. But I was wrong. We had a huge fight. He screamed at me to get out, that I was only after his money. That I was a conniving... a conniving..."

"I get the drift," I said. "Then what happened?"

Irma drew a deep breath and exhaled heavily, shoulders slumping forlornly. "I'm a year older than Zuly. When she arrived at the foster home, I was used to that life. But it was all new to her. She cried herself to sleep every night over the photos in that shoebox. It made me angry that her uncle had done that to her. When it would have been so easy to take her in and give her a home.

"I came back to Leafy Hollow as an adult to live in my parents' house. Noah had rented it out occasionally on my behalf, but the rent money barely paid for the maintenance that old place required. And there was a mortgage on it, naturally."

"Noah probably skimmed money off the top," Zuly said with a scowl.

Irma patted the sofa repeatedly, pursing her lips, before continuing. "When Oskar called me those names, all those memories welled up inside me. The nights I spent listening to a young girl cry. The string of foster homes, one after the other. The artwork that wouldn't sell. The foreclosure notice... and then, on top of it all, the gallery that was supposed to turn everything around was never going to happen. I tried to explain that to the old man. I tried. He laughed at me. Then he told me to get out."

Irma gripped the fabric of the sofa until her knuckles turned white.

"I was angry. I lashed out, and ended up hitting a stack of magazines. It fell over before I could stop it. That toppled the next stack, and the one after that, and then..."

She shook her head. "I knew he was dead," she whispered. "And I was glad."

Zuly awkwardly wrapped her arms around her friend.

I would have offered them both a tissue, but my hands were still tied behind my back.

Impatiently, Irma pushed her away. "I was in such a hurry to get out of there, I forgot about the shoebox. Hours later, when I'd calmed down, I went back for it in Henri's car. That's when I saw Mickey leave the house with it under his arm. I assumed he'd report the body. And possibly hand those photos over to the police." Irma rubbed the back of her neck, sighing heavily. "For two days, I paced the floor, expecting the police to come for Zuly. Instead, she got a message from Mickey, asking for money."

"What did he want the money for?"

"That photo of her and Oskar, taken when she was a child. Zuly was Oskar's only heir. It wouldn't have taken much digging to discover he abandoned her. That she was living in the village under an assumed name. That she knew where Oskar lived. And that he died in suspicious circumstances."

I had to admit it looked a bit dodgy.

"But what does any of this have to do with me?"

"All we wanted were the photos. We would have left you alone, Verity. But just now, in my house, you remarked on the *startling resemblance to a person we both know.* It was only a matter of time before you figured out what happened to Mickey."

"You killed him because he was blackmailing Zuly. He thought she killed Oskar."

"Obviously," Irma said.

"Leave her alone," Zuly said.

I ignored her. "But Irma, if you hadn't done that, the police would have assumed Oskar's death was an accident. If you'd left Mickey alone—"

"Don't you get it?" Irma screamed, her face contorted in anger. "The money Mickey took from Oskar should have gone to Zuly. She was his *heir*. And Mickey took it all." She glared at me, her expression black. Then her face relaxed, and that shy half-smile was back. "We have to wrap this up before the lights come back on." She rose to her feet. "It won't take long, and it will be painless. Mostly."

Great. I'd been twisting my wrists for the past twenty minutes with nothing to show for it. Duct tape was hard to dislodge without a sharp-edged tool. There were knives in the kitchen, but I doubted the girls planned to walk me out that way. Boomer's teeth were sharp, but he'd already proved he was useless at tackling would-be killers. In fact—I scowled at him—he was pawing at Zuly's leg, hoping for another treat. "Traitor," I hissed under my breath.

"Let's get her out of here," Irma said, stooping to pick up the flashlight.

"What's the plan?" Zuly asked. "Whack her first, then drag her out? Or make her walk down the road, and whack her there?"

All this talk of whacking was making me nervous. "Girls," I said. "This is never going to work. You don't seem to have any kind of feasible plan. Preparation is the key to a successful operation. If I was doing this—"

"Shut up," Irma said, brandishing the flashlight menacingly.

I shut up.

"It's only a matter of time before that chestnut tree beside the road comes down," Zuly said. "If we leave her body underneath, it will look as if it fell on her. Boom."

"I like that. It's simple."

"But she should have her parka on. And boots. Otherwise, it might look suspicious if she's found out in the cold without winter clothes."

"We can put her boots on later, but the coat might be a problem." Irma studied me as if she were a window dresser, I was a mannequin, and the biggest shopping weekend of the year was coming up. "We can't put it on with her hands taped behind her back like that."

Inwardly, I brightened. These idiots would have to cut my bonds, and the moment they did, I'd take them both out. Mentally, I scanned my repertoire of Krav Maga moves, searching for the most painful.

"We'll do it later. After she's dead."

No help there, then.

"*Mrack?*"

I turned my head to look down. The one-eyed General languidly swished his tail.

"*Mrack?*"

Catching his eye, I jerked my chin a few times in the direction of my assailants, who were ignoring the tomcat while discussing their options for gutting me and stringing me up—or whatever their latest plan was. "*Get 'em,*" I mouthed silently at the General, jerking my head again, remembering an earlier attack of his that had handily distracted an assailant.

The old boy gave me a curious look, pointedly turned his gaze on the dog—as if to say, *you made your bed, lady*—turned, and walked away, tail held high. If I got out of this in one piece, I was definitely changing his name.

"On your feet," Irma said, grabbing one of my arms while Zuly yanked on the other one to force me up. We walked to the front door three abreast. Irma threw open the door.

A gust of wet wind swept in, making me narrow my eyes. Without boots or a coat, it would be deathly cold outside. I might not last long enough to be killed by a falling tree. Or whatever the current plan was.

"Zuly," I said. "You haven't killed anyone. Yet. Stop this before it's too late."

Irma rapped me on the head with the flashlight. "Get moving."

I grimaced, wishing I could rub my scalp. If I survived this, I was going to have one heck of a headache. I stepped on to the porch, cringing as my stocking feet sank into cold, wet snow.

"Wait a minute," Irma yelled over the wind, yanking me back. "Cover her mouth with duct tape. Otherwise, she'll scream."

"Who's going to hear her?" Zuly shouted.

"Just do it," Irma hollered back.

We returned to the cottage long enough for Zuly to slap tape over my mouth. Irma stood over us with the flashlight, watching.

"We can't hit her with that thing," Zuly said. "It will leave the wrong kind of marks. We need a branch."

"There are plenty outside. They're falling off the trees like hammers."

Outside, a loud *crack*, followed by a *swish* and a *thud*, announced the arrival of yet another deadly implement.

"After that, we'll leave her on the road. The snow will cover everything up."

By the time we reached the end of the driveway, my teeth were chattering under the duct tape and my non-duct-taped skin was raw from sleet splattering against it. My socks were stiff and frozen, cutting into my feet like razors.

"That way," Irma yelled, pointing with the end of the flashlight.

We set off toward the massive chestnut that leaned over Lilac Lane. The partially uprooted tree was tilted even more menacingly than when I'd given it a wide berth on my walk home.

The power line beneath it sagged and creaked under its thick casing of ice. The hydro pole nearest the tree was leaning. I noticed a crack running up its side.

Irma pointed again, this time to a two-foot length of broken branch on the road. "There's a good one." She studied me, almost as if she were assessing the size of my head. "That should do it." Irma handed Zuly the flashlight before setting off at a trot toward the branch.

I considered making a run for it. But in which direction? My feet were so numb I could barely walk. Zuly would whack me over the head before I made any progress.

A flashing blue light reflecting off the snow caused me to jerk my head around. A snowplow was thundering down the road that led to the subdivision over the hill. It was nearly a block away, and heading in the other direction, but it was the only chance I had.

I hobbled in that direction, my feet slabs of ice and my

hands tied behind my back. Even though I couldn't wave or shout, the driver would see me if I got close enough.

"Get her," came a muffled shriek from behind me.

I darted and swerved, but in the end, a simple rap with the flashlight knocked me off my feet, ending my escape attempt. Groaning, I tried to lift my face out of the snow.

"Get up."

I struggled to my feet. With Zuly at my back, I slogged toward Irma's position under the giant chestnut.

Horror-struck, I halted.

A smirking Irma was waving the broken branch at us. Completely oblivious to the tree toppling above her.

It took only seconds, but those seconds were the longest of my life. The chestnut slowly toppled over, its roots soundlessly ripping out of the ground, until its trunk smacked onto Irma's head. Her neck snapped back at a strange angle, and she crumpled soundlessly to the ground, arms drifting out to the sides as she fell into the snow, pinned under a massive branch.

The tree's collapse stretched the power line taut. The cracked hydro pole leaned, but stood its ground, halting the line mere feet from the snowy ground.

Beside me, Zuly raised a hand to her throat and made a strangled sound, inaudible over the wind. Then, with an anguished scream, she darted forward. "Irma!"

I threw myself at her before she could reach the live wire. We hit the ground with a thud.

Zuly—struggling to get out from under the dead weight of a duct-taped woman with frozen feet—finally gave up. Helplessly, she reached out an arm toward her friend.

A gale-force gust roared up the lane, breaking off more branches. The hydro pole split with a loud *crack*.

We froze, unable to breathe, staring as the power line broke and plunged to the ground. It snapped and cracked like a circus whip around Irma's body.

There was a loud *pop* and a flash of light.

And Irma's parka burst into flames.

EPILOGUE

THREE WEEKS LATER...

It was with great surprise that I stepped aside on the threshold of the 5X Bakery to let the proprietor of Lucky Lentil step out.

"Talk to you later, Emy," Rick Armstrong called over his shoulder before nodding at me. "Verity."

I nodded back, mystified. "Rick."

After watching him cross the street to his restaurant, I stamped my boots on the mat and continued to the counter, where Emy was already pouring me a tea.

"There you go," she said, handing it over. "Chocolate croissant with that?"

"Croissant? Is that new?"

"No. They've been making them for centuries in France."

I made a face at her while lifting the mug to my mouth. "Never mind the pastries. Tell me what the competition was doing here."

"If you mean Rick, he's not the competition. In fact, we're planning a joint sales campaign."

I spurted tea onto my parka, hastily putting down the mug. "What? How did that happen?"

"He suggested it. Right after explaining how those reviews ended up online."

"Did he write them?"

"No. It was Gloria."

"Lucky Lentil's Employee of the Month? Who wanted to check out the wallet owners on social media to see if they were cute?"

"That's the one. She bribed the delivery guy—he also delivers to the Lentil—to plant that butter vat in my storage room and take a photo of it. Turns out Gloria had a crush on Rick, and believed that would get his attention."

Rebecca. Shanice. And now Gloria, I thought, shaking my head. *Were there any women in the village who didn't have a crush on Rick?* "And did it?"

"Yes, but not in the way she hoped. When she told Rick what she'd done, he fired her. And came over here to apologize."

I picked up my tea and sipped it, mulling this over. "It's not a bad thing to have another vegan shop across the street. Economists call it 'clustering.' If shops selling the same type of goods locate near each other, the added choice draws more customers overall."

Emy plucked a chocolate croissant from the display with a pair of tongs, dropped it on a plate, and slid it across the counter with a grin. "That's what Lorne says. They covered it in his business courses. Rick and I are planning a village-wide promotion."

Tearing off a chunk of pastry, I popped it into my mouth. I hoped there would be no guerrillas involved in this marketing venture. Leaning against the counter, eyes closed, I savored the burst of chocolate filling, grateful that Emy hadn't given up butter at the 5X.

"Did you hear about Noah and Rebecca?" she asked.

Instantly alert, I swiveled around to place both elbows on the counter. "Tell me."

"They're on a one-month cruise to South America. Left yesterday. Apparently, it's Noah's last-ditch effort to, you know—"

"Save his marriage?"

"Exactly." She paused. "He bought Rebecca a new designer tote bag, too."

We both chuckled, and I nibbled at my croissant. In Eco Edibles next door, the doorbell tinkled. "What can I get you?" we heard Shanice ask.

"She's still here?" I whispered, eyebrows raised.

"Why would I ask her to leave? Shanice was only trying to protect the bakery. And she's promised to restrict her butter sculpturing to the fall fair."

"What about Rick?"

"He's completely devoid of female companionship at the moment."

"That won't last."

"I know." We stifled our laughter when Shanice popped her head through the passage to say, "Verity—I thought I heard your voice. How are you?"

"Great," I said, adding a friendly wave. "And you?"

"Couldn't be better." She withdrew her head, I assumed to return to the customer.

I swallowed the last of my tea, set my cup on the counter, and zipped up my parka. "Time to walk the dogs."

"How's that going?"

"Pretty good. Although, every once in a while I have to return somebody's wallet."

"What about your investigation agency?"

I grimaced. "Jeff was not happy about the outcome of my first case."

"What do you mean?" Emy smirked. "You cracked that case wide open."

By the time I'd walked the dogs and returned home with Boomer, Jeff was lifting a huge cardboard box out of his pickup truck in the driveway. Holding the box, he leaned in for an awkward kiss.

"Is this where I say, 'Honey, I'm home?'" I asked, after stretching over the carton to manage a peck on his cheek.

"No. That's my line."

"Already you're bossing me around." I pointed to the box. "Is that the last of it?"

With a nod, he followed me inside—where he dropped the box on the floor, shucked off his parka, and wrapped his arms around me for a lingering kiss. Afterwards, I leaned my head against his shoulder, inhaling the scent of his Old Spice, comforted by the embrace of his arms, willing that moment to last forever.

Until I noticed the cardboard boxes stacked in the foyer. And the hall. And—as far as I could tell from where I was standing—the dining nook, the bedroom, and the kitchen.

Springing back, eyes wide, I gestured at the cartons. "We agreed on clothing only—plus any kitchen stuff you absolutely had to have. What's all this?"

Apparently amused, he grinned. "Clothing—and kitchen stuff I absolutely had to have."

"I meant your clothing, not the entire neighborhood's. In my whole life, I've never owned this many clothes."

He grinned. "I've been meaning to mention that."

"I wouldn't if I were you." My lips were twitching, and it was hard to maintain a stern expression. Glancing around, I added, "Are you going to put this stuff away?"

"Absolutely. But first—" He shoved aside a couple of boxes to reveal two printed with the familiar logo of a Scandinavian self-serve furniture store. "I have to put this wardrobe together."

I stared, unable to speak, panic welling in my throat. "Jeff," I wailed finally, pressing a finger to the throbbing vein in my neck. "You're not moving in. Not really. This is only a trial run. So that you don't have to go home to change your clothes. And now—you're putting furniture together?"

"Come here." He held out his arms. I snuggled into them, trying to breathe. "Everything will be fine," he whispered. "Don't forget. I love you. And I always will."

"You better."

He tightened his grip.

Much later, I curled up on the sofa with Boomer tucked in beside me. The General—unaware I'd observed him touching noses with the enemy—perched on the back of the sofa, pretending to be indifferent. From the bedroom came the occasional whirr of a power tool, followed by hammering, followed by a muttered oath. The curse of the Norse furniture gods, I assumed.

Smiling, I turned the pages of *Sleuthing for Beginners—A Handbook*. Maybe my first case had been a disaster, but that didn't mean I was ready to give up.

My cell phone beeped with a text. It was Emy at the bakery.

EMERGENCY. GET DOWN HERE.

WHAT'S WRONG? I texted back.

STRANGER. ASKING FOR VERITY THORNE.

My stomach ran cold while I stared at the screen. Hawkes was my mother's maiden name, and the one I'd used since childhood. Few people in Leafy Hollow even knew the other one.

B RIGHT THERE, I texted. And vaulted off the sofa.

"I'm going to the store, Jeff—I'll be back soon," I called as I hurriedly tugged on my boots with one hand and opened the front door with my other.

He stuck his head out of the bedroom, looking harried. "Okay." He disappeared again.

After pushing open the door of 5X Bakery, I shot Emy a raised-eyebrow glance from the threshold. She tilted her head in the direction of a man standing by the far wall. He was studying the notices pinned to the bulletin board with his back to us. The waxed canvas field coat he wore was totally inadequate for the weather.

I slammed the door closed, causing the overhead bell to jangle loudly.

He turned around, focusing laser-blue eyes on me. His face was heavily lined and deeply tanned. A grim smile briefly cracked his skin, but vanished just as quickly.

Emy, pretending to dry glasses behind the counter, watched intently.

I swallowed heavily, willing my stomach to settle before I spoke his name.

"Hello, Frank."

"Verity."

We exchanged glares.

Finally, "Why are you here?" I asked.

"I need your help. It's a matter of life and death, or I wouldn't have come."

"You've got a lot of nerve coming here, asking me for help."

He shrugged.

Still glaring, and without turning my head, I spoke again.

"Emy. This is my father."

ALSO BY RICKIE BLAIR

The Leafy Hollow Mysteries

From Garden To Grave

Digging Up Trouble

A Branch Too Far

Muddy Waters

Snowed Under

The Grave Truth

Picture Imperfect

The Ruby Danger series

Dangerous Allies

Dangerous Benefits

Dangerous Comforts

When not hunched over her computer talking to people who exist only in her head, Rickie spends her time taming an unruly half-acre garden and an irrepressible Jack Chi. She also shares her southern Ontario home with two rescue cats and an overactive Netflix account.

Made in the USA
Monee, IL
31 May 2020